My Lover, My Friend

My Lover, My Friend

True-life Stories of Lesbian
Romance Between Friends

Edited by
Lindsey Elder

alyson books
los angeles

MANUFACTURED IN THE UNITED STATES OF AMERICA.

THIS TRADE PAPERBACK ORIGINAL IS PUBLISHED BY ALYSON PUBLICATIONS,
P.O. BOX 4371, LOS ANGELES, CALIFORNIA 90078-4371.
DISTRIBUTION IN THE UNITED KINGDOM BY TURNAROUND PUBLISHER SERVICES LTD.,
UNIT 3, OLYMPIA TRADING ESTATE, COBURG ROAD, WOOD GREEN,
LONDON N22 6TZ ENGLAND.

FIRST EDITION: JUNE 2003

05 06 07 08 09 **a** 13 12 11 10 9 8 7 6 5 4 3

ISBN 1-55583-724-7
ISBN-13 978-1-55583-724-2

LIBRARY OF CONGRESS CATALOGING-IN-PUBLICATION DATA
MY LOVER, MY FRIEND : TRUE-LIFE STORIES OF LESBIAN ROMANCE BETWEEN FRIENDS /
EDITED BY LINDSEY ELDER.—1ST ED.
 ISBN 1-55583-724-7; ISBN-13 978-1-55583-724-2
 1. LESBIANS—BIOGRAPHY. 2. LESBIANS—SEXUAL BEHAVIOR—ANECDOTES.
3. FEMALE FRIENDSHIP—ANECDOTES. I. TITLE: LESBIAN ROMANCE BETWEEN FRIENDS.
II. ELDER, LINDSEY.
HQ75.3.M93 2003
306.76'63—DC21   2003041858

COVER PHOTOGRAPHY BY KLAUS LAHNSTEIN FROM THE STONE COLLECTION.

Contents

Introduction

More often than not, women are drawn into the world of lesbian desire through the touch of a trusted friend. Perhaps it was the girl next door who shared your tree house and borrowed your sweaters, the one you dreamt about but never knew she felt the same way until she snuck in late one night to kiss you. Or maybe it was your college roommate or a stranger who became such a fast, intense friend that you started believing in reincarnated love. Whatever the situation, we all share the passionate memories of a friend turned lover, even if it only lasted for one kiss.

My Lover, My Friend is a diverse collection of stories from women who have crossed the line. You've probably had an experience similar to one of these authors, or you're wondering whether to take the next step with your best friend—either way you'll find comfort and excitement and, in some cases, a release of emotion as you travel with these writers down your shared path. You'll feel those old butterflies again, or remember the smell of her hair, or wonder how you can get in touch with her again, or maybe even gather the strength to finally tell her how you feel.

Since the beginning of time women have bonded and crossed the line. We've been coupled in Boston Marriages, written Sapphic poems or Steinian stories, turned the radio up a little louder in our dorm rooms, and nowadays stand before our friends and family to be married. Sometimes, as a few of these stories reveal, the risk doesn't play out and we lose the friendship in trying to become lovers, but as one author writes, "Hey—you can't win if you don't spin!"

So take a spin—whether down memory lane or into a flight of fancy—and sit down and enjoy these sexy love stories that span all generations and locations but share the common bond of friendship, love, and what happens when the lines blur.

—Lindsey Elder

Sagebrush
Jesi O'Connell

Isabel cut her hair short the week after we trained together.

"I can't imagine having long hair in this job," she told me, contentedly watching in the mirror as her long brown locks fell to the floor at the hairdresser's.

We had just completed a weeklong training for a wilderness adventure program that involved trekking through the southern deserts of Utah with a group of teenagers in search of adventure, personal growth, and enlightenment. Backpacking, no showers, hot meals only if we built the fire ourselves—it was a fun job that would prove to be demanding, emotional, rewarding. I had spent all of my high school and college years in similar jobs: river guide, adventure program instructor at summer camps, rock climbing instructor, outdoor survivalist. This was Isabel's first experience in this industry, but she was a nature woman at heart and fit in as if she'd been doing this kind of work all her life.

I knew I was attracted to her the moment I met her, but I picked up fairly obvious clues that Isabel was straight. She mentioned past boyfriends and a recent bad breakup that involved Tahiti, an emotionally unstable man, and lots of drama. So I tempered my lustful fantasies and concentrated on being her friend.

We clicked almost instantly, spending the entire week as hiking buddies, shivering together in the enormous amounts of snow (it was January), and volunteering to be on cooking and cleanup details with each other. When we finished the rather grueling training, the trainers asked if we wanted to be on the same shift since we so obviously had become friends and could clearly work well together. Naturally, we jumped at the chance.

Isabel with short hair was even more attractive than Isabel with long hair. Shaped bluntly, framing her pixie face with a scattering of freckles across her nose and cheeks, her hair defined the new Isabel, she said.

"No more bad relationships!" she told me. "No more chasing men who are completely wrong for me! No more working at jobs that don't express the real me!" And she laughed, a deep, full-bellied sound that belied her delicate name.

Of course, the first thing she did, about two months after the training, was to find a man who was so completely wrong for her it was laughable. Sadly, she was the only one who couldn't see his faults. Six weeks or so after she started dating him, Isabel showed up at my door, crying nonstop, asking if she could come in for a few minutes. It seemed there were people gathered for brunch with her roommates at her house and she couldn't face them quite yet, as she had just driven down from the boyfriend's place in Park City after leaving at the crack of dawn. He had dumped her the second she showed up at his house the evening before, after she arrived all smiles in anticipation of another perfect weekend with him. Since Park City was a good four hours from home and she was too tired and stunned to turn around and drive right back, she had spent a mostly sleepless, lonely night on his couch. *What a schmuck*, I thought as I welcomed the sobbing mass of Isabel into my arms. She had a sprig of pungent silvery-green sagebrush tucked behind one ear, crushed into the individual hairs, and as I inhaled it I felt almost dizzy with a rush of desire. *I could be so much better for her*, and the thought startled me even as it titillated me.

"Jesi, I can't believe I did it again. It's like Mark in Tahiti and Rick in D.C. and Grant at school," she sobbed, her voice sounding alluring even though the tears clogged up her voice and nose.

"Cry it out, girl," I encouraged, making tea, handing her tissues, sitting close to her on the couch. I put my arm around her shoulder, let her sniffle on my shirt, stroked the glossy cap of her short chestnut-colored hair. I was struggling not to feel attracted to her at this moment because it was inappropriate, but I finally gave up. Something about the muscled runner's legs, the nicely-defined arms, the tanned nape of her neck under the shorn hair, and the knowledge of her quick mind and good humor just conspired to turn me on, and I finally simply let it lead me blindly.

"That feels good," Isabel murmured after a while, the crying slowing to an occasional hiccup. "Thank you." She looked up at me with her lovely face, still wet with tears, and both my heart and clit thumped alarmingly. A slow heat spread through my hips and washed over me like a rising tide; I suddenly felt light-headed.

When she nuzzled her face into my neck, tentatively, almost as if she was merely adjusting to a more comfortable position, I almost stopped breathing. Unsure of how to read her movements, I held myself still, waiting for some sort of signal from her. Her slightly sweat-tinged skin, the enticing perfume of a physically active person, tickled my nostrils and sent little sparks of excitement dancing along my veins.

"Mmm..." came the faintest of sighs to my ears, and I swallowed. Had I really heard that? Well, time to find out.

"Isabel," I said softly. I dropped my hand to her shoulder, bare but for the skinny strap of a tank top. Caressing the strong muscles, the smooth rise of her collarbone, the pulse beating rapidly on the sides of her neck, I slid my lips onto her head in the gentlest, least offensive way I could. Lightly kissing her hair, I still stroked her shoulder, her arm, all that bare warm skin. This was turning into my fantasies, except that it was deliciously real.

"Please," she breathed, and she turned her face up to mine.

"Please what?" I said in reply, my face hovering inches over hers.

"Please—do this. Don't stop, please. I want you," she whispered, and arched her head toward me, sought my mouth with her moist hungry lips, kissed me until I gasped for air.

She was a little awkward, a little unsure of herself, but, oh—she tasted *so* good, like wildflowers growing after a storm, like slow heavy molasses and sweet cinnamon. *Isabel, Isabel, my lovely strong Isabel* went inanely through my head like a litany, a confirmation, a long wet desire. I was definitely losing control of my senses and enjoying every second of it.

Hardly believing this was happening, right here, right now, on my couch in my house, I eased myself up over this amazing woman and spent a moment looking at her. Dark eyes shone back up at me, her face serious, her lips open and deep red from being kissed by my suddenly insatiable mouth. She parted them more, to speak, but I shushed her with a finger drawn slowly across her cheek, her mouth, up to trace her eyebrows.

"Tell me if I need to stop," I said rather hoarsely, and she nodded, still looking up at me, her eyes widening when I sat up and pulled off my shirt, my sports bra, then stood and removed my shorts and my underwear. I stood before her in my living room, the morning light streaming in from my south-facing windows, and let her look at my naked body until she began to tremble, began to breathe faster, gestured for me to come back to her, reached out for me with her hands.

Her clothes came off easily, and her supple, toned body took my breath away. She had the sleek physique of a well-disciplined runner. I could not wait to touch her; I had been dreaming of this moment for so long that I felt like a virgin fumbling during her first time. But Isabel was the virgin, in the sense that she had never felt the touch of a woman's hand on her breast before. I thought I should be the one taking the lead in this thrilling dance.

Slowly, giving her an out if she wanted one, I reached down and touched her. I traced the taut russet-colored nipples on her generous breasts with my fingertip and listened to her moans, watched her close her eyes and arc her back toward me. My lips followed my fingers, drawing a strangled little cry, which made me pause to gauge whether or not to continue. She opened her eyes, smiled at me, and pushed my head back toward her breast. I took that gesture as a yes and went full steam ahead.

"Beautiful," she said in a throaty whisper, which sent a throbbing clench right between my legs. "Incredible…it's so soft, like I'm being kissed by the sun," and then she was quiet again as I swirled my tongue over her nipples, between her breasts, down to her taut stomach which was trembling under my ministrations. Her belly button shyly peeked up at me, and I kissed it, dipped my tongue into it, tasted the sweetness of her skin. My head felt like it was exploding with little steaks of colored light.

Isabel suddenly shifted beneath me and raised her hands to push at me. Scared that I was doing something wrong, I sat back, giving her freedom to leave if that was what she wanted. My anxiety must have shown in my eyes because she gently laughed at me and caught up my hand to kiss it slowly, lips against the sensitive palm, bright eyes locked on mine.

"I want to do this. I want to make *you* feel good," she said, her voice barely above a whisper. Then she rolled over so she was on top, pushed me down into the couch, and started kissing me everywhere in a way that literally made me breathless. My belly felt hot and tingly, my thighs were sweaty and sliding against hers in a way that made every inch of my skin feel alive and desperate for the teasing touch of her fingers and mouth.

"Jesi, can I touch you?" she asked, and I was confused. My sagebrush-scented woman was already touching me, everywhere, madly, turning me into a frenzied ball of lust. Was there more? There sure was. Her hand was abruptly between my legs, gently pulling at my hairs, running fingers over my swollen lips, dipping a finger inside.

"Isa-bel!" I groaned raggedly, shocked, and absolutely driven over the edge. Her finger swirled around inside me, and I felt myself getting wetter and wetter, if that was even possible. My clit pulsed in anticipation, and I eagerly ground against her hand, begging her with my body to touch my clit, to stroke it, to rub until it burst, make me come so hard I might pass out.

"OK, OK," she said, laughter shaking her voice, and I realized I'd spoken out loud. I was too deep into lust to feel inhibited any longer. Besides, it was still Isabel, my friend. I trusted her implicitly.

Her fingers worked magic on my clit, doing exactly as I had apparently asked, fluttering on second, the next rubbing so hard it almost hurt. The more she went on, the more loose and eager I became, and I swore that once she even murmured "little bitch in heat" into my ear, although that could simply have been the blood roaring and pounding in my head.

Somewhere in the back of my head I was startled that she was so forward, so expert with my body, and I wondered if she had perhaps been with a woman before. But right now it didn't matter because her lips were suddenly down on me, then they were kissing and sucking my wet fullness, and I was saying words I could hardly understand. My head really did feel like it would fly off my body, and the room whirled around me. The smell of sagebrush and sweat and the outdoors surrounded me and made every nerve in my body scream for release. Her tongue darted deep, and it was so incredible that I came just like that, the second she entered me with her tongue, that simple and easy, and I shrieked with my head thrown back. I hoped the neighbors couldn't hear through the open windows.

When I came gently spiraling back to earth, Isabel was smiling down at me, pushing her damp hair behind her ear. The sprig of sagebrush had disappeared, probably crushed somewhere in all the flailing.

"I'm feeling a lot better now. Thanks for cheering me up," she said. My eyes focused on her sort of hazily. She ran a questioning finger down my slick chest.

"But maybe you could cheer me up a little more," she said in a teasing voice, yet her eyes were serious.

I grinned as she came into clearer focus.

"Anything to make you feel better," I said, and I have to admit that I made very good on that assurance.

That was three months ago. We're still friends and are working very hard on exploring every bit of our friendship as often as possible. After all, what are friends for if not to make each other happy?

Lovers Like Butterflies
Bernadette Rafferty

I met Justine at the Great Moscow Circus when it came to Cairns, Australia, in 1994. We were both backpackers—me an Aussie with itchy feet who had just returned from three years in Europe and who, at the age of 23, had decided to explore her own country; and she a 19-year-old from Surrey, England, who had come to this big country alone when her traveling partner had bowed after becoming pregnant.

We had both turned up at the Big Top for an interview along with about 200 others. We were two of the lucky few who ended up getting a job. I was employed as an usher; Justine landed the job of ice cream and beverage seller. At the end of the first night, our mutual friend Kim introduced us.

Although I had never been attracted to a woman before, I was instantly attracted to Justine. She had an infectious smile, beautifully clear skin, and aquamarine eyes that sparkled mischievously. The weather was extremely hot, and Justine was wearing a pink T-shirt and very short denim shorts.

That night a group of us circus recruits went out for drinks at a club called The End of the World. I was talking to Justine and sipping on a vodka and orange when she asked if I wanted to dance onstage with her.

"Sure," I told her, and put down my drink. Up we went. Justine was a bit of an exhibitionist, and so was I. From that point on we were inseparable.

A few weeks later Justine moved into the unit I shared with my brother. At this stage in our lives she and I were both straight. Justine had started dating an English backpacker and I was having an affair with a man. One morning I got up late and walked through the lounge room where Justine slept. She was fast asleep and totally naked from the waist up. I looked at her lying there—she was beautiful. And those curves! None of the hardness of a man's body. I felt guilty for gazing at her, so I lowered my head and went into the bathroom. From that moment on I never looked at her in quite the same way. I dumped my boyfriend and gave Justine all of my attention. I began to fantasize about her. I wanted her, but I didn't have the courage to do anything about it.

During the next four months Justine and I went through a lot together. It was a stream of nonstop parties, adventures, and laughs. Soon, though, I had to return to Sydney, settle down, and find a "real" job. Worst of all, Justine, my new best friend and secret fantasy lover, was leaving Australia and going home to the U.K. And I still hadn't told her how I felt.

It was a long lonely time without Justine. I missed her terribly. But fortunately, six months later she returned and moved back in with me and my brother, who'd come to Sydney with me. It was like a breath of fresh air; there was a spark of energy around the place. Once again each day became exciting, something wonderful to look forward to. She brought a bit of mischief and intrigue into my life.

But all too soon Justine's travel visa expired and her money ran out. And so did our time together. I hadn't told her I was attracted to her, that I got butterflies in my stomach when I looked at her, that I wanted to kiss her. But Justine was a woman. What was I thinking? I was confused and even ashamed of my feelings. I hadn't told a soul what was going on. But somehow I had a feeling that Justine was attracted to me in the same way.

During our time together, Justine and I had shared many lingering looks at each other. Words went unspoken. And now we were sitting in the airport, sharing a container of chocolate ice cream. I had waited this long, and now we only had a few minutes left together.

Between mouthfuls, I mustered my courage and asked her, "Are you a lesbian?"

"No," she replied.

"Are you in love with me?" I couldn't believe I was asking her this.

"Yes," she whispered.

My heart raced, but I was too scared to ask her anything else. Those were the last words spoken before Justine got on her plane and was gone.

After that conversation, she made another trip to Australia to see me. I hadn't confessed my secret to anyone, and neither had Justine. We were both treading new ground.

It was during this trip that Justine and I shared our first kiss. I had just broken my back in a boating accident and wouldn't be able to walk again for three months. Justine sat on my bed, talking to me and stroking my hair.

When I was in grade school, my friends and I would do the "frigid test" on one another. This involved one girl running her finger from the forehead down the face and rest of the body of another girl until her "victim" yelled "Stop!" If this occurred somewhere around the breastbone area, the girl was proclaimed frigid. As soon as I told Justine this, she put me to the test. Her index finger touched my forehead at my hairline and slowly made its way down the bridge of my nose. When her finger reached beneath my nose, I parted my lips and gently took her finger into my mouth, biting it teasingly. I lifted my eyes to look into hers, and as I did she leaned forward and kissed me. It was the most amazing kiss I had ever experienced—it was so gentle, and her skin and lips were so soft. It felt like the most natural and beautiful thing in the world. Never had I dreamed that kissing a woman could feel so good. I felt complete, as if I had been kissing Justine all my life.

"Do you know how long I've wanted to do that?" Justine whispered.

I gulped. My God, she was sexy.

After this, Justine and I decided we wanted to be together. She went back to England to tie up loose ends and pack up her life, with plans to move to Australia in a few months. As soon as she landed back home in England, she got a job. She took all the overtime that was possible and saved up to come back to Australia. We wrote each other almost daily. Our letters were full of the excitement of our newfound love for each other. We were having a long-distance love affair, and we hadn't even slept together yet.

We spoke on the phone often. Justine usually phoned me on her cordless while she was taking a bubble bath (the only privacy she could get in the house, away from her parents and sisters). I'd be sitting at the kitchen table, shivering in the dark cold of morning at 5 o'clock, hands shaking and butterflies fluttering around my insides, my brother asleep in the next room.

Four weeks and one day later, I got the wonderful news. "I'm coming back in two months," Justine told me. My heart leaped.

But those following months were the longest two months of my life. Each day dragged on, and I begged the sun to set, time after time, just so I'd be a day closer to Justine's arrival. I slept in the middle of the day sometimes just to while away the hours. I had a huge photo of Justine stuck to my wall that I looked at all the time. I read and reread all of her letters.

At long last it was time for me to go to the airport and meet my love. My new life as a lesbian was about to begin. A sea of faces poured out of the international exit. And there she was. We ran toward each other, and Justine picked me up and swung me around and around. And we kissed. Two women kissing in public. Right then we were the only two people in the world.

We squeezed each other tightly as we headed into the cold night air, then threw Justine's luggage into a cab. I gave the driver the address of the hotel where Justine and I planned to spend our first night together as lovers. We sat in the backseat, holding each other, touching each other, talking and kissing and kissing and kissing. My girl was finally here.

When we got to our hotel room, Justine opened her suitcase and showered me with Hershey's chocolate kisses. Then she kissed me. First on my face, then my neck. She carefully removed my clothes and kissed her way down my body.

My heart was racing, my breath catching in my throat. My chest and cheeks flushed as Justine spread my legs apart and leaned forward to taste me for the first time. Her first time. And mine. God, she felt good.

Once the initial fear was over, I relaxed and enjoyed myself completely as Justine gave me the finest orgasm I'd ever experienced. It rumbled up from the depths of my soul and made my whole body tremble. When Justine sat up, she winked at me and said, "Mission accomplished." We both fell back on the bed and laughed till we cried.

Justine was also fearful about this whole new sexual experience, and consequently she told me a big fib: She said she was having her period. (She admitted the truth to me months later, and I chased her around the lounge room and pinned her down as punishment.) So for an entire week I was completely and utterly spoiled with orgasm after orgasm after orgasm. Each night we didn't go to sleep until around 5 A.M. And although this whole lesbian lovemaking was certainly beautiful, we were both getting nervous about the change that would occur when Justine finished her phantom period. Justine was nervous while I thought she was an absolute lesbian professional who knew all of my secret spots, and here was I, a mere novice.

When the week was up, it was my turn to pleasure her. I was both excited and scared. I wanted it to be just right for Justine. And so, with butterflies in my stomach, I dimmed the lights and laid her down on our bed. We lay there kissing and I ran my hands down her curvaceous body. And then I went down on her in the best way I knew how. She tasted so sweet and delicious.

For the next few months we were insatiable. We did things like run out into the pouring rain barefoot to make love in the park. Once we were playing some CDs in the lounge room when Justine tore off my pants and took me till I screamed the house down. I was still gripping the empty CD case tightly in my hand when my legs finally stopped quivering.

Justine and I recently celebrated our sixth anniversary together as lovers and our ninth as friends. We are lucky in many ways: Our families have been extraordinarily accepting of our relationship, we found true love at a young age, and due to the recent lesbian relationship ruling in Australia, Justine has been granted permanent residency by the immigration department. We bought a house together in a small beachside town two hours from Melbourne and live there with our two dogs, three frogs, and a rabbit.

We love each other like crazy.

The Bride's Wedding Night
Monica S.

When I woke up early Sunday morning the day after my best friend Andrea's wedding, my limbs felt fluid, graceful, and tired. A bittersweet afterglow reminded my body of its forbidden desires. Andrea had just married her partner of four years in a very traditional wedding ceremony, and she and I had spent a brief part of her wedding night tangled together in ecstatic passion. As I recalled some of the details, I turned to my pillow and silently wept into it, careful not to wake my own lover beside me. Stirring in her sleep, she reached out a muscular arm to pull me close to her, and I forced my tears away.

"Christa, I'm sorry," I whispered, but she didn't stir. She didn't hear me, and she would never know.

When I first met Andrea in eighth grade, it was immediately apparent that we would be best friends. We both played field hockey, we were both on the swim team, and we both loved math and hated Latin. We were both slightly mischievous but never cruel. If Sister Agnes turned from her dusty chalkboard in dreaded Latin class to find all her students giggling at her, it was often because Andrea and I had managed to plaster a large sticker of a smiling frog or cat or even once a metallic guitar on the back of her habit as she passed by our desks frowning at our work. Andrea and I would chuckle with the class and obediently accept Sister's stern look and the subsequent punishment of various prayers. She and I also teased our classmates and played practical jokes on them, but it was always tasteful, never meant to truly harm. Once, an assembly was held in which our friend Barbara was slated to accept an award for perfect attendance. Along with the winners of the journalism award and the athletic award, she was granted a few minutes to speak. Andrea and I replaced the handheld mike they passed off to Barbara with a fake one so instead of hearing her inspirational ramblings, everyone heard Pink Floyd's "We Don't Need No Education" blaring through the auditorium. Andrea and I giggled in the back, holding the real mike squarely over the speaker of our tape recorder.

Andrea and I both tentatively explored our sexuality during our senior year, although not with each other, and firmly declared ourselves lesbians after our first semester in college (which we attended together in upstate New York). It is strange and bittersweet (though much more sweet than bitter) to think back now about how our beautiful, respectful, and loving friendship culminated in one night of the most incredible passion I have ever experienced. Not even, I admit shamefacedly, with my Christa have I ever been both so satisfied and yet still hungering for more erotic play, more gentle loving, more raw and unbridled sex. It was all that and more with Andrea, and neither of our partners could compare.

When Andrea and I were seniors in college, she met Jane, her future wife. The term *wife* was something we had always argued over—a wife is someone subservient, quiet, mainstream, I told her. Lesbians don't have wives—they have partners. But Andrea was starry-eyed over Jane, and Jane wanted to be a wife, so wife it was.

"It doesn't matter what she wants to be called," Andrea told me over the phone a few years after graduation, when were living on opposite coasts, separated for the first time since eighth grade.

"Will you be my maid of honor? Or partner of honor, or friend of honor, or whatever? Will you be in my wedding, Monica?"

"For you, Andi," I said, "anything. As long as you don't play Pink Floyd when I open my mouth to speak." We both laughed with the familiarity of longtime friends.

When Christa and I flew to Boston for Andrea and Jane's wedding (their "Boston marriage," Andrea's friends jokingly called it), I was nervous. I hadn't seen Andrea in a year, and I wondered if our friendship would feel different. Of course, I shouldn't have worried. She met us at Logan Airport, all long legs and sparkling reddish hair and big laugh as usual, fussing over us both and herding us to her car like a mother hen with her chicks.

"My best friend is going to be in my wedding," she said as she maneuvered through the sometimes terrifyingly narrow streets of Boston to the house she shared with Jane in Brookline. "I've imagined this since we first met in Sister Ursula's—"

"Pre-algebra class!" I finished, and Christa smiled along with us, happy to see me enjoying myself with my best friend.

The wedding ceremony went very smoothly. Andrea and Jane had a Catholic friend of theirs read the vows and bless them. Although the Catholic Church wouldn't recognize their union, they were determined not to let their faith shut them out completely. I had a hard time saying my own lines since I was crying. Christa always says I get soppy at the drop of a hat, and it's true. Seeing Andrea float down the stairs of Jane's parents' house dressed in white, looking like nothing less than an angel descending from heaven, was enough to make many jaws drop and tears to flow around the room. At least I wasn't the only one.

The most amazing night of my life began at Andrea and Jane's reception afterward at a gorgeous rented mansion in the Back Bay that catered to wedding parties. I danced all night long with Christa, with Jane, with Andrea. "Monica, can you believe it?" Andrea called out as Jane whirled her around the dance floor. Her tone was free, silvery, and utterly joyful. "I'm married!"

Around midnight, when many of the guests were three sheets

to the wind and too euphoric to notice if the bride disappeared for a minute, Andrea grabbed my hand and pulled me up from where I was taking a rest with Christa at a table.

"Girl talk," she giggled and winked at Christa, who waved her hand expansively at Andrea and helped me up.

"Have your girl talk and come back to me soon, lover," Christa said with a smile and her lips pressed to my hand for a second. I thought for the thousandth time how much I loved her and how lucky I was to have her before Andrea dragged me away.

"Where to, Miss?" I asked in my best chauffeur impersonation.

"The Star Room. It's in tower up there somewhere." She giggled and pointed to the oak-paneled ceiling.

"Star-gazing on your wedding night? Shouldn't you do that with Jane?" I helped Andrea find the stairs as we ascended up and up through the century-old house.

"I have the rest of my life to share with Jane," Andrea said as she stopped still, looking at me. Her voice was suddenly very clear. "You are going star-gazing with me now."

"Sure," I said, and I began to wonder how serious this "girl talk" was going to be.

Once we found the Star Room, which was indeed in a tower and windowed on all four sides to afford an amazing view of the city, Andrea abruptly sat down on a cushioned bench and pulled me down with her.

"Hey!" I cried as I lost my balance and fell on her lap.

"Hey, yourself, best friend," she whispered, and then she kissed me. It was not a little, friendly peck on the cheek or a dry lip-to-lip kiss. This was a real, heart-thumping, tingle-inducing, full-tongue kiss, and it caught me so off-guard I could only instinctively respond to it.

Andrea's hands touched my back, slowly at first, then firmly. She stroked my skin, my neck, tangled her fingers in my loose hair, nibbled her way to my ear, groaning my name with each breath.

I finally managed to pull back a bit and hold her arms still for a moment. "Andi, what are you doing?" I said. "Your wife is down-stairs, and I know you don't have permission to do this." My voice was trembling. Jane and Andrea didn't have an open relationship, and this was not typical Andrea behavior. I had never cheated on Christa and had never planned to. I was shocked—but suddenly very aroused. This was Andrea, this was forbidden, and this was breathlessly exciting.

"You're my best friend," Andrea smiled. "I trust you more than anyone in the world, Monica. I've always wanted to know what it would be like with you—and I'll never get another chance or feel able to do this." Her coppery hair flowed around her flushed face. "This one night, and never again."

"But it's your wedding night."

"Yes," she said simply, looking at me with almost feverish smoky green eyes. "That's why it has to be tonight. Right now, and then we go back down there and never tell a soul. I love you, Monica, I do. You're my best friend forever and ever, and just once I want to make you come, make you scream my name, make you thrash around beneath my tongue. I've dreamed about it. Please." She leaned forward to kiss my suddenly pliable lips.

Andrea's words turned my limbs weak and shivery, made a hot spot leap between my legs with a savage desire that took my breath away. Had I always wanted her over the years and simply told myself no because she was my best friend, and friends could not, should not, be lovers? Had I squelched my need for her because of Jane, because of my beloved Christa, because of a thousand reasons that were too late to change? Or was this really a surprise, an unexpected sexy secret in our relationship?

It was getting hard to think.

Just this one night, I told myself, *there are no rules*. And I kissed my married best friend on the lips.

Andrea groaned again when I plunged my tongue deep into her mouth and lightly slid it across her lips. She tasted like cham-pagne. I felt dizzy, and I swayed in her grasp.

"Lie back," she ordered, and her eyes were dark with a need

that made me breathless. I obeyed, and the bride knelt on top of me, the small circlet of flowers and ribbons on her brow pushed back, her white wedding dress spread over. It felt naughty and yet natural—and so very good.

I barely recall how my dress got pushed up over my knees, silk slippery on my thighs, above my arching hips. I don't remember Andrea pulling down my underwear, satiny soft against my skin. What I do remember is her lips, hot and wet and questing over my body, licking and sucking and kissing every inch of skin from my calves up to my thighs then between my legs, tongue flickering, seeking and finding my clitoris, drawing a long gasp out of me as she settled down to work. She knew my body like it was her own, as if she and I did this every night, as if she and I knew each other better than anyone else in the world. My fingers clenched her hair as I came, and I screamed her name as I thrashed in gloriously suspended ecstasy beneath the relentless expert attention of her tongue. Never in my life had anyone been able to coax such an ardent response from me. I lay still until I recovered enough to turn my attention to my friend, who was gazing at me with eyes dark with desire.

Andrea let me brush her nipples with gentle fingers, let me nibble her neck, let me push up her dress, allowed my tongue to freely roam over her shaking, beautiful body. She called out my name, first in a low voice, then in a steadily rising pitch, a chant that rose and soared and finally burst out above the lights of Boston. I licked her until she was quiet, until she pulled me up to her chest and held me for a long time, stroking my hair, saying nothing.

We straightened up our clothes and hair and went back to the party without another word. We didn't have to speak, although we did hold hands all the way down until we entered the reception area again and separated—Andrea going over to her new wife while I headed for Christa.

Andrea and I never spoke of that part of her wedding night again. We're still the closest of friends, and we're still each with our respective mates. Do I feel guilty sometimes? Of course I do. I am Catholic after all. Do I still want Andrea sometimes? Do I fantasize about her? Of course. Do I regret that brief night I shared with my best friend? Never. I cherish it, and it has made us even closer. It's a secret that binds us, and one I plan to take to my grave.

One Purple Kiss
Jules Torti

The story begins with one purple kiss…

I stood naked, despite being fully clothed. My heart pounded like a team of wild horses racing across the savanna. My palms were clammy, my armpits sweaty, and my tongue felt fat and swollen. Words seemed unfathomable right then. My knees buckled with my skyrocketing estrogen level. Wow. She had the most beautiful eyes.

She was the one; I knew this instantly. It was like the first time I saw the Grand Canyon—that incredible overwhelming feeling of awe. That's how I felt with her. Between us it was spontaneous combustion. We had known each other for years, and then one day, *blammo!* It happened—as if we had sipped a secret love potion and fell, mesmerized, into a lovers' trance. Our hearts consumed by an innocent kiss. One purple kiss…

Kate and I hadn't seen each other for months and decided to meet at an AIDS roller-blading fund-raiser in town. Upon greeting each other, we embraced and she kissed me, leaving a little purple smudge on my cheek. Something had definitely changed between us. We roller-bladed for hours, oblivious to the distance we covered. I felt her eyes undress me and mine undress her. We finished the course breathless…from anticipation?

"Let's get some wings and beer," Kate suggested.

We headed for the Sub Tub. The place was a dive, a very red-neck bar. It smelled like stale cigarette smoke, fried onions, and Old Spice—but it served great barbecue wings. The crowd was predictable: a bunch of drunken Sub Tub baseball players stuffed into too-small uniforms that constricted their chubby beer- and french fry–enhanced stomachs. Sitting across from Kate, I sipped my beer, distracted, almost unaware that anyone else was in the bar. Her smile was perfect.

Poking pieces of celery and carrot into a plastic container of blue cheese dip, we carefully avoided eye contact. I guess I've failed to mention that Kate's partner, Jan, had come along with us and was sitting on the stool beside her. Was our attraction to each other noticeable? I smiled shyly when our carrots accidentally bumped together in the dip. What we were both feeling was undeniable. This wasn't supposed to happen. We were old friends, and Kate had a lover. Regardless, I felt myself leaping into the canyon headfirst. No inhibitions. I kept trying to reassure myself that these emotions were innocent.

While crunching on a celery stick, Kate excitedly talked about the upcoming Mudcat Festival in her hometown of Dunnville. "Mudcats are catfish," she explained. "Dunnville celebrates in good fashion with a fishing derby, a fish fry, fireworks, and a dance at the local fire hall. Do you have any plans next weekend?" Her beautiful eyes rested on me.

I was scheduled to work, but my vulva was screaming, *No! You don't have any plans!* So I calmly replied, "No, I don't have any plans."

Kate and I had partied before without Jan around, and that's what we planned to do at the Mudcat Festival. Jan was vaca-tioning up north that weekend at a colleague's cottage, and he wasn't at all suspicious of Kate's motives in inviting me to the festival. I wasn't suspicious either, yet a part of me, the part div-ing headlong into the canyon, knew what I wanted to happen. On Saturday night Kate was having a barbecue with a bunch of her baseball friends, but what about Friday night? Kate was listening to her vulva as well.

I cycled to Dunnville Friday afternoon with no intention or expectation of sleeping with Kate. Yeah, I would jump at the chance—but realistically, I never thought I'd have the opportunity. Kate and Jan had been together 13 years. I pedaled up Kate's driveway, sweaty and exhausted. She was relaxing on the back deck, awaiting my arrival. I accepted a cold beverage from her and joined her on the lounge, sinking my tired body into its comfort before taking a shower.

After my shower, when I reappeared from the bathroom, I was surprised to find the dining table set for a candlelit dinner. Kate smiled from the kitchen as she stirred the bubbling pasta sauce. Uh-oh. I was seduced already. All she had to do was smile. An open bottle of red zinfandel sat on the counter, and I eagerly poured two glasses. We made a toast to the Mudcat Festival, and enjoyed the eye contact we'd tried to hide at the Sub Tub.

During dinner, before my first mouthful of gnocchi, I felt a warm hand gingerly touch my inner thigh. I took a deep breath, resisting the urge to touch her all over. The Grand Canyon feeling returned. Was I standing a little too close to the edge? I knew the risk...I knew the danger. But still, I wanted to jump.

My body responded to her touch. Endorphins coursed through my veins, my heart pumped hard, my breath grew fast and shallow. I hardly remember eating; my body was just going through the motions. I had left my inhibitions somewhere. Somewhere far from here. Jan was nonexistent.

We left the table and moved into the living room. Blond hair, blue eyes, golden skin. Reminding myself to breathe, I sat at the opposite end of the couch. Muscular legs, strong arms, firm breasts. She gave me a come-closer look. Suddenly the cat had my tongue. I had butterflies in my stomach. A frog in my throat. And the cow jumped over the moon. I watched as she slid surreptitiously in my direction.

One Purple Kiss

We kissed tentatively. Soft, gentle, tender. Then uncontrollably. Her passionate kisses transformed me into a blabbering fool. I was captivated, conquered. She smiled and caressed my cheek. We had fallen in love over chicken wings and blue cheese dip, consumed by the innocence of one purple kiss.

And so the story continues…

The One That Got Away
Karen T. Taylor

I didn't meet my first real lesbian until 1988, three years after I graduated from college. That might sound bizarre, but you have to understand my definition of "real lesbian." I mean a woman who openly expressed her sexual interest in another woman. As in "Look at her legs—she's really hot!" which is what my best friend Sharrin had said about a woman walking past us when we were having lunch outside on a busy street in Seattle's gay neighborhood.

Sharrin and I had been friends for almost a year. I hadn't had a best girl friend since fifth grade, and I delighted in every moment I spent with her. We talked for hours when we were together, then we would get on the phone and talk some more. She talked to me about wanting a girlfriend, and I talked to her about wanting to dump my boyfriend. I helped her study for her graduate degree, and she encouraged me in my own studies. We went everywhere together and talked about love, religion, feminism, homophobia, and anything else that intersected our lives. I loved her dearly.

And now I felt ready to launch my own lesbian life. At that point I had been living in Seattle for three years. I had just dumped my boyfriend and was working for a lesbian and gay organization. My lesbian boss, however, wouldn't even kiss her lover in front of me. The only lesbians I knew were earnest, jeans-wearing, ultrasincere women who were willing to process at the drop of a hat. I had no idea what they did in bed together, because while I knew they hugged each other a lot, I never saw them actually kiss or touch intimately. My only visual idea of what lesbians did together came from cheesy straight-oriented magazines filled with photos of blond, Waspy, thin women with wickedly long red fingernails. I was a short, plump, brunette who bit her nails. Sharrin was shorter and rounder than me, Jewish, and had red frizzy hair. Hearing her openly express an interest in other women delighted me.

"So, you really find women hot?" I asked her one day, knowing immediately from her rolling eyes and accompanying snort that I had asked a stupid question. "Look," I explained, "in college the only lesbians I knew were busy talking about politics, not sex. I never knew if they actually had sex."

Sharrin grinned, then laughed out loud. "Well, I've been having sex with women since high school," she said, a glint in her eye. "And I really, really like it."

Was she flirting with me? I certainly hoped so. I'd been interested in having sex with women ever since I'd cochaired the lesbian and gay alliance on my college campus (another long story), but I never knew how to approach the lesbians in the alliance. They seemed deeply offended by my enjoyment of sex with men. At the time I couldn't really articulate that my enjoyment was with sex, not necessarily with the particular gender of the person. And then, of course, that admission would put me into the dangerous bisexual category, which turned off even more lesbians. But Sharrin never seemed bothered by it. Of course, that might be because I had never let her know how attractive I found her. After all of that internal debate, I decided to take the plunge.

"I'd like to find out what it's like," I told her. "I mean, with someone who really likes to have sex. How do women like me find out?" I hoped she'd pick up the hint.

"Well, I'm wary of straight girls who want to experiment," Sharrin said. "I've been hurt in the past. I know lots of other lesbians who feel the same way. So it can be hard for women like you."

Well, that's not fair, I thought. For me, having sex with men was more a convenience than an orientation. I did have the good sense not to say that out loud, knowing it would only create further misunderstanding and hurt.

"I'm not interested in experimenting," I said. "It's more like my launching a new chapter in my life. The chapter where I finally find out what I'm supposed to be."

Sharrin didn't answer then. She just smiled and drank her iced tea. I wasn't sure whether she got the hint. And while I wasn't shy about a lot of things, I was definitely shy asking Sharrin about sex. It's hard to imagine now, 10 years later, living happily in a committed relationship with another woman, why talking to Sharrin about lesbian sex was so difficult. The reality was I knew men and women had very different ideas about sex. I knew straight men were pretty easy: It was all about penetration. But with women? Well, touching, kissing, penetrating, sucking, licking, fingering—all of these were possibilities. I just didn't know how to approach the subject. It wasn't just the generic "How do lesbians have sex?" question, it was the "How does Sharrin want to have sex with me?" question. It might also mean answering the reciprocal question too. And I had never had to ask those questions before. I wasn't sure how to begin without sounding ignorant or silly or offensive.

I finally got up the courage to ask Sharrin out. On a real date. Dressing up and everything. I remember being so excited about it: I called my mother to tell her I was dating a woman. She took it surprisingly well. When Sharrin drove up, I felt like I was back in high school on my first date. And when she came to the door, I was blown away.

Sharrin is a curvy woman, and she wore a beautiful black dress that plunged at the neck. I could tell immediately that she was wearing a corset underneath because her cleavage was more pronounced and the dress swayed very provocatively from her hips. In heels, she was my height. I had butched myself up à la Radclyffe Hall, with a scarlet-lined Chinese smoking jacket and black satin pants. I smelled Sharrin's perfume, and my nipples tingled.

We went to a French restaurant richly overdecorated in red and gold. Discretely gay. It was all terribly romantic. We drank wine and ate expensive food, then returned to her place. We retired to the couch and began to kiss each other. The smoking jacket was discarded, corset unlaced, and soft silky lingerie brushed erotically across ours faces, hands, and breasts. It was everything I'd hoped it would be.

Up to that point.

Because, well, we never went any further that night. Somehow, just like in high school, we got stuck in that kissing and fondling stage. From the waist up only. This is not to imply that we weren't having a good time—we certainly were. But somehow the next critical move, the one that would have taken us into the bedroom, never happened.

I wasn't really disappointed. As far as I knew, this was probably the way real lesbians acted on their first date, saving the sex for later. It seemed very old-fashioned, even romantic. But I hadn't dated in a long time—I just had sex a lot. So when I called Sharrin a day later, I confessed that I wasn't certain how to proceed with her.

"Considering your extensive experience with men," Sharrin chuckled, "you shouldn't act so unsure. We're not that different. Think of the things you like and how *your* partners know. Believe me, you'll know when you're doing something I like."

I didn't know how to tell her that this well-meaning advice wasn't very helpful. I'd never had a male partner who asked me what I liked, and I had never really thought about it. If I didn't have an orgasm during sex, I waited until the guy went home or went to sleep and quietly jerked off. If someone asked me what kind of sex I enjoyed, I would have stared at them blankly, or maybe thrown out a flippant remark like "lots of it."

But I wasn't worried. Sooner or later we'd get to the sex part, and I was certain that Sharrin, the experienced lesbian, would take the lead and teach me what to do.

We got together a few days later, this time for a more informal video and popcorn night. No dressing up—although I do remember Sharrin wearing a very sheer blouse and my own shirt plunging rather dramatically. We giggled, cuddled, and kissed, and while we giggled, cuddled, and kissed, we got each other's shirts and bras off. The giggles segued into sighs and even into moans. I was bolder on this date, cupping Sharrin's small breasts in my hands, brushing my thumbs across her nipples, kissing her deeply and passionately. Then she was kissing and sucking my nipples, her hair tickling my stomach, which made my whole body arch from the need to come. We grew hungrier, and I even dared to run my hand down to rest on her beautiful round ass. I hoped this gesture would lead her to understand that I was ready to be taken under her wing and introduced to the joys of lesbian sex.

A few hours later we untangled ourselves, still dressed from the waist down, and I stumbled home. Obviously, something wasn't going right. So the next day I called her to find out why.

"I don't know," she sighed, sounding as exasperated as I was. "Couldn't you tell I was ready? All you had to do was just take my hand and walk me to the bedroom. You're the top, after all."

(This outburst calls for a brief aside: In addition to our other mutual interests, Sharrin and I were exploring other forms of sexual identity and visiting the local S/M discussion group together to bolster each other's courage. Back then, Sharrin considered herself more submissive, and while I enjoyed my masochistic tendencies, I was clearly a more dominant personality.)

"But—" I stopped. I wasn't sure how to admit that I was hoping *she* would take the lead and take me into the bedroom. If I told her that it might make me sound like I was reluctant and bring back that whole "straight girl just experimenting" image. This lesbian sex thing was more complicated than I thought. I decided to take the more indirect route. "Sharrin, I love you, I want to be with you, and I want this to work between us," I told her.

"So do I," she confessed. And we had another of our long discussions about sex and love.

A week or so later, Sharrin called me. "I think I have a solution to our…problem," she said. "It's Lynda." As she described her plan, I laughed. It could work.

Lynda was one of the better-known tops in the Seattle leather dyke community. She was also an active member in the local S/M group, often called upon to lead workshops on flogging, waxing, and other S/M activities, and always showed up with a beautiful femme on the back of her motorcycle in the annual Pride parade. If she couldn't help us, no one could.

I went to Sharrin's house on the appointed day, decked out in black and whatever leather I owned at the time, carrying the only S/M implement I had—a riding crop. I arrived just as a large, loud motorcycle pulled up. Lynda looked like a leather-clad Wonder Woman in her tight chaps and big boots. Her chestnut hair was wavy and shoulder length, softening her face and drawing attention to her predatory smile. Lynda favored black and red, with flame designs licking across her leather jacket and bike. Rather than a golden lasso at her belt, Lynda was wearing matching black and red floggers on each hip. I was immediately intimidated but perked up when she wrapped a friendly arm around my shoulder and said, "Well, let's see if we can jump-start this little thing you and Sharrin have going, shall we?"

We went into Sharrin's house, and I saw she was wearing black as well, but something sheer and easy to pull off. Lynda wasted no time in ordering Sharrin to undress down to her black lace panties and to bend over a footstool. Lynda ran her nails across Sharrin's back, and I watched as my best friend shivered and moaned. Then I caught Lynda looking at me, and at her nod, I joined in as well, scratching lightly, then more harshly across Sharrin's back and shoulders. She moaned as I reached up to wrap my fingers through her hair. Incredibly turned on, I tugged her head back. Sharrin twitched her butt, and Lynda spanked it lightly at first, then harder. I tugged at Sharrin's hair again, then jerked her head back to kiss her. "I'm going to beat you," I murmured, and she hissed through her teeth and grinned at me.

Lynda graciously offered me one of her matching floggers, and together we began to work on Sharrin. I draped the tresses of the flogger seductively over her shoulders and across her back, then pulled back and smacked her briskly, finally moving into a steady rhythm. I knew from our many nighttime talks that Sharrin enjoyed being flogged. And I was quickly discovering how intensely satisfying and horny a good whipping could make me, and I was certain I could make Sharrin feel that way too. Lynda had been alternating strokes with me, catching Sharrin more and more frequently on her ample buttocks, raising little pink welts with the tips of her flogger's tail. All three of us were sweaty and horny, and the ripe smell of arousal was filling the room and increasing our drive. Lynda placed one of her boot-clad feet across Sharrin's ass to keep her still as I reached under her to pinch and twist her nipples. I kissed her hard, and she responded hungrily, pushing her tongue into my mouth.

Lynda removed her boot from Sharrin's ass. "I think you two know where to go from here," she grinned, picking up her floggers and leather coat. We barely noticed the motorcycle starting up as our Lynda drove off into the sunset.

I pulled Sharrin up by her hair, kicked the footstool away, and lay her down on the floor. I pressed myself down on her, twisting her pebble-hard nipples to make her moan and beg, my knee pressed hard between her legs, tongue deep in her mouth. Sharrin arched her back, her hands clawing at me, moaning and making pleading noises.

You can guess what happened next. Or, maybe you can't.

There we were, Sharrin and I, sweaty, horny, just steps away from her bedroom, and once again we never made it in. Who would take the lead? Me, the dominant partner in this hot kinky scene? Or Sharrin, the pro who knew what good lesbian sex would entail? The scene quickly deteriorated. Our passionate embrace became another warm hug, our kisses less urgent, and digging nails turned to light back scratches. Finally, pleading a full bladder, I got off the floor and headed to the bathroom, where I cursed myself in the mirror and splashed water on my face. When I returned to the living room, Sharrin was gone.

"Sharrin?" I called out. There was no answer, but I heard a rustle in the bedroom. I felt awful—she had probably burst into tears and left the room. And it was all my fault! I tiptoed to the door and knocked lightly. "Come in," she answered, and I found her in the bed under a pile of quilts, her eyes slightly closed.

"Sharrin, I'm sorry," I said, certain she had been crying and wanted me to leave. "I know I act like a top, but really I have no idea how to have sex with a woman. I keep waiting for you to make the first move. I know that's unfair. I know it's a mixed message. I know it's just like those nightmares about getting it on with a straight woman who then runs back to men, but that's not what I'm going to do. I'm just scared that I don't know what to do with a woman and I was hoping Lynda would show me, but then she left and I just really wanted you to just take over and show me..." Tears welled up in my eyes. When Sharrin didn't respond, I was certain our friendship was over. "I don't know how to make this work," I admitted, my voice small and shaky. I stood there, waiting for her to burst into tears or yell at me.

Instead she closed her eyes tightly, shook her head, then sighed deeply, opened her eyes, and grinned. "Me neither, but this time I decided not to go to sleep frustrated," she said, pulling her Hitachi Magic Wand out from under the covers. "Damn, I feel much better now." She leaned back against the pillows, patting the covers next to her as an invitation. I sat down and looked at her. Then we both burst out laughing. We knew then that while the sex might never happen, the friendship would last forever.

Missing Alice

Beth Greenwood

When, exactly, did I first meet Alice? I used to think she'd always been there, somewhere in my life—even places she never could have been, like cheering me on from the wings of a kindergarten play. Alice was like that. Once her orbit intersected yours she was somehow always in view.

Until she was gone. Then there was a hole, a gap, where she'd been. A big hole, because that was Alice. Not that she was a big girl (even though she sort of was), but because Alice never did anything simple or small.

Everyone I know has a story about Alice. We used to trade them. Alice and the drive-in: She'd rented a huge old projector, found a vacant lot somewhere, and for a night projected cheesy old movies onto the side of the office building next door. Alice and the morning high tea: Yes, the invitations said 9 A.M. for English tea, so we all climbed into tea dresses and scarves and trucked down to her place to have high tea, because at that instant it was 4 P.M. in Great Britain. Alice and the ski trip: Thermometers were boiling all over town; it was too hot to do anything but groan about how hot it was; and suddenly there was Alice, her station wagon crammed with skis and snow gear. We never found any snow, of course, but it was cooler up in the hills, and that was good enough for us. Alice and the baby party: Can a gaggle of butches and femmes have a grand old time playing Pin the Tail, Twister, Candyland, and Mousetrap? Do you really have to ask? Alice and the boating party: The nearest water was a half-empty reservoir, but that didn't stop her. Where she got the boat and trailer was anyone's guess, but she did, so we had grilled fish and a lovely white wine, all of us packed into that little rolling dingy. The party ended very late with the singing of bawdy sea shanties, and the cops showing up to tell us to stop. Alice and the strippers: When she heard that a few of us had never seen another girl take her clothes off to music, she hired a troupe of women to do just that—turning her little house into a nightclub for the night. She even had a sign made up for the evening. A friend kept it, proudly displaying PUSSYCAT PLAYGROUND in her living room.

There was something special about Alice, and not just her mischievous sense of fun. Other people, other girls would have done those things, and it would have been forced: theme-party screams for attention. But Alice didn't wear herself that loud. You knew she was enjoying herself—that was obvious—but it was a cry of fun and never for approval.

Alice was a big girl, as if a tiny little body couldn't contain her internal chemistry. In my past there were other big girls. Some of them smiled, some of them laughed, but there was always a desire to have their bigness vanish, if just for a little while, so they could be just like the other girls.

Not Alice. Alice was big in all kinds of ways. It suited her. In general, I wasn't attracted to big girls. That is, not until Alice. All the other ones? Underpants like a doll's. Tiny sports bras on the floor in the morning, sex like a workout. One of them actually said, "As good as 20 reps on the hip abductor," when we finished having sex. They were nice; I had no complaints, but afterward we'd end up staring across the bed or dining table at each other. One of them talked about an ex-girlfriend for two hours; another about her mother for three. I thought seriously about going celibate for a while, if just to save myself from awful postsex chatter.

For a long time I only saw Alice at weird little events or when I was taken to her parties. Then I started to get postcards in the mail: dates, times, orders (or requests). She made them by hand, all paint and glitter. It must have taken her days of work for one little bash, but that was Alice. Nothing cheap and easy or small. Getting that first invitation was a step, one I was surprisingly proud of. My first Alice party was something Roman and uproarious, a heckle fest to *Caligula*: a dozen sheet-draped dykes and a cheesy big-budget porno film. I don't remember many details, just laughter from the living room as Alice and I sat in the kitchen, drinking red wine and talking.

We talked a lot after that. Alice would show up at all kinds of times just to chat or to haul me off to some little café, bookstore, toyshop, or party. One time we had a breakfast of pancakes and cheap coffee at a little diner, then spent the day at a gun and doll show. Another time it was fresh picked blueberries and cream and a day at the museum. Once she left a 15-minute message on my answering machine, reading me a "delicious" part of a book she was reading.

She could have driven me nuts, of course, and after she woke me up at 3 A.M. just to say how pretty the moon was looking right then, I really started to worry that she would. But Alice was saved by being Alice. She knew when she had pushed too much, had crossed the line from wonderful eccentric to pain in the ass.

I became fascinated with Alice. I've always been reserved, skeptical and serious, cautious and methodical. I don't think I was boring, but I was hardly the kind to have a rooftop party where the main event was dropping watermelons onto a bed sheet target—with smashed melon daiquiris after. Even my relationships were carefully thought out, dating laid out with all the passion of a military campaign; and when they ended I even planned out a careful step-by-step series of moves to recover my crushed self-esteem.

Alice was everything I wasn't. For example, I remember one summer—the Godly Summer, us Alice-watchers called it—when she tried on one religion after another, going from Born Again to New Age in the span of a few months, trying out the lives they recommended. In the end she finally ended up giving away all of her books, Bibles, candles, and crystals in a Holy Garage Sale, proclaiming that if there were a god or a goddess one thing was certain: He or she was really confused. By contrast I always treated religion as something sacred, and I was always being bushwhacked by one zealot or another, too respectful to tell them to go to their respective hells.

Some of the Alice watchers confessed to me that they were waiting for the crash and burn. I looked in their eyes and saw a kind of anger at her, that she could take big bites while they choked on nibbles. These were hangers-on who were just sitting in the stands waiting for the crash.

I wasn't one of them because I knew Alice had a large heart to match her appetites. I found out firsthand when I was spectacularly dumped. Her name was Ellie and she was a fitness trainer at my local club. She seemed to offer more than anyone else I'd dated. Right in the middle of our first few weeks of love and lust she started talking about picking out china, buying a cat, and moving in—and then she abruptly left. I ran into her a month or so later at a street fair, with a lithe little femme on her arm. With a cold sneer she told me she hadn't ever been serious about the two of us, that it was all a game to get her "real" girlfriend jealous. Laughing, they'd faded back into the crowd.

Some of my friends called, offering their support. One took me out to dinner, but all I could do was play with my food and sniffle. Alice rang my doorbell, grabbed me by the arm, and hauled me out to her station wagon, the one covered with crazy daisies and outrageous bumper stickers. She took me way into the hills, barely saying a word. Finally, we ended up at the foot of a deserted hillside. Silently she got a big stuffed animal from the mountain of stuff in the back of the car and ran up the hill, balancing it against an old burnt log. Also from the back of the car came a battered leather case. In the case was an antique shotgun. Her father's, she said.

I'd never fired a gun before and probably won't again. But that day, it seemed like the thing to do. The rest of the day we shot at that poor big purple cat, until the hillside was dotted with wisps of cotton stuffing and purple fur. When she dropped me off she kissed me on the cheek, just once.

It was about that time that I realized I really loved her. She was probably the best friend I'd ever had. Then she vanished.

Alice was mercurial, so it took quite a while for us to realize she hadn't just gone to Burning Man, or New York City, or taken a leisurely drive through the Southwest. Some Alice watchers guessed that she'd followed something shiny out onto the road and would return when the sheen wore off. Others just shrugged off her absence, claiming it was "an Alice thing to do," to just pack up and disappear.

Without Alice the world was dull, monotonous, predictable. Some Alice watchers tried to re-create her parties and flare, but their efforts were clumsy and forced.

Her little apartment was empty. The manager didn't know where she'd gone. Her mail, mostly catalogs and a few scattered bills, was piling up. Rather than just have him throw them out, I took them, promising to give them to her when I saw her. The bundle of cellophane windows and brightly colored catalog covers sat by my phone for a week, like a promise that she'd come back and get them.

After a month, even the envious Alice watchers started to grow quiet. One of them, a baby dyke named Jackie, whispered to me one breakfast as the other girls were laughing and clapping over some catty joke, "I hope she's OK." Her soft brown eyes said that she too felt the big hole Alice had left in our lives.

I put ads in the local queer papers. I didn't expect a response, but it was better than doing nothing. I tried to find some relatives, thinking maybe someone had gotten sick, had an accident or something, but her last name turned up zilch. I thought about calling the police, but a cop friend said they wouldn't do anything unless there was proof of foul play—which there wasn't. I filed a missing persons report anyway.

Some nights it got very bad. I'd come home to my neat little apartment and stare out the window. Laughter made me think of her. Color made me think of her. I wanted to talk to someone, anyone, about how much I missed my friend Alice, and then got even more depressed when I realized the only person who'd understand *was* Alice. I tried to talk to the other Alice watchers about how much she meant to me, how much I missed her, but all they did was pat my hand and say how much they missed her too—but obviously not as much or as deeply.

One month became two, then three. I kept asking people about her, running my ads, and even going as far as putting up posters in a couple of bookstores. Nothing as extreme as MISS-ING, just in case she really had just gone off on some kind of wild "Alice quest." The posters had a photocopied picture and said MISS YOU, the bottom edge lined with tear-off tabs with my phone number.

I knew it was bad when a few of the old circle took me out to dinner to ask me to just "let her go." It was the first time I'd ever had an intervention for missing a friend.

That night I looked back on the times we'd had together. I remembered her smile, the way she jumped up and down when she laughed. Her various hair colors and styles. Her Western phase, her punk phase, her dyke phase. I remembered one particular New Year's kiss. I remembered how she'd rubbed suntan oil on my back.

I suddenly realized how stupid I'd been. She'd wanted more between the two of us. Maybe she'd gone because I hadn't taken that extra step; I'd been blinded by our friendship, blind to the lover she wanted to be.

But worse was that when I looked back on all those times together, I realized I'd been frightened of stepping outside of my usual box. Alice was more than what I needed in a friend—she was what I wanted in a lover.

And she was still gone. The ache got even worse: Now it felt like I was missing my girlfriend.

Luck was something Alice believed in. Sometimes, when she had the choice between two things, she'd flip a coin or roll some dice, happy to let fate pick a place to eat, a place to go, or who to follow out the door. I didn't believe in it myself. It was just averages, another law like gravity or inertia. Luck didn't know what was best, didn't work it's magic to lead you down the best path.

Maybe. But that doesn't explain why, as I sat there in my dark apartment, tears running down my cheeks, missing Alice so bad it was a deep ache in my chest, Alice chose *that one instant* to pick up the phone and call me.

She came over. I tried not to appear too eager but couldn't pull it off. When she drove up—her station wagon packed full of all kinds of strange stuff—I was intently peering out the windows like a nosy neighbor. She bounded out of the car and up the steps, almost running.

My heart was pounding in my chest. I wanted to kiss her, scream at her, "Where the hell have you been?" then throw her onto the bed and have a fast, desperate fuck. I wanted to cry for missing her so much. She beat me to all of them. When I opened the door she kissed me quick and hard on the lips and said, "I'm so sorry."

"That's OK," I stupidly said, when it was hardly that. "We were worried about you."

"Liar!" she said, tapping me on the nose as she scooted by, stepping quickly into my living room.

"Seriously, Al—we were worried sick. What happened?"

"Nothing," she said, standing with her back to me, looking out the window. "Nothing at all. I just hit the road for a few weeks to see who'd miss me." She turned around, smiling.

I wanted to say, "You bitch!" and slap her across the face, but I didn't. "Alice—" I started to say, my anger making my chest tight.

"I really am sorry," she said, sitting down on my leather sofa, looking small, lost, and alone. "Really. I was just so alone—and no one seemed to care. I needed to just…I don't know, get the fuck out of Dodge or something. That wasn't the worst, though."

There was something in the way she sat there, the way she seemed—smaller, as if she'd been diminished by her time away. My anger faded, making me dizzy. I walked over and sat next to her.

She put her head on my shoulder and spoke softly, almost in a whisper. "I didn't miss anyone," she said. "I could have just drove and drove and drove till my wheels fell off. Once I got out of town I didn't want to turn around. I didn't need to. There wasn't anything here that made me want to come back. I was scared."

My face grew hot, emotions mixing. It all got caught in my throat. I said, "That's OK," again and instantly regretted it.

"No, it's not," she said, pulling away from my shoulder. Her face was wet with tears.

I'd known Alice for…how long had I know Alice? Forever and a few days? I'd never seen her cry. I couldn't say anything. Instead I did something I've never done before—I did an Alice, something spontaneous and quick, something not thought but felt. I kissed her. I kissed Alice.

It was a short kiss, but it was a good kiss. I felt myself melt, just a little, and she did too. She broke it, smiled, and tapped her own nose. "Liar," she called herself, softly. "I came back."

"I hoped you would," I said, again without thinking. It felt good.

"I made sure everyone had a good time," she said, looking down at her large soft hands. "But no one did the same for me. I was everyone's good time, but not in a way that mattered. They loved me, darlin'," she said, "but they didn't *love* me, did they?" Her shoulders sagged as she took a deep, ragged breath.

I wanted to say a lot of things, but more than anything I want-ed to kiss her again. My thoughts were wild, banging around in my skull. I took my own deep breath and said the first thing that came to mind: "But you came back."

"No," she said, turning her head to look hard into my eyes. "I came back to you. I missed you."

Now Alice has been here a long time. So long it makes me feel like she's always been here. It's no longer my place, her stuff or my stuff—it's all just ours. We picked out the cat together, a butch little tabby that likes to attack our shoelaces when we get dressed in the morning. Last month we picked out china together, the month before that we bought a nice, sane, sensible sofa.

It's good. It's very good. The best it's ever been with anyone. I wake up in the morning next to her, her warm, soft body making me smile—even today. We go to movies every now and then. We go out to dinner occasionally. We have a nice little life together, full of slow days and good loving.

But sometimes I sit in our living room, where we watch sitcoms and laugh along with them, and I miss Alice, the wild Alice who left and never came back.

Truth or Dare
Lee Ann McCann

I was 20 when I met Susan during my sophomore year of college.
She was a friend of a friend, and until I'd met her I'd never once
considered having a relationship with a woman. In fact, I was dating a man at the time. We were introduced on the sidewalk outside one of the college dorms. I'll never forget her beautiful dark
eyes, noticeable even under her hazy purple sunglasses. She had
beautiful olive skin and luxurious mounds of shiny sable curls.

Her curvaceous frame reminded me of those great baroque
paintings you see hanging in museums—paintings from a time
when women could have flesh on their bones and still be considered beautiful. How easily she could have stepped out from one
of those paintings, poised and confident. She wore a pair of old
sweatpants and a T-shirt cut at the waist. I think I fell in love with
her at that very moment. It would take months, however, for me
to find the strength and opportunity to tell her how I felt.

That opportunity finally came on a Saturday night at a house-
warming party Susan was hosting. Having spent her first year of
college living in a dorm full of 18- and 19-year-olds when she herself was a nontraditional student of 32, she was delighted to be in
a place of her own now. The night was filled with good friends,
good food, and good wine.

Susan was a talented artist, and her work lined the walls and shelves of her two-room apartment. I made it a point to always express my appreciation for her talent, not only because I loved her paintings but also because I loved how my comments brought a radiant smile to her face.

By midnight, only a group of us, the Five Musketeers, remained. People called us that because we were always the last five people left at any party. It all started innocently enough when my friend Christine wanted to play Truth or Dare. Since she had come out a few months earlier, it had suddenly become her favorite game. The truth questions started out fairly harmlessly: Who was your first true love? Have you ever committed a felony? When did you lose your virginity? So when it was my turn, I said, "Truth."

"Have you ever had a sexual fantasy about a woman?" Christine asked me.

Her question hit me like a slap across my face. The four other Musketeers were cheering. Why hadn't I said "dare"? I couldn't speak—all I could do was look at Susan.

"Well, come on, have you?"

I knew everyone expected me to say no. I was Miss Innocent. I mean, I had just lost my virginity to a man less than six months before. Still, the answer came out of my mouth before I could think of its implications or the questions that might follow.

"Yes," I told her.

"Doesn't surprise me," Christine calmly replied, but I knew I was in trouble when that evil grin spread across her face. "So who have you been fantasizing about?"

Part of me wanted to shout out Susan's name, but a bigger part of me wanted to make up a name so I wouldn't have to face the possible look of horror on Susan's face. I knew Susan had experimented in the '80s with women, but that didn't mean she wanted to do it again.

Christine was relentless. "So who is she?"

"Someone I know."

"Really!" Now Christine looked surprised. "So, you've been fantasizing about one of your friends. Do we know her?"

"Yes."

Again a surprised look from the group.

"Who is it?"

"Susan." Had I really said that? Did that just come out of my mouth?

All I could do was look at Susan, as the others erupted into applause and laughter. Susan was blushing and smiling. That was good—a sign that she wasn't repulsed by my confession.

"Me? Why me?" Susan asked me. "I mean, I know I've been with women before, but it was just sex, and well, you and I are friends."

"So you wouldn't do it? I mean, with her?" Christine pressed on.

"That's not it," Susan explained. "It's just an experience that has to take place at the right time, in the right place, and when both people are comfortable with everything. But I'm sure if anything *did* happen between us, it would be a wonderful experience."

Again laughter from the other Musketeers as I sat there feeling relieved, scared, elated, and nauseous all at once. I had just told another woman I had fantasized about her and she was fine with it.

The rest of the night was a blur. After my answer, the game died out. One by one the Musketeers went their separate ways until only Susan and I remained. In silence I helped her carry plates, silverware, and food into the kitchen. As we cleared up the last of it, I told her I should get going because it was getting late and I had a long drive home. She smiled that smile that took my breath away. "You can stay here if you want," she said.

Normally this wouldn't have unnerved me at all. I'd slept on Susan's couch many times, but after what had gone on that night, it seemed like more of an *offer*. I didn't know whether she meant "You can stay here on my couch" or "You can stay here with me." Still, I didn't care how she meant it; I wanted to stay. I always kept an overnight bag in my trunk, and I practically fell over her trying to get out to my car.

When I returned she was sitting on the floor in front of the couch sipping a glass of wine. I went into the bathroom and changed into a T-shirt and boxer shorts, then sat down on the couch with my knees hugged to my chest. Part of me prayed Susan would just say good night, hand me a pillow and blanket, and disappear into the bedroom. That way I wouldn't have to face the possibility of my fantasy becoming a reality.

"I'm flattered you could think of me that way," she said, a slow smile spreading across her face. Her words, although music to my ears, frightened the hell out of me.

"Well, you're a very beautiful woman." Again my mouth spoke without my brain's consent.

"Thanks," she said. "Have you ever wanted to be with a woman before?"

"Not until I met you."

"It can be a wonderful experience if two people really want to share that with each other."

I couldn't speak. I just nodded. Somehow Susan moved so she was kneeling in front of me. I don't remember seeing her move; all I remember is looking into her eyes as she spoke. "Can I kiss you?" she asked.

"Yes." I didn't think about my answer—I just knew there was no other possible reply.

She pushed herself up so her face was inches from mine. I felt her breath on my face before we kissed. Her lips were warm and soft against mine. I tasted the sweetness of the wine in her mouth. I felt everything come alive for the first time. My entire body responded: My heart felt as if it were trying to break free of my rib cage, my pulse raced blood through my body, my head spun, I felt like I was falling. Then it ended; she pulled back and smiled at me. "Excuse me," she said, then stood up and headed to the bathroom.

I don't know if she really had to go or if she just wanted to give me time to think about what had happened. Either way all I could think about was that kiss. My whole body tingled. I knew at that moment I wanted this woman more than I'd ever wanted anyone.

When she returned, she took my hand and led me to the floor. Her lips again found mine as we embraced passionately. I was lost in the new sensation of her kiss; I wanted to explore every corner of her mouth.

When her hand dipped inside my boxer shorts and her fingers found the wetness between my legs, I untangled myself from her as a new sensation of pleasure coursed through my body and a sigh escaped my lips. Her fingers moved over me, then inside me, and then...then there was nothing. Nothing but the movement of my hips, nothing but my cries of pleasure, nothing but the fire inside me that built up until I thought I'd lose consciousness.

How long did it last? Seconds? Minutes? Hours? How long until I cried out her name as a storm shuddered through my body? How long didn't matter. All that mattered was the way I felt at this moment. I'd never felt so fulfilled, so complete as I did lying there with Susan wrapped in my arms as I tried desperately to catch my breath.

"I want to touch you," I told her, my voice shaky. More than anything I wanted to make her experience the same unimaginable pleasure she had just given me.

"Tonight is about you." She kissed me tenderly. "We can talk about me tomorrow."

"But—"

She stopped my protest with another kiss. Then she stood up and offered me her hand. I took it and she pulled me to my feet and led me into the bedroom. As I lay beside her in bed, she curled up into the crook of my arm and nestled her head onto my chest. I wanted to tell her how wonderful she was, how beautiful she was, how amazing she made me feel. I wanted to tell her I loved her, but she was fast asleep only seconds after she placed her head on my chest. So instead I settled for holding her in my arms all night, watching her sleep, watching the rise and fall of her chest, the flutter of her eyelids. I was too awake to sleep. Too awake with the reality that my life had just changed forever. I knew who I was—a woman who loved other women, or at least one woman in particular.

Although neither of us had ever had a long-term relationship with a woman, we fell madly in love. That night happened almost seven years ago. Today my love for Susan continues to grow stronger every day; she's everything I've ever wanted in a woman. She's my lover and my best friend. This story is my gift to her so she will know that as we reach our seventh anniversary my love for her will never fade.

Sex and Candy
Rachel Kramer Bussel

A mutual love of sex and candy brought Caroline and me together. I was visiting Washington, D.C., and being the nerd I am, I was checking my E-mail at an Internet café. I decided to post to an E-mail discussion group that I run. The list's topic? Sex. I wrote that the band Belle and Sebastian was playing on the sound system of the café, and that, it being Easter time, I was thrilled to see those deliciously gooey Cadbury creme eggs on the shelves of drugstores everywhere. I found something distinctly erotic about their overly sweet creamy centers.

I was bored and wanting to meet new people, so I left my phone number in case anyone would be around when I returned to New York. Upon checking my voice mail later in D.C., I was pleased to hear a giggly girl's voice introducing herself as Caroline, telling me she liked my posting and got my random connections. She also said she would be visiting New York the following week. I liked her perky voice and the way she was able to follow my train of thought; any girl who also found something sexy and wicked about something as innocent as Cadbury creme eggs was my kind of girl. I called her back, and we agreed to meet up the next week in New York. I was excited to make a new friend.

When we met the following week, she was even cuter than I'd

expected. Her short, dirty-blond hair and bright-red lipsticked smile, along with the strawberry tattoo copied from a Beat Happening album cover that lay right above her breast, endeared her to me. We did that instant bonding thing girls like me tend to do, talking our heads off about crushes, makeup, music, candy, and gossip. She was only two years younger than me, 20 to my 22, but her girlie look made her seem even younger. I felt like we were two teenagers with our gossip and giggles.

We discovered we had a lot in common and became fast friends. We didn't run out of things to talk about, and I liked hearing her tell me about her life at college. She was refreshingly different from most of my friends, who were so bogged down in their serious careers and problems that they didn't have much time to just relax and enjoy life. Caroline told me about her plans and dreams but was much more focused on the here and now, and that was a delight.

After talking for a while, we headed over to a lecture by a feminist sex writer. While the writer, dressed in a cute top and tight leather pants, talked about her sexual experimentation and favorite porn videos, Caroline and I ate candy and giggled, trying to keep our voices low so as not to disrupt the whole lecture.

After that, we went back to my dorm, where we stayed up late talking about music, mutual friends and enemies, our families, and our sexual interests. I felt like I'd known Caroline forever, and she felt the same. The fact that we were both single and bisexual made it easy to talk and share our most private moments.

The next day we went shopping for porn magazines, two cute girlie girls amidst the dirty racks and old men. We held them up to each other, debating the pros and cons of each and reminiscing about our favorite porn stories and models. I eagerly grabbed a copy of *Barely Legal* while she dove right into *Nugget*. We giggled our way through the racks, perusing every offering lest some tempting smut pass us by. At a nearby drugstore we bought some Cadbury creme eggs, smirking as we did so, to eat later on, then stopped in a fancy lingerie store. We fingered the lacy bras and delicate teddies, holding them up against our plump bodies, knowing the prices were much too extravagant for items we both hoped we'd be in a hurry to remove later on.

We went back to my apartment and pored over the mags, huddled together on the floor. She told me about a story she'd had published in a 'zine that had inspired two people to have sex, which I thought was really hot. A guy friend of hers was there with us, reading music magazines, but he was sitting on the other side of the room. I was a little surprised that someone as seemingly sweet as Caroline was into *Nugget,* with its whips and chains and wax. The juxtaposition of all those kinky images and Caroline's perky, smiling face, was adorable.

We stayed up late into the night talking. At one point Caroline began lightly touching my arm. We started touching each other cautiously, holding hands or stroking each other's arms, but we didn't dare do anything more with her friend there. This gave us extra time to get to know and observe each other, and it also built up our excitement for what was to come that night.

At 2 A.M. we were laughing and messing around in our sheer nighties. We were the kind of friends who could talk about anything, but we also knew there was a mutual attraction simmering just beneath our easy talk. I wished that we lived closer together so we could hang out more often. I also wished we had more time together, but the next day her parents came to pick her up, and my only souvenirs were the porno mags she left me with.

Caroline and I E-mailed throughout the rest of the year, catching up on each other's lives and musical interests and dating habits. As we got to know each other better, I started to get a crush on her and could sense that it was mutual. Because she lived so far away, it was safe to fantasize about her. I'd think of our wonderful night together and imagine taking things a step further. She was my dream girl, the one I thought about when I was lonely and wanted a happy face and cute girl next to me.

The next time I saw her was a year later, when she was making another visit into town. Things hadn't been strained, but I wasn't sure how it would be when we saw each other—casual or flirtatious or something else. I was thrilled that she still wanted to see me, and when we got together I knew my uncertainty had been totally unnecessary; it was like we hadn't been apart at all. We picked up where we'd left off, but we were a little closer now, getting our photos taken in a bar photo booth and going down first-concert memory lane. This time though, we'd upped the ante by flirting with each other from the start. All our talk about our sex lives gave us insight into each other's sexual tastes, and we weren't as shy as we'd been the first time. After sharing the details each of our various recent sexual adventures, and making out in an underground bar and flirting with its patrons, we took the subway home, stopping to get some food along the way. When we got home we ate our noodles quietly, tired but eager to get into bed after teasing each other all night.

When we finally moved into the bedroom, it was nothing like the last time. While we still smiled and giggled, there was a definite tension in the air; we were much more than friends now. Caroline surprised me by being much more aggressive than I'd expected. She'd obviously been paying attention to my E-mails, because once we were both naked she immediately climbed on top of me and started spanking me. At first she did it with a slight laugh in her voice, teasing me, but then she was spanking me in earnest, and for a pretty small girl she did it very well. We didn't have any inhibitions, and we each spent plenty of time getting to know each other's bodies and making each other come. Caroline acted older than her years, and I reaped the benefit of her sexual experience. She was sweet and sexy, just like the Cadbury eggs that had brought us together.

I knew she'd have to go home the next day, and even though I was thrilled to be with her, I liked that we were only taking our friendship to another, deeper level, not starting a big dramatic relationship. We fell asleep naked and warm and happy, and even though it was close to 4 A.M. I didn't mind the missed sleep.

She left me a note the next morning near a small box of chocolates, and I knew we'd have more nights like this. We just can't resist the sweets.

Possessed by Demons

S. Katherine Stewart

In my life, Renee is the only thing I regret. Really regret. The kind of guilty regret that keeps you up at night. The kind that makes you think—even when you're enjoying yourself, even when you have your moral high horse at the ready and your self-righteous armor on—that you'd take it back if you could, that you would've never done it. It makes me need a God to ask forgiveness from.

I met Renee in 1994. I had just moved into the bottom half of a barely standing old house in a Midwest college town when I spotted a middle-aged woman in the house opposite mine. She was painting her walls Pepto pink and unself-consciously singing to the opera roaring from her stereo. She looked like someone's mom but acted like a character in a John Waters film. I was 21 at the time, just starting grad school. I'd moved to this new town with my about-to-be-ex-girlfriend, and I thought, *This is a bizarre omen.*

I was right, in a way: It was an omen. But I was a little wrong about Renee. She was different but not exactly bizarre. She was fascinating, if secretive. It took a long time for her to talk about her past, and I swear I'm still in the dark about a lot of the details. She was larger than life, flamboyantly dressed, never shying away from sequins, satin, or the occasional feather boa if she could get away with it. Her status as a costume design grad student gave her end-less opportunities to play the kind of oddball diva-ish role she rel-ished. I couldn't help liking her. She was so much more fun than I was: She played dress-up; she didn't care who heard her sing.

"I went to college after my divorce, after all that time as a wife and mother and a strict Mormon," she told me one afternoon. "I didn't know there was a life outside my family or the church. And when I got into the theater department here, it was like I was allowed to have all these other feelings too. I don't think I could have realized that I was attracted to women any other way."

Serendipitous? It seemed to be. Our neighbor was a recently former heterosexual, fleeing from Salt Lake City to the gay-friendly graduate theater department at our big Midwestern school. How lucky was it that just a few feet away lived a young lesbian couple? How impossible not to be fast friends?

I thought a lot about her past—that hermetically sealed social vacuum she'd escaped—and how different her experience was from my own radically secular identity that seemed so much sim-pler by comparison. I often think it was her complexity that made her interesting to me, made me want to know her better. She was older, and in that sense knew more and seemed wiser. But she was a queer neophyte and I wasn't (or, like many 21-year-olds, so I thought). It gave a balance to our connection, made me feel we each had wisdom to share.

But the complexity that interested me also made the friend-ship complicated. She was so reticent about sharing her feelings about her past, about specifics, even about what was going on in her present. It was three months before she told me how many children she had. Three months for something as simple as that.

Our connection was cemented rather tenuously by a teasing and, eventually, flirtatious banter. I remember hassling her about a young woman she was screwing around with—a woman with an out-of-town girlfriend, whom I spotted leaving Renee's at 7 o'clock in the morning. I made a beeline to her door. "Hey, who was *that*?" I asked her.

"Um…pizza delivery girl?" she blushed.

After that I stuck Pizza Hut coupons in her mailbox for a month and teased her mercilessly. But that's typical of the way I discovered anything about her. I wonder now if I taunted her so ruthlessly out of a perverse sense of indignation: Why didn't she just admit these things to me? Why didn't she trust me? I wonder how much of her obscurity was a strategy to get some attention from me (or anyone). Probably neither. Perhaps it wasn't that she didn't trust me. I think secretiveness was simply a part of her chemical makeup, or more likely an emotional souvenir of her life as a Mormon matriarch.

Things changed when my girlfriend, and I split up a couple of years later. Jesus, those days were miserable, though predictably so. I moped for months and generally felt sorry for myself. I'd been humiliated, felt unattractive, insecure, unloved. I got involved in a long distance relationship with a woman more than twice my age.

I needed security, stability, the reassurance of someone who knew from experience that I'd survive this. But it was probably about power as much as it was about being taken care of in an Oedipal way. I'd been cheated on, and she did it with a man, of course. Lesbians hate to admit the kind of insecurity that can lead to.

The power of a young body makes up for a lot. And there are reasons an older woman desires a 23-year-old, and precious few of them involve her sparkling wit and well-earned wisdom. When Elaine, my older lover, ran her hands over my thighs, when she kissed my neck and sighed, I felt invulnerable. It was good for my bruised sexual ego. And I slept with other women as well. A lot of them—anyone, really, who could make me forget for a couple of hours that I felt two inches tall, empty, and unfuckable.

Renee and I grew closer, and without my girlfriend in the way, more flirtatious. It seemed innocent enough. During the fall and winter of '96–'97 we'd go out to eat a few times a month. I'd drink too much wine—as I did a lot that year—and we'd go to her place or mine, sit and talk on a couch. She was living in this beautiful house at the time, one of those places with glossy hardwood floors, furniture with a gay man's sensibility, and lots of wall hangings. I'd prop myself on one side of the couch and rest my feet on her thighs. "Why don't you sit on my lap?" she'd tease.

"OK, but I can't promise to behave." I swear it seemed innocuous, even if in retrospect it appears almost ridiculously risky. "Snuggling's not sex. It's just what friends do," I'd say. Was I saying that to justify my need to be desired? Probably. Then we'd talk. Mostly I'd complain, I guess. And I'd kiss her cheek or her neck before I left, or she'd hold my hand and pinch my thigh. Things like that—dumb high school stuff.

But flirtations progressed. Holding hands became a regular thing. And one night, after too much wine again, I kissed Renee on the lips. We'd been looking at each other, and after a long, silent moment I leaned over and kissed her. Light pressure, my right hand on her cheek, for a few seconds only, but so much more than a kiss goodbye. An invitation, clearly.

I felt better afterward. I liked the way she looked at me after that kiss, like a mother and friend, but like a lover too. And it felt easy and—I keep saying this, I know—innocent, light, and airy, nothing like the stiff throb of love I'd felt for my ex, the painful longing that had left me hurt and angry. I simply assumed Renee felt the same.

A week later we had our usual dinner date. It was a mild winter that year, but cold that night and very dark in the restaurant. She was quiet. I felt bold after our kiss, and kept teasing and pestering her. "Renee, we have *got* to get you a girlfriend," I told her. You are just too good a catch to be going out with me on Friday nights."

She smiled, a little derisively, lips more pursing than grinning. "Maybe I don't want one."

"Don't be cheeky," I said. "Everyone wants a girlfriend."

"Maybe I don't like anyone." She was fiddling with her fork and not looking me in the eye.

And it may seem more than a little dense of me not to pick up on what she wouldn't say, but I didn't. When a woman looks at you that way, under her eyelashes across a table, and when she *won't* look at you when you bring up love and relationships, you really ought to realize that she's thinking of you when she goes to bed at night. And you ought to realize, especially if she's your friend and you don't feel the same, pursuing the topic or pursuing *her* is selfish and dangerous. But I continued nagging her anyway. "There's got to be someone. Come on, I know there is, just tell me. Out with it."

In my defense, and this is the only thing I really can defend, this wasn't the first time she'd kept something from me for (I thought) no apparent reason. Like I said, she was secretive and it really bothered me. I was tired of her keeping things from me; I wanted to be closer to her, and she never let me in. *Why can't she just trust me with one damned little emotional fact?* I must have been thinking something like that when she looked up, and in the quietest, most deflated voice I've ever heard, said, "It's you."

I don't know how long it took to register—10, 20 seconds, maybe more—and when it did I blushed and looked away. I felt a little pang in my chest, half triumph, half defeat. Why hadn't I seen this? Expected it? "Renee," I said, a little sheepishly, "you know I love you, but you're my friend. I can't—"

"I know that," she smiled, I think bravely. "It's fine."

But it wasn't fine. And it got less than fine, because whenever I'd see her again that feeling of half triumph—a tempting feeling—would always win, and I'd flirt with her, kiss her, each time more passionately, graze the side of her breast with my fingers, touch her neck lightly just at the hairline. Why? Didn't I know I was setting this up for sex? Didn't I know I didn't want the relationship she did and that sex would hurt her—if not immediately, then later? Wasn't I lying to everyone else about the relationship—even to Elaine, who had every right to expect I'd be monogamous at that point?

It didn't matter. If this had happened in the Middle Ages, I'd claim I was possessed by demons; but it was the 20th century, and even my fragile emotional state at the time can't absolve me of what has to be understood as selfishness. I liked that she loved me. I liked that I didn't love her back. I liked that she had no choice when I kissed her or when I refused. And I gave her as many reasons to hope as I could.

The perverse way it happened was this: I was on the phone and she was on the bed with me some late winter afternoon in my room. Bare bulb for light, thick Asian carpets masking the linoleum, quilts, and prayer rugs on the walls. Cozy, but we were very conscious of the potential, had in fact breathed it in when she arrived earlier in the afternoon. We'd been fooling around for weeks, but there was nothing consummated, nothing I couldn't take back. A friend had called after Renee had come downstairs with me. I was pretending to talk while I teased her a little. Nice to be pretending, I thought. She was holding my hand, running her fingers against my palm, up and between the digits and their creases. I cradled the phone against my shoulder, touching her thighs through her jeans, smiling—wickedly, I suppose.

She unbuttoned my shirt, and I didn't stop her. It was perfect—the conversation on the other end was keeping me from looking at her too carefully. I couldn't say anything. It meant, somehow, that I wasn't responsible. I didn't hang up, and I didn't stop Renee from leaning me back against the bed. I didn't stop her from taking my small breasts in her hands, unbuttoning my shirt, unhooking my bra, taking my nipples in her mouth, nestling her face and tongue in the grooves of my stomach and ribs.

I kept up a halting conversation on the telephone. Renee and I grinned at each other, feeling naughty and coupled in our dangerous game. I'd catch my breath, move the receiver away from my mouth so that my friend on the other end couldn't hear me gasp. Her fingers found the buttons of my jeans, well-worn and easy to pull open. She teased at the band of my underwear, pulling gently at my hips, slipping a finger just underneath but pulling away. I stifled a groan and kissed her quickly, struggling out of my jeans and panties altogether.

She was on top of me then, me keeping up only a pretense of a conversation on the phone. Our thighs were brushing against each other in mad friction. And when her fingers finally slid deep inside me, I said, "I'm sorry, I've got to go. Bye." The phone clattered into the corner of the room. She had one, two, maybe three fingers inside me. I wrestled her over, on top of her now, keeping her fingers with me. I don't know in which order I took off her clothes. I cupped her full, soft breasts, sucked them, felt her inside me, found her clitoris, her vagina. We were inside each other for long moments, moaning, then coming.

And the whole time I knew. I knew. I knew I shouldn't do it. When I felt her tongue touch mine, her hand possessively spread my thighs, I knew. I knew that I was: (1) cheating on my girlfriend; (2) lying to Renee, even if she claimed to know that I didn't love her; (3) fucking her over the whole time I was fucking her. What I had done before was bad enough, but when I felt her under me, felt her breathing so hard, that openness and wetness that comes from a passion that is so much more than sexual—I didn't stop. And I should have.

When it was over she smiled very weakly, kissed me, and held me for about a half an hour. We didn't say much. She left, making some excuse about her dog. I asked her to stay. I think I really did want her to. If she'd stayed, I could have pretended it was OK. That I hadn't just screwed up. But Renee, despite all her weakness, was at that moment so much stronger, finer, better than me, and wouldn't stay in my bed, pretending this was the start of anything. We both knew it was an ending, not a beginning. I had just allowed our friendship to be ruined. It had been up to me—she'd given me that power, or I'd demanded it—and neither of us was ignorant or confused about what had happened.

There were no fireworks. No shocking accusations or passionate speeches of moral outrage. We actually slept together again, maybe twice more. Once in her bed, her clinging to me the way a terminal cancer patient clings to hope—with a sort of defiant indifference. I looked into her eyes and all I saw was resignation, not passion. She was taking what she could get, pulling my clothes off and painting me with her hands and tongue so slowly. I think she may have loathed herself and me a little for it. She wasn't a beggar by nature or creed, and I made her feel like one.

That spring she graduated and got a job with an actors' company in Tennessee. I broke up with Elaine and moved away for six months, taking time from my bruised life, trying to heal. We called and wrote each other half-heartedly.

When she heard about my new lover some months later, she wished us all the best. And that amazing woman actually meant it. But after that, I didn't hear from her again and still haven't. I don't even know where she lives, and I don't have the guts to find out.

I can't remember when I started to feel guilty; for my sake I hope it was immediately, but I'm not sure. At the time, I was grateful for the distance and natural attrition of our communication with each other. It made it easier, and Renee was always terrific at making things easy for me.

I've made it nearly impossible for myself to contact her, even though I think about it a lot. I'm more weary now when I think of what I did, when I massage the wound of guilt. I even wonder if I enjoy the feeling, like a child loves fidgeting with a loose tooth that is painful at the gums. I like to think I've learned from it: It's easier than you think to become the villain in your own life story.

Just Like Old Friends
D.M. Gavin

I had received a letter from Angela a month prior to New Year's telling me she was coming home for the holidays and wanted to spend a weekend with me. Since we'd made these annual reunions a tradition, her letter came as no surprise.

We had been friends for nearly a decade. We met when I was young and married. Angela was even younger and had just finished high school. Now she was living a state away and made treks to visit me every few months. By this time, I'd admitted to myself that I was a lesbian and had left my husband to live with a woman. It didn't take long for Angela to realize the same about herself and become involved with a woman she had met in Colorado, 2,000 miles away. In a little more than a year, she dropped out of college and moved across the country to be with her lover.

I felt attracted to her the first time we met, and my feelings had grown stronger over the years. I didn't want her to leave the East Coast, but I lied to myself about why, since I was in a long-term relationship. At times I was inclined to think she felt the same way about me, but I convinced myself it was just my overactive imagination telling me again what I wanted to hear. To complicate matters, I had begun to realize I wasn't as happy in my relationship, which was now in its seventh year, as I should have been. Things between my girlfriend, Lyn, and me weren't as good as I wanted to believe, but I had refused to admit it to myself. Lyn had become surly and withdrawn. She had grown comfortable with our relationship and no longer tried to work to make it successful. She constantly brushed me off whenever I voiced my concerns.

Since Angela left the planning of our weekend together up to me, I reserved a suite in an elegant hotel in downtown Baltimore so that the three of us could enjoy a long weekend, including New Year's Eve, together.

Lyn and I arrived first, having driven the two hours straight from work that Friday. I was excited. It took less than a half hour for us to unpack and get comfortable before heading downstairs to wait for our friend in the hotel lobby. We didn't make it. On the first stair landing, we came face to face with Angela. Our eyes met, and we both knew this visit would be different. Lyn seemed unaware of the chemistry.

I hadn't seen Angela in a year. She looked incredible. Had she always looked this beautiful? She stood before me with her dark curls framing her face, pink from the cold. Her inviting smile was aimed at me.

I tried to bury my inappropriate thoughts as the three of us headed out into the cold. We stopped at a liquor store to buy wine for our stay, and then we moved on to a gay bookstore where we browsed and laughed over a display of sex toys. Angela and I agreed instantly on which ones would be fun to try, while Lyn turned away, repulsed by any kind of sex that didn't involve a mouth or fingers.

There was an indefinable difference in the way Angela and I interacted that night. We were more intimate with each other and seemed more at ease than we ever had during our long friendship. Giggling like teenagers, we cracked jokes only the two of us thought funny. I could tell that Lyn prided herself on being the mature one as Angela and I laughed. The more boisterous we became, the more Lyn crawled inside herself.

We headed back to our rooms, our arms laden with our purchases, and settled in for a catching-up session. While Angela and I shared a bottle of burgundy, Lyn slammed down beer after beer. Maybe she sensed what was coming and wanted to be oblivious for the occasion. Before long, Lyn was too intoxicated to remain upright and went to bed, where she passed out for the night.

Angela and I stayed in the living area, relaxing on the sofa, and resumed our discussion. The bottle of burgundy was soon emptied, and our conversation waned. Angela must have felt the electricity of the emotions flying around the room. Out of denial, or avoidance, she rose from the sofa and made a long-distance call to her ex in Colorado. My heart sank as I stretched out on the couch, wanting her to come back and devote all her attention to me. The burgundy was going to my head. During her conversation, I floated between varying levels of consciousness, some words clear, others too fuzzy to make out.

I was barely cognizant as Angela hung up the phone and came over to where I was lying. Resting her hand on my shoulder, she shook me gently and told me to get up so she could go to bed. I'm not entirely sure I knew what I was doing when I raised my hand, eyes still closed, and rested it on her side, stroking tentatively. The sound of her breathing immediately took a rougher, quicker cadence. Taking this as a sign of encouragement, I removed my hand and placed it under her shirt, rubbing the bare skin where my hand had rested seconds before. There was a sharp intake of breath on both of our parts.

"What are you doing?" she asked in a throaty whisper. Fearing rejection, I refused to answer and kept my eyes closed. She, unfortunately, took this as a sign that I was not fully conscious and that I was mistaking her for Lyn.

"Who am I?" she asked. Instead of answering, I removed my hand from her bare side and placed it behind her head, attempting to pull her toward me in a kiss. She resisted.

"Who am I?" she asked again. Finally, convinced I had been

wrong about any mutual attraction, I gave up and lay still on the sofa. Angela pulled me from the sofa onto the floor, saying she needed to open it into a bed for herself. I lay on the floor in a desolate heap, convinced I had ruined my one chance.

Once the bed was open, Angela turned off the lights and climbed inside. "Get in," she whispered. I didn't have to be asked more than once. I tiredly climbed from the floor, using the streetlights streaming through the windows as a guide, then slipped in beside her. Leaning on my elbow, I looked into her face, unable to read what she was thinking, and kissed her as softly as I knew how. I was encouraged that she let me, but disheartened that she didn't kiss me back.

I lay back on the pillow and stared at the ceiling as we began to talk. I confessed that this attraction for her had been growing within me for at least the past five years and that somewhere along the line it had grown into love, a fact that surprised her. We talked some more, and after we had cleared the air about what we were feeling and she was sure I wasn't drunkenly mistaking her for someone else, I tried again, and my insides melted as she kissed me back.

We pressed our bodies together as I kissed her, tasting the wine still on her lips and breathing in her scent. My hands touched her face, hair, and neck. I was so overcome by what I was doing, by what I had wanted to do for years but never considered a possibility, that the room began to spin, and I had to lie back again with a deep sigh. We held hands.

"I feel so guilty," I confessed. I had wanted this moment, had dreamed about it for years, and now that my wish was fulfilled, I was racked by a combination of elation and grief. "I've wanted this moment for so long, but I never thought it would come to this. And my lover of seven years is in the next room," I agonized.

Angela stroked my hair away from my face and murmured reassuringly. Suddenly, the guilt and alcohol proved too toxic a combination to bear, and I headed for the bathroom, where everything came up in a rush. I stumbled back to the sofa bed and lay weakly in Angela's arms. "I should go to bed now. She's going to wonder where I am if she wakes up," I said, pointing to the next room. Angela sent me off with another kiss. I forced myself to sleep as excitement, mixed with guilt and wine, made my stomach flutter.

The next morning was New Year's Eve, and I experienced my very first hangover. After waking up, it took me a grand total of five seconds to remember what had happened the night before, and my stomach began flipping again. I felt as if my punishment for being unfaithful would surely be death by a severe tongue-lashing. I tried to decide whether or not I would confess to Lyn when we got home. Would she forgive even a kiss? She had told me several times over the years that the only thing that would make her leave me would be my cheating on her.

Lyn woke up and was more interested in watching a football game on TV than tending to my hungover body—another obvious sign of her disinterest in me. Angela woke up and joined us on the king-size bed, stroking my hair lovingly and every few minutes asking me how I was feeling. Finally, at Angela's urging, they both went downstairs to find something to ease my stomachache. After the previous night, it felt strange for them both to be alone together, but they returned within minutes with herbal tea and water, and urged me to hydrate my body. I sipped the water doubtfully, sure I would die before the day was through, but it worked wonders, and I was able to get up and dress so we could all go out for lunch.

My insides screamed the entire time. I felt reprehensible for what had happened, but it was also killing me that Angela and I couldn't get a moment alone to talk about it. She appeared so calm and normal while I felt nothing but turmoil. Is she sorry about last night? I wondered miserably. Nothing in the way she looked at me was different, and I began to believe I might have imagined the entire incident.

At the restaurant we ate and carried on as if nothing had happened. My earlier paranoia that Lyn suspected something soon disappeared as the three of us talked and laughed, although I still felt an urgent need to be alone with Angela. What was she feeling about our encounter?

The opportunity came finally when Lyn offered to stand in line to pay our check and Angela went outside for a cigarette. I followed her out and stood with her in the subfreezing cold, my arms wrapped around myself—as much for support as for warmth.

"Are you all right?" I asked, unable to make eye contact. She smiled.

"I'm fine. How 'bout you?"

"I'm fine now that my stomach's settled," I answered. "What about last night? How are you feeling about what happened? Tell me what you want."

Angela took a drag from her cigarette, smiled, and responded, "More."

A slow grin captured my face, and I returned her stare. "OK. We'll need to get her drunk again. There's a liquor store across the street," I suggested, nodding in Lyn's direction as she stood inside the restaurant. My guilt disappeared and was replaced by intense deviousness.

Horribly enough, we headed to the liquor store, where we eyed the merchandise closely, suggesting to Lyn liquors with the highest concentration of alcohol. Stoli. Cuervo. Seagram's. Malibu. Crown Royal. Old Crow. I was determined to pursue a relationship with Angela. Lyn had to have known something was up, since I usually discouraged her from drinking. She became obnoxious when she got drunk. Regardless, she settled on whiskey after making a fuss about drinking again after last night. We headed back to our room.

The hotel package deal included a complimentary dinner at a Polynesian restaurant. After dinner we were meeting a friend (who had just been named Mr. Mid-Atlantic Leather) at a leather bar. Fully aware of how I wanted this evening to end, I took extra care getting ready. I styled my hair and applied makeup carefully before slipping into a black crushed-velvet dress and heels.

I smiled as I thought back to earlier in the week when I had told a friend at work about the dress I had bought for New Year's. She smirked and asked if I had bought it to make an impression on "Miss Colorado," as she referred to Angela. I feigned ignorance, but my blushing cheeks gave me away. I had bought the dress with Angela in mind.

I finally began to relax when we got to the restaurant. Angela sat across from me, and Lyn sat next to me. More sure of myself now that Angela had been blunt about her feelings, I looked at her longingly across the table. She would see my looks and glance away, unable to return my gazes because she was also facing Lyn.

When Lyn got up to use the rest room, Angela and I talked openly but still shyly about the evening ahead of us. I reminded her that we had to drink enough to not cause suspicion, but not enough to damage our sobriety.

"The last thing I want is for you to be the one to pass out," I admitted.

We finished our meal, left the restaurant, and headed toward the bar. Arriving earlier than our friend Tom, we ordered drinks and took in our surroundings. After the first round of drinks, there was a commotion at the entrance as Tom and his lover walked in. They mingled with everyone in the club while Angela and I stood in a corner, looking more obvious than we should have.

Lyn spent most of her time with Tom, meeting his friends and having a good time. I think she had some suspicions about what was transpiring and tried to spend as much time away from me and Angela as she could. The men at the club certainly succeeded in keeping her mind off us, which was fine with me. I took the opportunity to occasionally whisper in Angela's ear how attractive she was and how I couldn't wait to get back to the hotel to continue what we had begun. Lyn only returned to where we stood when midnight struck. She kissed me as Angela looked on.

Ready to end the long evening, we called the hotel and asked for the limo to pick us up. The ride back was fraught with tension—on all sides. Back at our hotel suite Angela and I were terribly obvious, encouraging Lyn to keep drinking as we nursed our own cocktails.

"Are you trying to make me pass out?" Lyn asked at one point. She finally gave in and went to bed after I promised I'd join her in a while.

When we were sure Lyn was asleep, we opened the sofa, turned the lights off, and crawled under the sheets. Our pent-up passion enveloped us as I took Angela into my arms and kissed her desperately. Our breath was ragged and hot as our mouths explored each other. I ran my hands through her hair. I kissed her mouth, her neck, eyes—any place I found exposed flesh. No longer afraid of how she might react, I ran my hands under her shirt and touched her bare skin. I raised my hand and took a breast into my palm, kneading her nipple while she moaned into my ear, sending chills through my entire body. I ran my tongue along her neck and moved up to nibble on her ear as she gasped and moved her hands under my shirt, raking her fingernails sharply along my back.

"Don't leave any marks, baby," I whispered, and she eased up.

I was afraid again. Lyn was in the next room. How soundly was she sleeping? Meanwhile, I was in bed with this person who may or may not wake the dead during sex. I had no idea what to expect.

"Can you be quiet?" I asked. Angela nodded her head and kissed me again, harder this time. My hands trailed her sides again and moved down until they met the waistband of her panties. I tentatively moved inside and rubbed my flat palm against her stomach, feeling the warmth radiate from below, but temporarily unable to go any further.

That's it, my mind warned. If you do anything else, you will officially cheat on Lyn, and you know what that means.

Angela interrupted my conversation with myself by grasping my arms and whispering, "Don't tease me."

Everything but the thought of pleasing her rushed out of my mind as I moved my hand closer to her center. I reached between her open legs, amazed at the moisture that met my touch. I moved slowly at first, listening to her soft sighs as my fingers explored her, then faster as her breathing quickened. Her hips rose to meet my fingers, and her hands grasped me and pulled me closer. I held her as I stroked her and brought her closer to the climax she was moving toward. She came all too quickly and stilled my hand with her own. I held her and whispered words of affection until she caught her breath and asked to do the same to me.

Afterward we lay grinning in each other's arms. My guilt from the previous night did not return as I kissed Angela again and told her I was in love with her. She smiled.

"I love you too." I climbed from the bed and returned to the bed I—sadly—was supposed to be in.

The following day there was a noticeable change in Lyn. She was catching on to us. We made every attempt we could to get rid of her. During one of Lyn's outings, I was bending over to kiss Angela as the door began to open. I moved away quickly but not quickly enough. Lyn saw me move away from Angela's mouth and went to our room, where I found her crying. I tried to comfort her. I denied everything. I was not only a cheat—I was also a liar.

Angela and I tried to be more sensible about our feelings and agreed to attempt to control ourselves around Lyn. Our last evening together was miserable. I would be dropping Angela off at her parents' house the next day, and she would be off to Colorado within a week.

After Lyn went to bed, Angela and I walked together into the main lobby and settled into the fat cushiony sofa at the center. Completely alone, I confided my feelings again and asked if there was any way we could be together. To my utter surprise, she beamed and said she wouldn't mind moving back to the East Coast. My heart hammered at what this might mean. I was thrilled we might be together but terrified at the prospect of ending my relationship with Lyn. We held hands and talked for almost the entire night.

Toward dawn some guests came through the back door and busied themselves in the lobby. Wanting to be alone, I took Angela's hand and led her to a space behind the main stairs, pulling her into my arms. Her mouth met mine with hungry kisses. Unable to do anything more and unwilling to take a chance in our suite, I merely held her in my arms.

The following day we dropped Angela off as planned. *How can I leave her and go home with Lyn?* I thought. I had realized by this time how unhappy I was with Lyn and how wrong our relationship had become. I realized she wasn't the Princess Charming I had created. I agonized over when I should talk to her, knowing Angela and I would not see each other again for another few months.

Once apart, Angela and I spent enough time on the phone with each other to raise suspicions not only in Lyn but also in Angela's parents. I convinced Angela to borrow her mother's car and drive the two hours it would take to see me. I had the entire week off from work. Lyn would be at her job. We would have the day to ourselves.

"I never got the chance to make love to you like I wanted to," I said. This reasoning was enough to convince her, and she arranged to borrow her mother's car two days later. I gave her directions to the house, and she agreed to arrive by 9 A.M.

Wednesday morning came and Angela arrived. She would be leaving for Colorado in just a few days, but having her near eased my sadness. I put some music on the stereo, took her hand, and led her upstairs. I kissed her chilled skin, wanting to warm her inside and out with my mouth. I hurriedly removed her clothes and then my own and pulled her forcefully into bed. Our kissed grew in intensity as our bare bodies touched for the first time.

I began making physical comparisons between Lyn and Angela. As my hands roamed her body, I thought of how different it all felt. Angela was smaller in every way: her waist, her breasts, her lips. It wasn't an unpleasant change, just different.

Holding her close, I kissed her neck. She moaned and grazed my back with her fingernails. I moved to her ears and sucked hungrily.

I wanted more, but I was suddenly shy. We had known each other for so long but never like this. I looked up at her comforting smile and moved down the length of her body, kissing her stomach and thighs along the way. Without warning, I opened her legs and took her fully into my mouth, delving into her warm taste and forcing another comparison into my brain.

She opened her legs wider and arched her back as I slipped several fingers inside her. With each moan, I thrust deeper and harder into her, until her entire body shuddered and a cry broke free from her throat. I smiled to myself as I remembered how, for years, I had known she would be like this. The smile remained as I moved up to hold her in my arms.

Before long her breathing returned to normal, and she was moving down my body, leaving scorching kisses in her wake. She teased me with her tongue as one, two, then three fingers entered me slowly. Soon we were following an identical rhythm as her fingers slid into me and my hips rose to meet her hand—first slowly, then frantically—until an orgasm tore through my body.

Instantly, I felt tears wash down my face and onto the pillow. The emotional ups and downs that had plagued me over the last week had finally surfaced. I had been trying to hide my feelings for Angela from Lyn all week. The turmoil I felt over what we were doing to Lyn, but being unable to stop myself from wanting to be with Angela, tore me apart. Besides, Angela was leaving to go back to Colorado in a little over 24 hours.

"What's wrong?" Angela asked, concern written in her eyes.

"It just hit me that you're leaving tomorrow. You're going to change your mind about being with me. I just know you will," I sobbed.

"No, I won't. I promise." She took me into her arms.

"You will," I continued, convinced this wouldn't last. I said I was sure that once she went home and told her ex about us, her ex would panic and do everything in her power to patch up their relationship.

"It won't happen. She's had the past several years to do that if she wanted." Angela held me until my tears subsided, stroking my hair away from my wet face and kissing my forehead in an attempt to comfort me.

"Don't spoil our time together worrying about that," she said. "Make love to me."

She brought her mouth to mine in a deep kiss, running her tongue along the inside of my mouth, planting an ache for her deep within me. I turned her over so that I was above her and kissed her neck before moving to her breasts. I took my time kissing and caressing each one before taking a nipple into my mouth and grazing my teeth over the swollen flesh.

I released her and turned over again, resting on my back and pulling her with me. She straddled my hips, and I moved my fingers between her legs, listening to her gasps as I entered her. She began to rock slowly, taking my fingers deep into herself with each movement. I watched her face contort in ecstasy, her head tipped back, her mouth slightly open as she rode my hand. My heart warmed and my insides melted as she came, murmuring my name over and over.

We continued making love throughout the day, never leaving the bed. Three o'clock came all too soon, and we both knew Angela would have to leave before Lyn got home from work. We slowly dressed and hesitantly moved downstairs before embracing one last time.

"Don't worry about what will happen," Angela reassured me. "Everything will be fine. I'll call you on your birthday." And then she was off, leaving me with only memories to tide me over until we would meet again in the spring.

Unfortunately, my foresight had been well tuned that day. Angela went back home and broke the news to her ex, who responded by begging for their reconciliation. It worked. Angela called me a week later to break the news. I was devastated…but not surprised.

I had confessed everything to Lyn the week before, only three days after the day Angela and I had spent together alone. She amazed me by forgiving me and trying to save our relationship by attempting to become a different person, one she thought would make me happy. The part of me that began the affair with Angela knew my relationship with Lyn wasn't salvageable, but I made a small attempt, even though I knew I should just end the relationship.

At the same time, Angela and I fought to save the friendship we once had. It was important to me, even through the pain, to keep the connection I had with her.

Just one month after our breakup, Angela sent me a Valentine's Day card, humbly explaining that she realized what a mistake she'd made by ending our budding relationship. My hopes skyrocketed, but my heart also sank. I was terrified of going through the gamut of emotions once again, only to be let down in the end.

It took several months to trust Angela again. I was afraid that if I resumed my relationship with her, she would hurt me once more. During those months we worked on our relationship long-distance. We talked on the phone and wrote several times a week. In July I moved out of the house I owned with Lyn and moved to Colorado to be with Angela. We've been together, happily, for more than seven years now.

Roberta: Dodging a Bullet
M. Damian

She was a kid, relatively speaking, when we first met—21 to my 32. She looked and acted like any of the other thousands of students who attended the university where I worked. And like any other student who swirled through the department on a daily basis, I didn't pay special attention to her. Not at first, anyway. It wasn't until summer session, when she hung out in the department killing time between classes, that we went past perfunctory politeness. By the time she left six weeks later for a European vacation with her sister, we had gotten pretty friendly.

The "kid" who came back had metamorphosed into anything but. Gone were the print blouse and Swiss polka-dot pedal pushers, no more Keds-style sneakers, two different earrings, and two different hair lengths. When she walked past me the first day of school, I saw she had a sleek new hairdo and was wearing tight khaki pants with a matching military shirt, opened provocatively to suggest the merest hint of young, firm cleavage. A very tasteful display, just enough to whet my appetite and wonder what had brought about such a drastic transformation.

Over the next two months our friendship strengthened, then one day in November she wanted my advice about her coach. Roberta was on the female varsity volleyball team and was having the devil's own time with her bullying female coach. After hearing her out, I offered my erudite conclusion: "She's after you." Roberta was shocked and didn't believe my assessment even though she knew I was gay. When she asked me why I thought she had been singled out from her teammates, I told her she was very cute. And she was. I was sure the coach had zeroed in on that and was trying to get attention from Roberta by constantly picking on her. Hey, it worked in grade school with little boys and girls; why shouldn't it work in college with two women?

Roberta asked if I would go to a practice so I could eyeball the interaction between her and the coach. I knew she doubted what I told her. Why would the coach want her? She was, after all, straight. I went to that evening's practice, watched, and left. When Roberta came to see me the next day, I firmly reiterated my original assessment of the situation. *Now* she paid attention. When she asked me for help to get the coach to cease and desist because she was definitely not interested, I told her what to do and voilà! Two weeks later, no more problem.

My advice to her had been to not be a doormat to the coach; in other words, sass her back, show a little spirit. The next time the coach went after her verbally, Roberta didn't just stand there and take it; she stood up for herself. After a few incidents like this, the coach called her into her office and said she admired her spunk. They eventually got to the point where they could even laugh together. Roberta came to me, all smiles, thanking me for my invaluable help.

Shortly after I solved this problem for her, Roberta offered me a ride home (we lived 10 minutes apart). I knew she owned a sleek gold Trans-Am, and as I have a thing for cars I readily agreed. Somehow during the 30-minute ride I also agreed to go to her house to see her collection of Coca-Cola memorabilia. She drove us to Manhattan Beach, a very expensive section of Brooklyn where she lived with her folks.

A few weeks after my oohing and aahing over Coke memorabilia from almost every country in the world (Roberta traveled extensively), it was time for Christmas break. I was driving my lover down to Georgia to visit her recently transplanted mother. As much as I was looking forward to the 1,000-mile trip because I love to drive, I was also hoping the time we spent together would help us stabilize our floundering relationship.

The university I work at is a presentation school, which means once a semester, students have to discard their jeans and sneakers for business attire to professionally present cases before professors and classmates. Roberta was scheduled to give her presentation on the last day of school. After her class, she appeared at my desk. "Can I talk to you a minute?" she asked in a subdued voice. Her demeanor made me think something must have gone wrong in class. "Can we go in an office?" *Wow,* I thought as I unlocked an empty office, *she must have really bombed out.*

We went in and I sat behind the desk with her in front. I waited silently for her to begin, not wanting to push, but she just sat there, looking down at her hands folded in her lap. Slowly, as if being manipulated by a puppeteer, her head came up, and hesitating briefly, she came out with it: "Remember all those things you told me about my coach?" I nodded. "Were they for her…" There was a very pregnant pause while her eyes drilled me into the chair. "Or for you?"

I sat there, staring at her in dumfounded amazement. She thought I… "No, no, no, Roberta," I answered, shaking my head emphatically, "I was telling you about what the *coach* saw in you, not me." Barely had the words left my mouth when she jumped up and ran out of the office, slamming the door behind her. I stayed there another five minutes, shaking my head in disbelief, trying to figure out where or how she came up with such a crazy idea. She knew I was with someone. I had never come on to her. What was this? When I emerged from the office, Carolyn, a coworker, looked at me and asked sharply, "What did you do to Roberta? She left here crying." When I related what had happened, she told me I should call Roberta at home to make sure she was OK.

"Why should I?" I protested. "I didn't do anything wrong." Carolyn just sat there, scowling at me. I sighed. Why did these things always happen to me? I went back to work, giving Roberta enough time to get home. Forty-five minutes after she had stormed out of the office, I called her, explaining myself again—and got hung up on. I stomped out and raged at Carolyn.

Eventually I calmed down and went back to finishing up some work. I was excited and happy about my impending trip, so much so that I began to relent in my harsh feelings toward Roberta. Aw, what the hell, I reasoned. Christmas vacation was here and I didn't want her to have hers ruined because of me. So I called her again—and got hung up on again. At that point, I didn't care what the fuck she felt.

Departure time for my much anticipated trip got delayed until the following evening because my lover couldn't score any blow. I don't use drugs, but Stella couldn't go anywhere unless she was snorting coke. This was one of the problems with our relationship.

After a night of fruitless searching, I dropped her off (we didn't live together) and got home at 6 in the morning. She'd try again during the day without me. I went straight to bed. At 1 P.M., my brother and roommate woke me up and told me hurriedly that someone named Roberta had called.

Oh, what the hell does she want? I thought groggily, blinking myself awake. I didn't need to be hung up on a third time. But again I relented: I didn't want to be the cause of any hurt feelings. I looked her number up in the phone book and dialed. Then we talked for two hours about how *she* wanted to go out with *me*. You could have literally knocked me over with the proverbial feather. Roberta? Straight little Roberta? When I asked if she meant *romantically*, she shyly answered, "Yes." She spoke so quietly I could barely hear her.

I knew to tread very delicately. Roberta was in a very fragile frame of mind. What she was proposing was major big-time for a straight woman. Choosing my words carefully, I assured her what she was feeling was natural curiosity, that a lot of heterosexual women had lesbian experiences. By the end of the conversation, we made plans to get together when I got back from Georgia.

Now, I don't claim to be anybody's paragon of virtue. Roberta coming on to me and the very real possibility of being with her were constant thoughts throughout my drive to Georgia, even though Stella was in the car with me. More accurately, because she was in the car with me; Stella was stupid drunk all the way down and bitchy mean all the way back, then she dashed any hope of repairing our damaged relationship when she invited her sister along for the ride. How were we supposed to talk about our problems?

When I dropped Stella off after we'd gotten back, she walked away, ignoring my request that we talk. I had made up my mind to break it off with her. Our relationship was past saving. Her ignoring me showed me what she thought of it too. I had no qualms when I called Roberta two days later.

When we met on Sunday afternoon, we were both nervous. It was a gray and gloomy day with temperature in the 30s. I had put a lot of thought into where we should go. Seclusion would be best for us, so I headed for the beach. We got out and walked the boardwalk, more to relieve our nervousness than to take in the splendors of the wild waves flinging themselves along the ramparts. We strolled from one end to the other, about a mile; when we got back to the car, I noticed her teeth were chattering. "Why didn't you tell me you were cold?" I asked, quickly turning on the engine and jacking the heat all the way up. "You're freezing." She sat in the passenger seat, arms wrapped around herself, shaking.

However or whatever I might have had in mind about initiating anything between us had just been handed to me. "Maybe I can warm you up," I offered in a soft voice, sliding over and kissing her. She didn't respond, but she didn't back away either. I kissed her again, just as gently, only a little longer, letting her get acquainted with my mouth. "Isn't this what you wanted?" I asked, looking into her eyes. She nodded. "Can I kiss you again?" She nodded again, shyly.

She warmed up (both literally and figuratively) right away. We front-seated it the rest of the day, taking breaks only when we went to get a bite to eat or change our venue (somehow we ended up in a park out in Queens). Once her initial nervousness was over, Roberta was fine with what we were doing, as evidenced by the way she squirmed when my hands and mouth were on her body. And by her comments: "Ooh, Marie, that feels so good. No one's ever done that to me before," she moaned breathlessly. By the end of the day, she'd let me slip my hand inside her panties eight times. Eight times.

We made a date for the next afternoon, New Year's Eve, when her parents were conveniently out of town. We both had plans for later that evening, so we'd only have a few hours together. I was expecting play like the day before, but when I got to her house I knew it was going to be different: She opened the door wearing a midriff T-shirt with no bra underneath and tight light-blue satin shorts. We immediately fell on each other, kissing deeply and passionately before she turned and led me upstairs.

Her room was cold. I pulled off her T-shirt. Roberta was a few inches shorter than me, so I sat on the bed and pulled her to me, fastening my hungry mouth on one nipple, then the other. My hands roamed over her slippery-satin ass. Her brown eyes were wide, innocent, trusting, tense as I eased her shorts down.

Gently I passed the pad of my thumb over Roberta's mound, which was feathered with dark chestnut hair. Her eyelids fluttered at my touch as her hands encircled my neck. I pulled her forward, barely grazed her mound with my lips. Her knees shook; she fell against me. I went with her weight, falling back onto the bed until she landed on top of me. I pressed my thigh up against her, and when I pulled it back I saw a wet mark on my pants.

I rolled over, pinning her under me and slowly, leisurely, kissed her mouth and neck. I blew hot, soft breaths into her sensitive inner ears, sucking her earlobes. Roberta moaned as I surfed her body—moving my palm from the tips of her erect nipples down her belly to her thigh. Whenever my hand skimmed her mound, she made a little sound. It was getting harder and harder for me to control myself. When she shivered a few seconds later, I gently eased open her legs and touched her until she fell against me, kissing my shoulder.

We ended up in a four-year relationship. She proved to be insatiable—we had sex every day, even though we never lived together. We back-seated, front-seated, lay on the sand, touched in the pool, boned on the tennis court, fucked in the Jacuzzi and in the basement watching television—no place was safe when we were around. After my former lover, who was very stingy with sex, Roberta should have been a treasure. And she was—until it got to the point that every time I saw her, I knew I was going to be between her legs. *Every* time. And it was only me doing the top work. Throughout our four years, Roberta obstinately refused to admit she was gay and held on to her straightness by not going down on me. She tried to, twice—and both times I stopped her, since it wasn't working. When she wanted to use her fingers instead to fuck me, I politely but firmly moved them, explaining that I wanted to feel her mouth, not her fingers.

Roberta knew that it wasn't fair to me, so one night when we were on a weekend away, after I made love to her, she suggested—insisted actually—that I find someone else to "do that." At first I demurred, stating I couldn't do that, but she kept insisting until I reluctantly gave in just to shut her up. I knew I wasn't going to do it; I'm not that type. But when she heard me say sure, she burst into copious tears, asking how could I do that to her? I couldn't win.

After four years it began to get to me, the one-sidedness of it all. Sure, the sex with her was plentiful, but it became rote, so much so that I dreaded seeing her because I knew I'd be fucking her before the night was over. I wasn't happy, but I wouldn't leave. She had committed herself to me and I wasn't going to break her heart over sex. I don't masturbate, never saw the point of it, so I stuck it out.

And then she dropped the bomb on me.

Roberta: Dodging a Bullet

Long story short: She dumped me. She said she hadn't been happy for the last two years of our relationship. I was furious—not because she left me, but because of the way she did it. She had started sleeping with the butch FedEx driver who had the evening run to her father's place of business, where Roberta worked. And I do mean *fucking*. Suddenly, Roberta knew she was gay. When we had the obligatory tearful breakup scene, she remorsefully relayed this info to me. "Funny, all the time you were with me, you were so-o-o sorry you couldn't go down on me, but now, you have no problem? Suddenly, *poof!* You're a dyke?"

Yeah...well. Whatever.

There is an epilogue with a twist to this story: Through the guilt she was feeling, Roberta wanted to stay in touch. Still the sucker, I agreed. I even met her new girlfriend Terry.

A couple of years after Roberta gave me the boot, I ran into Terry. I didn't even have to ask—she just volunteered the info. Roberta had asked her for a promise: Would she please stay in the background while Roberta got married, had a couple of kids, then got divorced?

I wasn't really shocked. Seems her sister Alicia had gotten married to a nice boy from Israel and was living there. It also seems that Roberta's family was not happy with her lesbian lifestyle and would be leaving most of their money to Alicia and her newly started heterosexual family. Roberta did not intend to be left out of inheriting her half of the family fortune. Hence her demand of Terry.

I don't know if Terry ever did it; I never saw or heard anything of her or Roberta again. But after meeting Terry that time, I didn't feel so bad about Roberta anymore.

Boy, did I ever dodge a bullet or what?

A Risk Taken, A Life Gained
J. Devon Archer

It was March of '89, only two months before I was to graduate from boarding school and move to another state for college. I'd known I was gay from a very young age, but I hid these feelings for the sake of my father, who was a minister. I lived in the women's dorm, so you can imagine how difficult this was for me. Being gay was a definite no-no, and I felt like I was going insane. The absolute worst was not being able to be true to myself.

Jordan lived in town, attending the boarding academy as a city student. It was a home-leave weekend, but because my parents were out of town I was dorm bound. Only a few of us were there that weekend, and luckily the resident assistants left us alone. A boring, lonely Saturday.

As I lay on my bed reading, wearing just underwear and a white sports bra, the phone rang. It was Jordan. Jordan and I had grown to be good friends over the short year and a half that we'd known each other. We often studied together, double dated with our boyfriends, went shopping, and played on the same sports teams. Once we even sneaked off campus to see *Lethal Weapon II*. Even though it was clear we were drawn to each other in many ways beyond friendship, we never mentioned our sexual attraction for each other. With both of us being attractive we had no trouble dating, so we always had our male counter-parts to help us play our sociably acceptable parts. But when we were alone, the world went away and we were secretly enthralled with each other. Still, we were held at bay by what we were taught to believe was damning.

When Jordan said that she wanted to come to my room later that night, as unbelievable as it was, I knew what she meant. I agreed and told her I couldn't wait to see her. I was so scared. What if someone caught us? Was I throwing away my future? What would my parents say?

Up to this point, I had always acted the way my head advised, but on this night my heart spoke much more loudly. My fears of expulsion and being shunned shrank away. I was ready. No mat-ter what happened, I knew my life would be forever changed by what was about to unfold.

I paced nervously around the room as I waited for Jordan to arrive. About an hour later I heard a quick knock at the door. I felt my heart pound in my chest. I moved to the door, trying to calm myself, then opened it. There she stood. This beautiful young woman who had as much to lose as I did was risking everything for one night with *me*. As she stepped inside and I closed the door behind her, we both knew this was ours alone to share. A smile spread across her face as she heard me lock the door. Looking around, she took note of the room. I had lit some candles and put on some quiet music. We were as alone as we could be and we had all night.

The first thing she did was wrap her loving arms around me. She just held me. I had been hugged many times before by women, but never like this. I felt everything she was saying with-out her speaking a word. She felt safe and warm. We both want-ed and needed each other but had never acted on it. My head was resting on her chest; I felt comfort and excitement as I felt her heart beat fast and strong. Her perfume was enticing. Being this close to another woman was home to me. We already knew what to do and what we wanted. The barrier had barely been crossed, and already I was happier than I had ever been. I knew I would I never return.

Jordan held me for a few minutes, trying to calm my trembling body. Her hand moved across my back and up to my face. She placed her finger under my chin, lifted it to hers, looked at me, and smiled. I closed my eyes, and our lips met. It was a soft kiss at first but quickly grew passionate in a way I'd never felt with men. Our lips parted and her tongue brushed against mine. It was then that I knew for sure we would have every part of each other that night. What I had always longed for was happening and it felt like someone had stripped away a lifetime of confusion and lies.

As we continued to kiss, my nervousness faded away. I moved Jordan against the door. She held me very close and untucked my shirt from my jeans. Her fingers slid underneath my shirt and up my back. I moved one of my hands to her neck while I slid the other under the front of her shirt. I cupped her round, firm breast. As I lightly touched her nipple with my thumb, she pulled her mouth away from my lips and let her head fall against the door. I felt her nipple harden in response to my touch. Her body was responding to me and it drove me wild. I kissed her arched neck; her skin smelled so much different than that of a man. I loved it.

In response, she moved her hands to the front of my body. For just a moment her palms rested on my chest, then button by button she opened my shirt. Her warm, delicate hands slipped past the material onto my shoulders. She pushed my shirt down my goose-pimpled arms; I shivered as it fell to the floor. It was then, for the first time in 20 minutes, that she opened her eyes. She said she liked the way the sparkle in my eyes danced in the candlelight. She gently pushed me back a little so she could take me in. The look in her eyes made me feel like the most beautiful woman in the world. All at once I started to cry. She brushed the first tear from my cheek with complete understanding and kissed me again. I had experienced a fair amount of sex in my life, but for the first time I felt like I was making love.

We continued kissing and touching with an absolute craving. Not another soul existed in our world that night. We only felt each other. I remember taking off her shirt and her unbuttoning my 501s. We kissed for what seemed like hours. I had to see and feel more of her. I reached around her back and unsnapped her bra as she did the same to me. Our eyes didn't open as our breasts met. I remember feeling her nipples against mine, so warm, so soft. We stood there holding, feeling, touching, kissing, and never wanting any of it to end. We were in heaven, about to unbind our wings.

By this time we were both so hot we couldn't get enough of each other. We started to move faster. She knelt in front of me, slipped her hands into my jeans, and moved them down my legs to the floor without ever losing contact with my skin. I had decided to surprise her by not wearing underwear. She looked up at me with this huge smile, then went back to kissing my stomach, sides, and breasts. She sucked my nipples until they were cherry red and satisfied. I ran my fingers through her hair and held her close to me.

Jordan stood up and moved me to the bed. I went to take off her jeans, but she wanted to do it herself. I watched the most beautiful creature tantalize me as she shed her garments, not once letting her eyes leave mine. We were now both naked and ready for anything.

She moved in front of me so I could kiss her anywhere I wanted to. I slid my hands down the back of her legs and around to the front of her thighs. She moved them apart and I placed my hand between them. I explored her with my hand and then delicately entered her with one of my fingers. She was so soft and warm. Her scent floated into my nostrils, and I thought I was going to explode.

As I penetrated her she gripped my shoulders with both hands, her breath quickening. She bent her head down and kissed me as I moved in and out of her with perfect rhythm. Her grip tightened as she came closer to coming, my finger inside her while my thumb rubbed her clit. After a few minutes she threw her head back, her legs started to quiver, and her hands nearly crushed my shoulders. I watched her face as she bit her lip to keep herself as quiet as possible. I felt the muscles inside her tighten and loosen on my finger and a soft warm gush filled my hand.

My being able to give her such pleasure our first time together made me cry again. I held her for a long time as we both took in what had just happened.

By this time we were both sweating, so I suggested we take shower. Jordan wanted to make sure that I had my turn, so she took my hand and led me to the bathroom. I turned on the water, keeping it at a cool temperature. When I stepped in I swear I could hear the water sizzle on my hot skin. I had never in my life been so aroused.

Jordan picked up the soap and started to wash my back. I stood there feeling her touch and for a moment thought it was all a wonderful dream, but then I felt her kneel down again. Taking my hips, she turned me to face her and the reality of what was happening came at me with full impact. I was incredibly wet with anticipation. She pushed me back against the wall of the shower, giving herself as much room as possible. I moved my legs apart and reached for the iron bar above my head for support. She took one of my legs and placed it over one of her shoulders and with little effort she lifted my other leg and put it on the other. Then she buried her face between my legs. Lingering for just a moment, she seemed to be memorizing my scent, then I felt her tongue lapping at me.

She began very gently, sucking my clit. Being very attentive to the reactions of my body, she seemed completely intent on what she was doing. I grasped the bar with all my strength, keeping myself as extended as possible. My legs gripped her back and I pulled her closer. I was careful not to hurt her, but the intensity made me want her close enough to pass through me. She caressed my clit, lips, and opening with her tongue until we were both exhausted.

I didn't come that night, but I'll never forget the effect Jordan had on me. Once again I knew more of who I was and who I was supposed to be. I was perfectly content.

We got out of the shower and held each other, still soaking wet. I took my towel and dried her off. Even though we both knew nothing would come of us, we were grateful for the trust and comfort of being friends and finding our way into our sexual identity. We kissed some more and fell into bed, exhausted. We slept naked, wrapped in each other's arms, all night.

That night had been a risk, but it was worth it. We woke up the next morning and got dressed before anyone came to my door. When they did I knew they suspected what had happened but couldn't confirm it. As they left Jordan and I looked at each other and realized what had happened was beautiful and that no one could ever take it away.

This is where my journey to find myself began. Jordan gave me the strength to begin my new life, and to this day I am grateful for everything we shared.

Whichever Comes Faster
Gina Perille

"Mom, I made plans with Jennifer Agnos for the Thursday night that I'm home, OK?"

"Sure, honey," my mother chirped over the phone. It sounded perfectly normal to her. "Will you need the car?"

I laughed. Ah, the joys of visiting the parents at age 29. "No, I think she's going to pick me up."

"Well, that's nice."

I said goodbye to my mother and checked my voice mail. Nothing except Jennifer's message from a couple weeks ago. I played it again. It was Jennifer all right. Goddamn. Jennifer and her gravelly Greek voice. Something had to be up. Jennifer never called me.

I called my best friend in Connecticut and left her a message. "Hey, Rachel. Get this. I am having dinner with this chick Jennifer Agnos when I go home to Chicago next week. Total blast from the past. She was my buddy from peewee softball back in my braces-and-glasses days. Call me."

Rachel E-mailed me that afternoon. "You idiot," her E-mail read. "You've told me about little Jenny Agnos 3,000 times. Did she really call you out of the blue? I thought this was the chick that kicked you out of her life before you reached puberty. What gives?"

"Charming," I wrote her back. "You are so charming. That's why I love having you as a best friend. She did kick me out of her life, more than once, I recall, but we managed to be friends again all the way through college and postcollege. She even met a couple of my girlfriends, remember?"

"No," was all Rachel wrote back. And then, in a new message: "Is she a hottie?"

I laughed out loud at my desk but didn't reply. It occurred to me that I had no idea whether Jennifer was a hottie or not. She and I had been summer best friends years and years ago. Skokie Youth Softball was the great demographic uniter, generating a lot of friendships across town lines and across schools. And even though we always went our separate ways when classes began, when each spring came, I'd start looking forward again to softball...and Jennifer. I remember the summer of 1987 quite clearly. We did everything together—talked on the phone all the time, bought Slurpees after practice, and spent hours listening to Whitney Houston, Chicago 17, and Richard Marx.

But there was one summer when Jennifer wanted nothing to do with me. I'll never forget it. It was 1988. Jennifer was 14 and I was 16. She didn't return my calls, didn't talk to me after games. She was gone with little explanation other than she couldn't give up all her other friends for me like she had in other years.

That was that. We weren't friends that summer at all. Jennifer was big into making proclamations. And, unfortunately for me, she was big into keeping them. I was devastated. I decided to try to stay in touch. I sent Christmas and birthday cards. Jennifer's mother and my father were friends, so I'd hear snippets about what was happening with her family now and then.

A few years later we got back in touch when Jennifer had transferred to a college near the University of Illinois, where I was going to school. I was in the theater department and had my first girlfriend. Jennifer was rushing a sorority. It sounded awful to me, but I drove down with my girlfriend to see Jennifer's campus, her dorm room, meet her friends, the whole thing. Jennifer didn't know I was dating the woman I brought.

More time passed. Jennifer disappeared again. I had finished college and was home in Chicago for six weeks between shows at the theater where I worked. In 1994 I called Jennifer while I was home, and we started to hang out again. It was fun and easy to be together. I had a new girlfriend—a woman who happened to be Greek and had a gravelly voice. No one ever seemed to notice or appreciate the irony in that, least of all me.

I remember coming out to Jennifer while sitting on my bedroom floor. I had no idea what sort of reaction my news would bring, but she was great about it. She told me I was her friend and nothing I could say or do would change that. We even took a road trip to see my girlfriend, the other gravelly-voiced Greek. Jennifer drove me there in her new purple Jetta. We talked the whole way down and back. We didn't turn on the radio once.

Then somehow we lost touch again. I continued sending Christmas cards and birthday cards for a while. Then finally I couldn't take it anymore and stopped.

Now, a few years later, I was sitting listening to Jennifer's voice mail message again. "Hi, Gina. This is Jennifer. Um, Agnos. I'm just calling to say hello and find out how you are, how you've been. Things like that. Give me a call."

It sounded like a perfectly normal message. I wondered how she'd gotten my number in Boston. I had moved several times since coming east and was about to move again in a matter of weeks. Good timing on her part. I called her the next day, not even feigning aloofness. I told her I was coming home to Chicago for the 4th of July and my dad's birthday.

"Do you want to get together? Maybe for dinner or drinks?" I asked.

"Absolutely."

"Well, I won't know my schedule until closer to the time," I said. "My mother likes to schedule me for things and I never know what's happening. You know how Toni is."

Jennifer laughed. "Gina, whenever you're free, I can be free. Just let me know. It'll be great to see you."

After Toni let me in on my agenda for my trip, I called Jennifer back and we set up a night. She called me at my parents' condo on Wednesday to confirm our plans for the next night. My dad answered. He asked about Jennifer's mother and what Jennifer's job was like. Her mother was doing well, having a lot of success as a lobbyist. Jennifer worked for a screw distributor, and, back in the day, my dad had worked for a screw manufacturer. Apparently she and my dad had tons to talk about.

Thursday night arrived. About five minutes before Jennifer was to pick me up, I found myself streaking around my parents' condo wearing only black pants and a bra. My mother popped her head out of the kitchen and asked, "Is this a late babe or a punctual babe?"

I stopped in my tracks, or as much as I could stop in socks on the tile floor. "There is no babe in this equation, mother. No babe. I've never gone out with Jennifer. This is not a date."

"OK, honey. But you're dressed like it's a date."

"I'm going to wear a shirt!" I stamped my heel on the tile. My mother quietly snickered as she returned to the kitchen.

Jennifer arrived exactly on time. *Punctual babe,* I thought. I had mascara on only one eye and slapped on the rest while she rode the elevator up to the third floor. I went out to meet her.

I saw her from the back first. She had started down the wrong hallway of my parents' building. All I could think was, *Wow.* She was in black capris and a tight white shirt that tied in the back— bare shoulders, very tan. We hugged somewhat awkwardly and headed back into my parents' place. My parents promptly pounced on Jennifer like puppies. It had been years since they had seen her. They peppered her with questions while I decided to take some preventative Advil and make sure I looked OK. When I walked back down the hallway, I thought Jennifer seemed a little nervous. Either that, or she was beleaguered by having to deal with my parents. I managed to pull them off her, and we made our way down to her car, across town, and into Evanston.

We went to dinner at a little place on Noyes Street. "Do you prefer red or white wine?" I asked her as I skimmed the wine list.

"Whichever comes faster," Jennifer said distractedly.

I smiled. She really was nervous. We chatted about this and that for a while. The waiter brought our wine. Red. He took our orders and disappeared. All at once Jennifer started talking. She told me all about being in therapy, how she'd been meditating, jogging, doing well at work. She said she sold screws for a living. I pretended not to understand.

"Like on a street corner?" I asked with incredulity.

"No, you jerk, like with a headset and a spreadsheet," she retorted. A beat. We smiled at each other. "And," she started again, "I was seeing a woman for eight months. Romantically."

All at once I understood. I totally understood. I smiled as the words came pouring from her mouth. "I realized one day that I was in love with my coach, Paula."

It took me a minute, but then I remembered Jennifer's high school softball coach. We'd had endless conversations about that crazy lady. I knew it had been a major crush for Jennifer, but Jennifer had never seen it that way back then. "And then I realized what a horrible, horrible friend I was to you. I put so much of my own process onto you. I can't believe how I treated you. And I am so, so sorry." She was crying. "So many times over the years that I wanted to call you," she went on. "I feel like you're with me everyday, giving to me everyday. I do. Gina, I am so sorry. You were always reaching out, and I never gave you anything."

We were quiet for a while. I refilled our wineglasses. We locked eyes. "Did you know?" she asked, almost in a whisper.

I spoke slowly. "I think I did. Or at least I had some inkling. Maybe I even hoped. Let's face it, I've carried a torch for you for years. I am so proud of you right now. And a little bit happy for me. Is it wrong to feel vindicated?"

She laughed. "It's been a hard road, but things are really good right now. I knew I had to find you. It wasn't even hard to do. I just picked up the phone and dialed. Well, I had to try a few different numbers until I heard your voice on the voice mail."

"Were you leaving messages all across Boston?"

"No, you idiot. I just mean that I was determined. You know, when I came out to my mother she asked about you."

"No way."

"She totally did, Gina. It's like my family always knew even when I didn't."

I smiled. "Your family knew what?"

Jennifer didn't answer. All she said was, "Ready to go?"

We left the restaurant, our food barely touched, and went for a walk so Jennifer could have a smoke. She looked as though she needed it. We walked slowly in the direction of Lake Michigan and the beach, with no real destination in mind. After about 10 minutes we found a stone bench on top of a small hill and sat down. Jennifer sat, legs crossed, sandals off, facing me.

She was rubbing my back with one hand and my arm with the other. I looked out at Lake Michigan and noted it was incredibly still. I turned my head toward her and leaned in a little. Her eyes closed. I stopped for a moment and then closed my own eyes and kissed her. Soft. Jennifer's mouth opened to mine immediately. I put my hands on her—her neck, her shoulders, her breasts— with the ease of someone who had done so before. But I hadn't. I had never kissed or touched her like this in my life. She was breathing heavily. One of us said, "Oh, God."

We stopped kissing for a moment. She was crying again. "I've thought of you so much and so often, Gina. I don't want to hurt you again."

I kissed her forehead. "Jennifer, we were *children*."

We sat watching the Chicago skyline for a while and silently decided to head back to the car. We chatted easily. It felt totally natural to be there with her, holding hands as we walked through the Northwestern campus toward Noyes Street. It was quite late, and we had to hop on and off the path in order to avoid the sprinklers that were running.

"Your sandals are kind of snappy," I cracked.

"Snappy? What the heck is that?"

"Well, you know, they make noise as you walk."

"Uh-huh. Is that a problem, Gina?"

She was practically growling. I think I liked it. I took a big step ahead of her, then turned around in her path. She was a couple inches taller than I am to begin with. Her snappy sandals also had heels. I had to stand up on the balls of my feet to kiss her. The evening was turning cool, but standing there kissing Jennifer was making me sweat. More of our bodies were touching now, and I noticed every point of contact.

Back at the car Jennifer fumbled with her keys. I tried to hide my smirk. "Don't even," she said while pushing me out of the way. We rode across Evanston in relaxed silence. The windows were down. She had her hand on the inside of my leg. Again, no music.

"Are you all right?" she asked.

"I think so. It's all a bit bizarre, isn't it? I was just sitting here trying to think of how long I've known you."

"Long time." Her hand moved off my leg and into my hand.

I turned in my seat to watch Jennifer as she drove. Every now and then she'd turn her head to look at me and give a crooked grin. We got to within a couple blocks of my parents' condo when I reached over and untied the string behind her neck, the string that held up her white shirt. We would later call this shirt the "cha-cha shirt" and what she wore that night the "cha-cha outfit." For now I just wanted it off her.

I slowly pulled the shirt down over her chest and looked at her body. Her breasts were perfect, round. As I rolled one of her very hard nipples between my thumb and forefinger, I said, "I think you'd better pull over, Jennifer."

"Working on it."

She stopped the car, put it in park, and turned to me. The streetlight was coming in the car through the windshield and across her body. I opened my hand to touch more of her breast. Jennifer put her head back on the headrest and closed her eyes for a moment. I saw her chest rise and fall twice with deep breaths. And then she turned to me. "You don't know how many times just thoughts of you have made me orgasm," she whispered.

She leaned forward and across to me. We kissed again. This time our kiss was much more intense and reckless. I still was stroking her breast when I felt her hand up behind my back. First I was reeling at the feel of her bare hand on my skin. Then I realized she had unclasped my bra. With the force of her kiss Jennifer pushed me back into my seat, lifted my shirt and bra up, and began sucking on my nipples. She left her hand on my chest and kissed my neck and slipped her tongue in my ear. I squirmed. "I've thought of all sorts of things to do to you," she said. "All sorts."

With that, she moved her hand from my chest down to the clasp of my pants. In very short order, she had my pants undone and zipper open. She paused for a moment, took a deep breath, and plunged two fingers into me. I arched back in my seat and gasped at how wet she had made me. I felt her exhale deeply beside me.

She was kissing and sucking on my neck, one hand pumped inside me while the other slid under my ass. She tipped my hips upward and pushed her fingers in even deeper. I began to move in rhythm with her. I pushed against the armrest on the door for support. Little sounds escaped my throat. I felt Jennifer's breath on my neck.

She pulled her fingers out of me and moved to my clit. Lightly. I lowered myself back down into the seat. My arms and legs were trembling. Jennifer was looking into my eyes. I was biting my bottom lip, holding her gaze as long as I could. I threw my head back as I felt the orgasm take control of my body. I said her name. She buried her face in my neck and gripped my shoulder with her free hand. It was a long orgasm. And hot. Temperature hot. It made me sweat. She made me sweat. My friend. My oldest friend. My dad's friend's daughter. Jennifer.

That night was the beginning of our oft-renewed relationship, but the first time as being lovers. And as Jennifer and I agreed, the first time she ever felt truly comfortable with me. "I think *comfortable* can be an emotion," she said later that night. I've turned that thought over in my head several times.

The structure of our relationship is still taking form. Yes, it's a long-distance romance right now, Boston to Chicago and back again. But the structure of our relationship is also supported by our long and deep personal history. Mostly it's the cause of a lot of laughter between us. My hope is that it will also be the force that brings us together. Finally. Lovingly. Comfortably. Forever.

One Night at Lizards
Brenda King

Wendy and I had known each other for two years, ever since ninth grade when we both were trying out for the soccer team. I was trying out because I had a crush on a senior, Jim Branson, who was a big jock on the varsity boys team. Wendy was trying out because her brother was a star on the football team and her parents were pressuring her to try out for a sport. But Wendy was clumsy and didn't care about athletics that much, she told me, so she picked the one sport that required the most coordination and that she knew she'd be terrible at. At least her parents would think she had tried to get on a team.

We'd met each other while we were both benched. It was hard to believe that you could get benched during a *tryout*, but every afternoon it would be just the two of us sitting in the hot sun watching the other girls on the field. It didn't take long before we were best buds.

It was the mid '80s, and I had just moved to Madison, Wisconsin, from Minneapolis that fall of ninth grade and hadn't made that many friends. I was pretty shy back then, but over time Wendy helped me come out of my shell. We soon discovered that we had a lot in common: not making the soccer team, not caring much about school, and listening to hard rock and heavy metal.

By the time our junior year rolled around, we were both thinking about dropping out and getting an apartment together, but we knew our parents would never let us.

There were a few underage clubs (16 and over) in town where we could dance to our favorite music—Bon Jovi, Whitesnake, and Poison. (OK, you can laugh, I told you it was the '80s.) Wendy and I didn't really have many friends at school because we were what you might call "burnouts." Back when I was in high school they actually had a designated area in the back of the building where students could smoke: It was called the smoking lounge, and we'd hang out there during lunch and free periods. Hard to believe now, I guess, but this was before it was illegal for minors to smoke. Wendy had teased blond shoulder-length hair and wore a lot of lip gloss. She also wore this black jean jacket that she had spray-painted with the logo for the band Ratt. We both thought it was pretty cool, but the other kids didn't. Most of them were either rich snobs, kids they bussed in from the south side of town, or drama-club geeks. I looked kind of like Wendy's twin, I guess, except I had dyed jet-black hair and I mostly wore long plaid shirts with black stirrup pants. We were kind of like Romy and Michele from the movie, except with way worse fashion sense.

The other kids had a nickname for us—the Metal Twins, and sometimes The Headbangers—and they teased us a lot and generally made life pretty miserable for us. But we didn't care that much since we had each other. And we fit in at the underage clubs, where we made friends with a lot of kids from other schools in the area.

One Friday at school during lunch, Wendy and I were in the smoking lounge sharing a Camel filter. She was wearing one of her dad's undershirts and some cutoff jean shorts.

"Hey, Brenda, I heard about this new underground club on Saturday nights. It's called Lizards. Want to go tomorrow night?" Wendy asked, a curl of smoke escaping her lips.

"Man, I wish," I said. "But I'm still grounded for four more days."

"That sucks big time. I'm getting kind of sick of Club 557. All the jocks and snobs are starting to take over. Pretty soon they're going to be playing Wham! or some other gay shit. You should just fuckin' sneak out!"

I took a long drag off the Camel and passed it to Wendy. "Yeah, right. You know how my mom—a.k.a. the Hawk—is."

Wendy smiled a devious smile. "I got an idea. Tammy—you know, that redhead chick we met at Hardee's a few weeks ago?— she said Lizards doesn't really get hopping until 10 or so. So just tell your mom you're not feeling so hot and pretend like you're going to sleep around 9:30."

"But I'm never sick. She'll know I'm faking," I told her.

"Stop being a wuss. Haven't I taught you better?" Wendy laughed. "I'll grab the ladder from your dad's shed behind your house a little before 10, and you just climb out the window and down the ladder. OK?"

"I don't know…"

"I heard Lizards is doing a Poison tape giveaway."

"All right, all right, I'll do it. But if my mom finds out, I'm dead meat."

All day on Saturday I sat in my room, sick to my stomach because I was so nervous about sneaking out. In fact, I felt so sick that I probably wouldn't have to fake it for my mom that night. I'd gotten grounded a couple of weeks before for staying out too late with Wendy on a school night. At least my mom hadn't smelled the grape Mad Dog 20/20 on my breath when I stumbled in around midnight. If she had, I would've been grounded for the rest of my life. My mom was pretty cool, now that I look back upon that time, but when you're a teenage girl, your mom is *never* cool.

So even though I was scared as hell to sneak out, I still followed Wendy's instructions. I had even taken the screen out of the window in my room earlier that day and shoved it under my bed to save time when Wendy came to get me that night. Luckily, my mom made Salisbury steak for dinner that evening, which to me was and is the nastiest entrée on the planet, so I could pretend I was sick from that. And she *knew* it grossed me out, but she'd never let me leave the table until I'd eaten at least half of everything on my plate. I bitched and moaned the whole time, but when she wasn't looking I stuffed half of the steak into a baggy I'd hidden in my pocket. (I did that a lot.) After she excused me, I went into the bathroom and flushed it down the toilet, then went into the living room and watched TV for a while with my younger brother, Mike.

Around 9 P.M. I started acting all sick, and by the time 9:30 rolled around I was in the bathroom pretending to barf. I even put a hot washcloth on my forehead just to pretend I was feverish from throwing up.

"You'd better go lie down, Brenda," my mom said when I came out of the bathroom. I guess my fake retching was pretty convincing. "Hold on a second…"

Oh, no, she knew I was lying!

"Here, take some of this Pepto Bismol," she said, opening up the bottle and spooning some of the vile pink stuff into my mouth.

After Salisbury steak, to me Pepto Bismol is the second nastiest entrée on the planet, but I downed the stuff anyway.

"I think I'll just go to sleep for the night," I told my mom, clutching my stomach.

I went into my room and shut the door, then heard my mom, dad, and brother laughing over some lame-ass sitcom in the living room. They'd watch TV for hours at a time, so I knew my mom wouldn't bother me, especially if I had the light off in my bedroom. I turned out all the lights in my room, except for a small lamp on my dresser, and got ready to go out with Wendy. I had just finished putting on my black eyeliner when I heard a noise outside. I looked out and saw Wendy throwing pebbles at my window to get my attention. She had already propped my dad's ladder up against the house.

"Hey, cute thing!" Wendy whispered. "Come on down!"

I grabbed my wallet and shoved it into my back pocket, took a quick glance in the mirror, opened the window, and climbed down.

"Lizards, here we come!" I said, and hugged Wendy, proud of my small feat but anxious about getting caught sneaking out.

Wendy and I walked around the corner to her beat-up Plymouth, then headed for Lizards, which was just a couple of miles away.

"Cover's three bucks," said the burly guy at the door of the club, a small converted warehouse.

Wendy pulled out a five and a one and handed it to him. "Tonight's on me," she said. "Since you snuck out and all." She grinned, and for some reason at that moment she'd never looked more beautiful.

Once we got inside the dark club, we immediately knew something was awry. The Smiths were blaring on the speakers, and the crowd wasn't your usual heavy metal–hard rock bunch. I didn't recognize any of the usual kids from Club 557. Everyone looked pretty New Wave: guys with poofed-up hair and bolo ties, girls with hair dyed orange and pink and blue and wearing all black. There were so many chains and dog collars, you'd think it was the city pound.

"I thought this was a heavy metal club," I said to Wendy.

"So did I," she said. "Maybe it's alternative night or something. Oh, well. Might as well stay for a while. It's not like there's anything else do to in this fuckin' town."

"All right. At least it'll be interesting."

Wendy went up to the "bar" (as I said, it was an underage club, so all they sold was soda and snacks) and got us two Diet Cokes and some corn chips. We grabbed a table near the dance floor and watched as kids undulated to Bauhaus and Siouxsie and the Banshees.

"Oh, my God," Wendy said. "Look at that guy. Like, could he have any more safety pins in his ears?"

"Yeah, we should go over and pin a note on his ear that says, YOU LOOK RETARDED."

"And what's up with that girl in that old-timey dress? Hel-lo! It's 1985. Go back to the prairie, Laura!"

Wendy and I were cracking up so bad, but when we both looked up we were speechless. Three feet from our table two chicks were actually *making out*. Now, when you're 17 and living in a small town in the Midwest in 1985, this is a *huge* deal. The only time I had ever seen two girls kissing was in the movie *Personal Best* on Showtime one night when my parents were out and my brother was in the basement playing Atari. I must admit it kind of turned me on a little, but I never told Wendy about it since I thought she'd freak out. We always called gay guys "fruits" and lesbians "bull dykes," but I was always just joking around. I didn't know what Wendy's opinions about gay people were, but that's just because I never really thought about it. I knew I liked guys—at least I always had crushes on them; on Jim Branson, for sure—and I knew for a fact that Wendy did, since she was always gushing over this one stoner guy at school, Dan Rudin.

"Oh…my…God!" Wendy and I both said in unison, and when we did, one of the girls, a tall, skinny chick with a shaved head and black bangs, looked straight at us.

"You got a problem?" she said, and she was all business. "Or did you want to join us?"

The girl she was with, a short redhead with Thompson Twin hair, piped in. "Why don't you go back to your trailer and leave us alone?"

"Um…we…uh…sorry," Wendy stammered. "It's cool, it's cool."

The two girls walked off, hand in hand, to the other side of the club. I was looking out of the corner of my eye at them, trying not to be conspicuous, but Wendy could tell I was watching them.

"What are they doing?" she asked me.

"The tall one has the short one pressed up against the wall," I told her. "They're *totally* going at it! Grinding and everything."

"Jesus!" Wendy said. "I can't believe no one's hassling them."

"Yeah, except for us. That was pretty lame of us, you know."

"I know—it just took me by surprise, is all."

"You mean, it doesn't make you sick or anything?" I asked her.

"Sick? Hell, no. I mean, we're freaks, right?"

"Yeah, and…?"

"Well, how the hell could we judge them when *we're* judged and made fun of every day at school by the jocks and snobs? Plus, my Uncle Gordon is gay. It's no big deal."

After a few minutes I got up the courage to tell Wendy about how I'd seen *Personal Best* that one time and how it had kind of turned me on. "But no way does that make me like those girls," I said. "It was probably because I hadn't had a boyfriend in a while. You know, some kind of hormonal thing." I laughed to cover up my nervousness, but Wendy looked all serious.

"Have you ever thought about kissing a girl?" she asked me.

I was looking down, a little embarrassed about where this was going, but I answered her truthfully. "Once I had a dream where I kissed Brooke Shields," I said. "But then she turned into Mel Gibson. Does that count?"

"What do you think it would be like, you know, to make out with a girl? You think it'd be the same as with a guy?"

"I don't know… I mean, I've never really thought about it," I stammered.

I don't remember exactly how it happened, but the next thing I knew, Wendy had her lips pressed to mine. And man, this wasn't like watching it on TV at all. I was tingling in places I didn't even know I had.

"Wendy!" I pulled away from her. "Someone's going to see us!"

"And you think anyone would care? Look where we are," she said.

I looked up and saw two skinny guys in fluorescent suits holding hands. Another glance revealed a rather masculine-looking woman wearing a T-shirt that read I SCREWED YOUR MOM. I'm *not* making this up.

"This place is crawling with gay people," I said, then cracked up. After a moment I got up the courage to ask Wendy the all-important question: "So, did you like it? You know, the kiss?"

"Yeah…it was…nice." Her lips were turned up at the corners, and she had a really sweet, shy look on her face. "What about you?"

"It was much…softer, you know, than kissing a boy."

"Want to do it again?" Wendy asked.

I just smiled.

"I've got an idea," she said. "Come on." She grabbed me by the hand and led me through the crowd to the bathroom.

"I don't have to go," I told her.

"That's not why we're here." She grinned and led me into an empty stall, locking the door behind us. "OK, kiss me like you'd kiss Mel Gibson—you know, kind of like a science experiment. Just to see…"

Wendy didn't need to make excuses—I was more than ready to do this. "OK, Road Warrior," I laughed, and placed my lips on Wendy's full mouth. But what began as rather tentative experimentation quickly became something more. The more Wendy and I kissed, the more turned on I got. For a full 15 minutes we made out in that bathroom stall, her tongue darting in and out of my mouth to travel down my neck and back up again. It felt so good that I didn't even stop to question what was going on. This was my friend, I loved her, and if I were going to make out with a girl, I couldn't think of a better choice than Wendy. Her slim body pressed against my more curvaceous one, and she rubbed her thigh up against my crotch. At one point she even started to put her hand down my pants, but I told her I wasn't ready for that yet.

"It's OK," she said. "It can wait."

When a couple of girls started screaming about needing to use the toilet, we got ourselves together and left the stall. We still looked all disheveled, though, and Wendy's lipstick was smeared across her face.

What do you know: It was the two girls we'd seen making out.

"Heh, heh," the tall one said.

"Guess the trailer will be rockin' tonight," the short one laughed.

Needless to say, Wendy and I were totally embarrassed, but it was kind of funny too, and I felt proud for some reason—like having those girls see us like that kind of made up for how we'd reacted to them earlier.

"Thanks for the lesson," Wendy said to the tall one, and then we bolted out the door and out of the club, laughing the entire time.

When we got to Wendy's car and were heading home, I turned to her. "Hey, how the hell did you know where the bathroom was? You dragged me there like you'd been to that club a hundred times."

"I have," she smiled, and grabbed my hand.

So, yeah, my mom did find out that I'd snuck out that night (she came to check in on me around 11 and found me missing), and I did get grounded for another two weeks. But it was all worth it. Wendy opened up a whole new world for me. She later told me that she'd never really had crushes on guys, that she'd made up her crush on Dan Rudin just so I wouldn't suspect anything. She also told me she'd had a crush on me since ninth grade and that she'd actually gotten benched during soccer tryouts on purpose so she could get to know me. Wow.

I know it sounds weird—me not really having any lesbian tendencies and then all of a sudden making out with my best friend. But it happened. And what happened after that was even weirder: Wendy and I dated for the next year and a half, until we both started college. I ended up going to a two-year community college and then transferring to the University of Wisconsin in Madison, where I got a computer science degree, and Wendy got a soccer scholarship to a big school on the West Coast. She joined the team her senior year of high school, and she was incredible, the league's highest scorer and team MVP. Our parting was sad, but we both knew it couldn't last forever, so we decided to cut our losses and move on with our lives. Today Wendy and I are still the best of friends, and we both live in Milwaukee. She works in telecommunications and has a partner, Julie, of eight years. They also have a 3-year-old son, Jake. I'm bisexual and date fairly regularly, but I still haven't found "the one." But thanks to Wendy and that first night we kissed, I always keep my options open and I know enough to never, ever take anything or anyone at face value. Thank you, Wendy, for that one night at Lizards...and the lifelong friendship that followed.

My Favorite Seduction
Margaret Green

Blue cashmere…boy, that took me back. Blue cashmere—a certain blue cashmere sweater. Memories zapped right across the ol' gray matter as I stood in the second-hand shop Cheap Frills on Melrose, fondling the $29.95 V-neck. Molly Sinclair's blue cashmere sweater…Molly Sinclair's blue cashmere sweater and Becky Iverson, who tried her damnedest to get inside it.

Well, the sweater was too expensive, so it stayed on the rack, but Molly and Becky stayed with me the rest of the day, putting a silly little grin on my face as I grabbed a tall at Starbucks (mea culpa, mea culpa, mea culpa for this corporate sin I committed) and got back to the gallery. Luckily, Cassandra, the lanky little black-clad girl I got to watch the place in the afternoons, had flaked out on me—probably too much virgin blood or something the night before—so I didn't have to explain my wistful smile. Probably would have been too much for that lace-and-velvet girl to know that good old Margaret—pudgy, middle-aged, (oh, my God) gray-haired, Margaret—was lost in reminiscences of adolescent seductions. Would've made her even paler, no doubt—as if that were possible—or make the poor little thing fade completely away in embarrassment.

Molly and Becky…what is it with adolescent girls that makes

them think they're masters of manipulation? Maybe it's all those years digging dollars out of their parents' pockets and batting long, luxurious eyelashes at teachers that makes them think a good dig and bat will get them anything they want. I sighed, one that echoed through the empty gallery (damn it, I have to pay my rent, somebody buy something): if only they were any good at it.

Becky Iverson. I can still close my eyes and see Becky, that little brown-curled cupid. Something about her eyes always made me think of Audrey Hepburn. I always a good time with Becky. I still remember the first time we met, that first semester at Brookwood—an Educational Establishment for Women. A fine one too—It did it's job so well that a majority of its graduates never married, though a lot of them moved in together.

"I get to be on top," were the first words Becky Iverson spoke to me, dropping her heavy luggage in the doorway and bounding into the top bunk. "On top is *great!* Don't you think being on top is *great?* Not that being on the bottom is bad—not at all—but nothing compares to being *on top*." Giggle, giggle, giggle. Becky made the giggle an art form. She had a giggle for everything: leaves tumbling down in the fall, the first snow, holding up my drawers that first day, cheating on math tests, putting a frog in the principal's office. Had Becky worked on it, she probably could have worked it so she never had to speak again—just giggle through life.

But when she did stop giggling for more than a second the words came out, an avalanche of words, like a giggle represented a thousand words.

That girl should have sold used cars for a living or something. She could talk you into or out of anything—like she did that first day in our room: At the end of it she was definitely on top (of a lot of things), had three out of the four drawers ("Can't stand wrinkles, not at all," giggle), and most of the desk. She even stuck up that poster—WAR ISN'T GOOD FOR CHILDREN AND OTHER LIVING THINGS—that didn't come down till it was time to cry and say goodbye four years later.

Naturally I had a thing for Becky. Who wouldn't? She might sound like a flake and a self-centered cow (which she was), but she was also Becky Iverson. Becky wasn't just a machine-gun giggle factory, she was also a great best friend. When I got detention one time for talking in class, she stuck around and helped me clean up the room. That one Christmas when my folks couldn't come, she dragged me off to her house and I had one of the best Christmases ever.

Becky was the first girl I ever kissed. Late at night, whispering to each other, we talked about movie stars I liked (and I kept bringing up Audrey Hepburn) until we got to kisses on-screen and how sometimes they looked icky (a torrent of giggles from Becky at that) but sometimes they looked sexy. "Sexy" was a new word, but one that had quickly obsessed us. Panties were sexy (except for mine, Becky claimed, as they were just simple cotton things); bras weren't. Eyes were sexy; noses weren't. Audrey Hepburn was sexy; Cary Grant wasn't.

Becky was sexy. To me, that is. When we kissed that first time, comparing different ways of doing it, I knew right then that I wanted more from Becky, but I didn't have an idea of what that might be. That was our first year together, and by our second I knew exactly what I wanted to do with Becky Iverson.

Closing my eyes…there she is, Sweet Becky Iverson. Brown curls, chubby little face. She was plump. Not fat, not that swollen kind of big you see sometimes, but just the right kind of juicy plump. She had tits. Oh, man, I wanted tits. I have them, of course, but I can't really call them tits—maybe, on a good day, a B cup. But Becky, she popped out and kept popping out. I used to watch her while she got dressed, looking as cautiously but studiously as possible. Her nipples, I remember very well, were very dark and inverted. I thought for the longest time that they weren't right, that maybe she'd lost them somewhere in some kind of horrible accident; but then winter came, and they came out. "There you are!" she said one morning, brushing her fingers across the hard points. She used to get dressed really slowly—really, really slowly in the spring when our room wasn't so cold. I used to watch her, wanting so badly to touch myself while she did, but I was too scared. I knew she was giving me a show, and I knew she liked me watching her, but there it stopped.

The problem was that Becky Iverson didn't want to do it with me. She was never rude about it, but I was just her pal. That was me, always a pal and never a partner. Undressing and dressing was one thing, and maybe the occasional practice kiss, but we were Mutt and Jeff not Audrey Hepburn and Cary Grant—though I would've killed to be Cary, even if we both thought he was ugly, since he always seemed to be kissing Audrey.

What Becky Iverson wanted was Molly Sinclair. I hated Molly Sinclair. I wish it weren't true, but Molly Sinclair was sort of my second kiss. Molly Sinclair: tall, thin, perky, bottle-blond (proud of it too, which made her even more of a cow), and sexy—or at least she thought so. The problem was, she was sexy—at least on the surface. You couldn't help watch Molly Sinclair as she walked by; there was just something about her. Of course, showering together didn't help things. It was like watching a piece of Greek or Roman statuary soaping up, rising off, and soaping up again. Then she'd look at you watching her, and she'd laugh and laugh and laugh.

That was Molly Sinclair—that and the blue cashmere sweater she wore all the time. Even though we had uniforms, she wore that damned sweater like it was her mantle or something, and even when the summer spiked the thermometer at 90-plus she'd still tie the thing around her waist. The only time she took the stupid thing off was for gym class.

Anyway, the kiss—I almost forgot, or keep wanting to forget. There was a lot of fucking around. We all knew that, or maybe secretly hoped there was, so there was like this crazy kind of steam over everything there. We could barely sit still in class for the hormones racing around. It was like trying to stand up in a hurricane.

I hated Molly Sinclair for her attitude, for her smarts, her money (though my folks were just about as well off as hers), her tits, and even that blue cashmere sweater—but that didn't mean I didn't look at her when she walked by. I wanted to get that naked soapy girl away somewhere and do…well, whatever it was that the girls did in those "special" books with the lurid covers that kept drifting between us: *She Liked Girls, Dykes in Love, The Maneater.* While my heart was for Becky, I certainly would-n't have turned down "a voyage into her nether regions where her sex steamed like a feminine boiler of desire." Whatever the hell that meant.

She knew it, of course—like I said, you could have cut it with a knife. So there I was in the library, trying to figure out what the average rainfall was in Brazil, when Molly Sinclair walked up. "Hi, Betty," she said, with a giggle in her voice—but not Becky's special giggle. All this giggle said was that she knew I was quaking in my shoes and it was all so *funny.* "I thought you'd be here." Then she kissed me hard, the whole tongue dance and everything. *Bang,* I was wet. *Bang,* my little tits were aching. *Bang,* my nipples were hard and tight. *Bang,* she slapped me. "Like I'd ever do you, cow," she said, laughing high and shrill as she walked away.

I hated Molly Sinclair. The problem was that Becky Iverson wanted Molly, even thought she might love her, and spent most of her time trying to get into that blue cashmere sweater. That wasn't the worst of it. The worst of it was that Becky thought she was this master seducer, this chubby little femme fatale, and so I had to spend four long years listening to Becky plot and plan how to get Molly. I didn't mind it half the time since I adored Becky and liked hanging out with her even if she was reading me sickly sweet love poems about the color of Molly's nipples, the softness of her skin, or how she dreamed of "tasting the woman nectar between her pale thighs." Damn those stupid books.

Finally, that last summer together, Becky had it all worked out. For all her snot and superiority, Molly was crashing and burning at geometry. That provided opportunity—especially since no one else could really haul Molly's ashes out of the fire. So a letter was written, surprisingly simple, considering Becky's florid and pornographic reading habits, and a date—though Molly didn't know it was one—was set. For the love of my friend, I promised to be elsewhere that night—though after Molly's cruelty I couldn't bear to go into the library again, so I told Becky I'd just bring my books to the cafeteria. "Don't worry about me," I told her. "Don't worry about my sadness and heartbreak. I'll be fine."

So I read Virginia Woolf and Jane Austen and waited. It was right after gym, so the rest of the girls were either in the library, down in the rec room, or off doing God knows what in their rooms. Me, I had Virginia and Jane. Virginia and Jane, while Becky hoped to get Molly. It just wasn't the same.

I waited for an hour or so, then went back, opening the door to the hard sounds of Becky's tears. It was bad, so bad she was on the bottom bunk, all curled up into a ball. Molly, it turned out, had cruelly chastised and humiliated Becky in the hall, accusing her of all kinds of things. Then she'd left, storming off in a fury.

I held my friend for a very long time, just letting her cry. Slowly the tears dried up, and while the giggles didn't return, at least she was able to talk. Poor Becky was heartbroken, her seduction in tatters. I felt bad, of course, really bad—and I ached like you wouldn't believe. "Tell me what you wanted to do," I whispered in her ear.

And she told me. Her words were simple, direct. It was touching, really, and while I still hurt deep inside I think it was good for both of us. And then we did little things: a kiss, long and tender. The feel of her plump breasts in my hands, the way her nipples poked out: one, two. The taste of salt on their tips. More kissing. Lots of kissing.

We didn't do a lot, but we did enough. I'm not even sure I came, though I definitely know I was excited. It was like the excitement was the be-all, end-all. Fuck, I'm not too sure we could have come—we were just too excited. It was nothing out of those awful books, thank God. No, it was more like two real good friends who decided to help each other take a peek over to the other side of friendship. That's what was so special about it—that little step from Frick and Frack to girlfriend and girlfriend.

It didn't last long. That was our last year at Brookwood. Becky went on, I went on. I saw her the year after that when I went to her place for Thanksgiving, but all we did was kiss and hold each other. Christmas cards, the occasional letter—eventually nothing at all.

In the end, I think it worked out for both of us, knowing that it's OK to sleep with your friend or to make a lover into a pal. I just wish it hadn't started with tears. Still, some tears were worth it—like those that snotty Molly Sinclair cried when she realized that someone had stolen her precious blue cashmere sweater, the reason behind her big tantrum. I threw it away the next day, stuffing it into a cafeteria trash can.

Blue cashmere. I hated blue cashmere. Sometimes, though, something you hate can bring you something wonderful.

Down Under
Katie L. Parker

'I woke up when a gentle pressure nudged my arm. The faint smell of L'air du Temps wafted its way to my nose, along with the even fainter, rather sweaty smell that long airplane travel ingrains in the body. Sweaty or not, both smells belonged to someone very dear to me. And although fear did not allow me to fully acknowledge it at the time, the salty-sweet perfume of this woman stirred some deep part of me that was as yet lying dormant. *Marlie,* I drowsily thought. I smiled and opened my eyes.

"Katie, look out the window," my best friend whispered to me. Excited blue-green eyes practically sparkled at me as she spoke. "It's Australia."

I sleepily looked out the window of the flying tin can that had miraculously transported us from San Francisco all the way to Sydney in the land Down Under. The ocean was vast and blue as it had been during most of the excruciatingly long flight, but finally we were closer to land. The city of Sydney appeared to be dotted with graceful white buildings set into green hills. I saw boats sailing in the harbor, gleaming little specks on the water being bounced up and down by gentle waves.

"I can't believe we're actually here," I said as I woke up more. That was really Australia outside my window, and that was really

Marlie in the seat next to me. "The land of kangaroos and koala bears, finally. Just a train ride from Sydney and we'll be at our campus in Melbourne."

"And together, like we planned back in Bramwell," she said back, squeezing my arm. Entranced by the city growing bigger and more detailed as we rapidly approached it, I only grinned and squeezed her arm back in reply.

It was February 1990. Sharing an adventure in the southern hemisphere for a semester abroad was a college experience Marlie and I had dreamed of since we were first-year students thrown together as roommates in Bramwell Hall at our small school in Northern California. Although the room drawing that had placed us together was random, we instantly clicked as friends and chose to remain roommates right up until our journey to Oz. Marlie and I had shared intimate confidences, late-night study sessions, and spontaneous trips to the campus coffeehouse for steaming cups of mocha and lattes to fuel our undergraduate experience.

While Marlie and I had several lesbian friends at college and were comfortable around our queer classmates, we ourselves had always dated boys, denying our physical attraction to one another. Marlie, in fact, was involved in a long-term relationship when we headed to Melbourne. She and her boyfriend had begun dating at the end of our sophomore year. I was lucky if I had relationships that lasted more than a month at the outside. But although we didn't realize it when we left for our semester abroad, our friendship was rapidly developing into something much more wild and passionate.

After we blearily accepted the greetings by the local study-abroad program officials, we were bought breakfast at an airport café, whisked off to the train station, and tucked into our car with cheerful goodbyes and wishes for a pleasant journey to our final destination several hours south. When we eventually arrived at Monash University in Melbourne (which, we discovered from seatmates, needed to be pronounced "melbun" if one did not want to be utterly disgraced as an ugly American), we were still thrilled but exhausted. More smiling officials met us, plopped us and our baggage in a car (which drove on the "wrong" side of the street, amusing us to no end in our slightly delirious state), and deposited us in front of the dorm, which looked remarkably like dorms at large American universities. Then we were each handed a different room key.

Marlie and I took our keys and stared at each other for a second.

"Wow," Marlie finally said, laughing a little. "This will be the first time in two and a half years we haven't shared a room together," she explained to the hostess, who smiled cheerfully and uncomprehendingly, told us when to be down for dinner, and encouraged lots of sleep in the meantime while our bodies adjusted to the enormous time change. Then she bustled off, leaving us together. *But not much longer*, I thought morosely.

"Well, I guess we needed to stand on our own two feet someday," Marlie joked, although her face looked anxious.

After a pause, I swallowed the abrupt feeling of desolation and brightly said, "It'll finally be easier not to cramp my style. Think of all the great Aussie guys I'll be able to bring over without having to use the code." The code was a small bathroom towel hung outside the door when one of us wanted privacy and requested that the other lose herself on campus for an hour before returning to our room. Hiding behind a professed attraction to boys sheltered me from facing my true feelings toward Marlie.

"Sure," my best friend said as she turned away from me and headed to her own room, alone. I watched her dark blond head move away from me and struggled against a crazy need to call out, "Just stay in my room." Biting my tongue, I went into my own room and shut the door.

A few months into our stay at Monash University, we were settled in and enjoying the local life. While her boyfriend was pining away for her in America, Marlie was steadfastly not dating other guys and therefore living vicariously through me. True to form, I'd already gone out on nearly a dozen dates and been seeing this one particular guy (bloke, as the Aussies would call him) for a week already. None of them interested me much, except for the tantalizing, somewhat terrifying fact that the ones I kissed only turned me on when I imagine their mouths soft and sweet against mine, their hair long and flaxen shimmering against my face. It was much later that I realized I whizzed through men like they were so many party favors because none of them ever measured up to the one person I truly wanted and was too afraid to reach for.

Marlie was in my room one evening, watching me get ready for a date with the cute bloke. She was helping me decide on an outfit, apply my makeup, and dispensing advice on how the evening should progress, as was our habit. On this particular evening, she was somewhat pensive as she watched me primp. Oddly enough, I also felt a little deflated. I didn't really want to go out with someone tonight; I only wanted to be with Marlie. The implications of my feelings, however, frightened me, even as they sent a bolt of hot lightning racing through my blood and igniting my skin. *Your best friend,* I mentally chastised myself. *And she's a girl.* It was scary but definitely electrifying.

"The blue, Katie," she quietly advised as she cast a critical eye over my choice of dresses in the closet. "Blue always brings out your eyes."

"But I wore it last Saturday," I pointed out.

"You could never look bad in it. Not even if you wore it every day for a year. It looks perfect on you." Her voice was solemn as she spoke, and I looked at her turquoise eyes to see the firm truth in them. Her dark golden hair, tucked behind one ear, fell over the rest of her face like a smooth waterfall. Taking a deep breath, I resisted the impulse to reach out and discover how soft that hair really was against my skin. *Think about the bloke,* I futilely urged myself.

"Katie, do you sometimes feel like you're in a fairy tale here? In Australia, I mean." Marlie's voice was faraway, dreamy, and yet somehow sharp. I could tell she was leading up to something, but I could not be sure what. My heart, though, starting beating double-time as I tried to be nonchalant.

"Sure," I agreed.

"As if we could do anything here, and it wouldn't count at home? I mean, like the rules at home don't count here? When in Rome, do as the Romans do," she concluded.

"OK," I said. My skin was beginning to prickle as she spoke. I wondered if I was crazy, getting ready for a date when my best friend clearly needed to talk to me tonight. *You mean, when you want to kiss her*, the thought popped into my head, and I almost gasped.

"Can we go for a walk before you met him?"

"Sure. Where do you want to go?" I reached for a light sweater to cover up my exposed shoulders from the slightly cool night air.

"Down by the kangaroo pens. To look at the stars," she said, sounding very blasé all of a sudden.

In the mornings, if you passed by the 'roo pens early enough on your way to class, you could sometimes see the large gray males boxing over the females, huffing and puffing at each other like prizefighters. Once, Marlie and I saw a baby stick its fuzzy little head out of its mother's pouch on her belly.

So we wandered out of the dorm. I was in an almost breathless state, wondering if Marlie was going to tell me she wanted more from me than friendship. It seemed crazy yet at the same time the perfect culmination of our years as friends. Or was I just wistfully dreaming?

"Katie, I want to talk to you about something very serious," she said to me as we walked through the night air of Australia. "I mean, what I want to say is—"

"Marlie," I interrupted. I stopped so I could face her. "Look up at the sky. Isn't that why you wanted to come out here?"

She looked up at the unfamiliar constellations, up at the dancing Southern Cross. I reached out my hand and grasped her chin. She lowered her eyes to look at me in the moonlight. Surprise was evident in her shadowed face, as was something else I had been longing to see—passion. Desire. Acceptance.

"Please, Katie," she whispered. "Stay with me tonight."

We kissed then, in the moonlight, under stars we didn't know, on a foreign land that had given us the freedom to explore what we really wanted. Marlie's soft, full lips, her silken hair gliding between my fingers, her warm breath on my cheek as she said my name between kisses.

We stumbled back to my dorm room, where I called the bloke and begged off with our date with an excuse about a migraine. Shutting off the lights, opening the window for the gentle breeze, Marlie and I tumbled together on my bed. She removed the satiny blue dress I wore, her hands eagerly caressing every inch of my skin that she exposed. Everything felt so right with her, so in tune. There was no question at all where this sultry night would lead us.

Her touch set my body aflame in ways it had never once experienced with a man. Marlie nibbled her way down the length of my body when my dress was off. Her teeth bit at my collarbone, my nipples, making me cry out in a sort of sweet agony. As her lips moved every downward, over my stomach, hesitating over my belly button, then determinedly kissing and licking in slow smooth strokes the skin just above my pubic hair, I thought I might pass out from the scorching pleasure.

My best friend, was perhaps my last coherent thought.

"Marlie, I've been wanting you for so long," I managed to raggedly say before her lips descended between my legs and I could no longer speak.

Marlie and I loved one another throughout the night, pausing only to look at each other in wonder, to giggle, to drink cool water before impatiently reaching out again.

Five years later, back in California, we are in a committed relationship, considering raising a child, and blissfully sharing every wonderful day and passion-filled night together. I met my soul mate when I met Marlie, and luckily I was hers as well.

Most importantly, we are still best friends.

Dinner and a Friend
Toni Rae Knight

We could be making love like finger sandwiches, one on top of the other…a layer of this, some of that…I could be touching you like a man with one hand, making you buck underneath my strength. Desire is so much like a stone sometimes, so hard and so indefinitely physical, like a flash of light: It is either there or it is not. It was there, even though sometimes I didn't want to believe it was there, me being the girl you most trusted, most adored…

You told me about Erik and how he did these things to you, and I smiled with my eyes all wide like a gleeful surprise, but it was more like a scream of jealousy. You told me everything, spilling it all in your hand, giggling over vanilla wafers while I munched in sync, my mood like a room with no air. Even with all the munching and giggling, guffawing and playful pinching, I couldn't think of any good excuse to lean over and stab you with my love. Over the crumbly sweetness I wanted to lick the sugar from the dip of your lips and do what is best said in a song with violent guitars. I never told you that I had slept with women a few times before—they were the kind of women that had other lives and preferred to return to them when the night was over.

When you think of best friend and lover, you think of oil and water, sugar and salt, polka dots and stripes. Still, I don't avert my eyes when we change in the same room, and I didn't turn my head when you flung off your clothes and gave me a full view of your naked body before diving into the lake two nights ago. My nights were filled with lakes and dreams of you naked, but this time there are no trees or darkness, just you, brown and fresh before me. Then your mouth comes like a confirmation of my desire and tells me; "I want you to go to a party with me tonight."

And then I am awake. "What?"

"Javin's party. I want you to go with me. It's supposed to be wild."

So we go, and as promised, it's a wilder night than most, but many of our nights seem wilder now that we're both old enough to drink. For me it is mostly television and adjusting my sleeves to wait for you. For you it is other people and random conversation as you whirl around Javin's two-story house. But bless your heart; you visit frequently to feed me grapes and hard bread. On the fifth visit you stuff cheese and round crackers in my mouth and hug me as if we had parted two months earlier. Then you send me to fetch two glasses of spiked punch, which I do. I will gladly be that for you—the one to fetch all you need and hold them before you, dripping and full of intention.

I've started to understand your quirky adoration of me, but by some desperate chance I'm hoping that deeper affections are not far behind. The evening slowly wraps itself up into a wayward bundle of heavy eyes and low voices. I want to go home with my arms around your shoulder as if we are escaping from a war. You grab my hand and drag me into the kitchen, where two men are stroking each other.

"Javin," You moan. "I am so-o-o fucked up. And Dee's been drinking too. Can we crash here?"

"Of course, hon." Javin eyes me with a smile, a muscular arm wrapped around his new "dish" for the night. These days his smiles are more of a knowing wink than an actual grin. "You girls just go upstairs to my second bedroom."

I haven't slept this close to you since we were much younger, but it seems like for you it's all the same feeling. For me it's so much more, although simpler than it used to be. When you begin to learn the implications of desire, you understand that there is nothing simpler than lust. And you understand why certain parts of you are driven for people you don't understand. It was more than sharing my days with you; I want you—that is evident now.

We're in Javin's guest bedroom, and I want to turn on the fan and perhaps forget the heat of your leg on mine, but more so I want to devour your lips with mine, without fear of your response. I want to have the courage to reach out and stroke your breasts, which are so close to mine.

It's Saturday night and we're both drunk. I'm on fire with a feeling like swimming, and the bitter heft of the sweetened punch is riding me long and dry. I could think about other places and other feelings, but your breathing is becoming a louder distraction than my own panicked burning. Turning my head underneath the blankets I see that you have moved and are now on top of them. You are hot, but I'm now realizing it has nothing to do with the temperature of the room. I follow the curve of your neck to the soft rise of your belly, where the movement of your hand leads me even lower. And that is when my memory of your naked body is forever changed from soft and beautiful to hard and animal and wet.

I am watching you shifting on the bed and then touching yourself, your fingers quickly learning the rhythm of your sudden arousal. Your eyes are closed and your head is tipped backwards as if to loosen your breathing. I watch your fingers disappear into the small mass of wiry curls between your legs before moving back out again to sink deeper still. The small space between us soon becomes damp with the sharp smell of your arousal. Perhaps it is the lack of real distance between our heated bodies or the combination of animal scent and scattered breathing that is causing my own breath to shudder through me in a frenzied mixture of anxiety and longing. I can't forget the soft sounds of your wet suction around the steady stroke of your fingers. I imagine my own fingers inside you. I want to teach you this feeling inside me. I want to fuck you into knowing the smell of me.

When you climax in the bed beside me it starts with a small squeal; an accidental outburst, and then you turn your head away. As you exhale loudly and furiously, my eyes are wet on the naked length of your legs, and the inner flesh of my own thighs are wet with my desire for you. Finally, slowly, you turn your head around to the right, where I am laying. You look at me as if just now remembering me laying here.

"I'm sorry, Dee. Did I wake you up?"

"No," I say, although you have, but in a different way.

"I guess I had too much to drink," you smile, winking at me.

For the next week or so, it's you and me as if nothing had happened, floating through our days as usual, bumping fondly into each other and chattering lightly. And you continued to cook for me. For some reason you live to feed me as I live to be nourished by you. I especially love lasagna night. But as you prepare the same delicious meal Friday evening I'm far from happy. Erik has joined us after being MIA for a couple of weeks and is lounging on the sofa, legs slung over the armrest, waiting. Why would you waste your culinary talents on an ungrateful oaf like him? He wouldn't lick the spoon like I would, wouldn't imagine the wicked reflection to be your tongue on the other side. It's not that I hate Erik—I don't know him well enough to have the pleasure—I just hate the way he hangs around, the way he can get so close to you after just a few months, and I've known you all my life and can only dream about feeling your mouth on mine. I'm sure he doesn't lie awake at night thinking of you.

You, Erik, and I are eating like starving hogs, and the wine makes us giddy. I'm lazy with the wine and ready to roll on the floor with you. But Erik is here, and I want to throw him out the door. He's grabbing at you with the smugness of being full and inebriated, and his touch turns from friendly to suggestively sexual. As he grabs for your breasts and reaches with wet lips for your neck, I fight the urge to shove him away. You playfully push against him, giggling.

Suddenly you change the mood of the evening. "I think Erik should let me strap it on and fuck him," you say. "What do you think?"

"What?" Erik laughs very loudly, rolling his eyes.

"I think all straight guys secretly want to be fucked in the ass." You raise your eyebrows at me. "Don't you agree?"

I shrug. "I suppose."

"What does she know," Erik guffaws. "She's a dyke."

You shove Erik. "Shut up. You don't know that."

He shoves you back playfully, chuckling, and then you go back and forth like that, drunkenly shoving and snickering at each other. He takes advantage of the silliness of the moment and grabs your flailing arms, pressing his lips against your laughing mouth. I don't think you notice me leave the room, but you must because your movements are suddenly more aggressive and you kiss Erik passionately. I disappear to my bedroom. For minutes I stand there staring at my bed, waiting for my jealousy and anger to push me down onto it. But I can't move.

And because I know what I'll see and because I cannot stay away, I go back in the hallway, letting my curiosity drag me to the scene of your tangled bodies. And there you are with your jeans around your knees, a couple thin straps of leather drawn tight around the curves of you buttocks. The your ass flexes repeatedly as you drive the plastic cock into him. You have a way of making people discover desires they didn't know they had. You are leaning into Erik, bending him with the strength of your thrusting as you fuck him from behind. I don't want to hear the crack in his voice as his heavy groans turn into whimpers of pleasure. My stomach tightens at the sight of your hand reaching below him, gripping the hard thrust of his penis, roughly tugging at its swollen length, pushing him into a deeper place. That's when I find it impossible to continue watching and return to my bedroom.

I change into a T-shirt and boxers before climbing into bed and pulling the covers up over my head. More than just anger and jealousy swirls hot behind the tight pressure of my closed eyes. More like disappointment? A desperate anxiousness? Several minutes pass, and then your voices are louder again, but it's a different sound. I know you're heading to your bedroom.

"I have to say good night to Dee…" I hear your voice again, almost like an afterthought. "See if she's all right…"

When I hear you come into my bedroom, I turn my head under the covers, hoping you'll think I'm asleep and won't lean over me smelling of sex and sweat.

"Dee, are you asleep?"

I remain silent, breathing deeper and louder. You don't get the hint. "You can't be asleep already. I know you were watching us."

And so I roll over to face you, not knowing what you're able to see of my eyes in the dark.

"Are you OK?" you ask.

"Couldn't be better."

"That's the worst lie I've ever heard."

"It's not a lie. I'm OK, really."

"Then why do you look so angry?" You lift the covers and crawl under them, nudging me over. I sigh. Suddenly the small space is filled with you, and my heart is filled with the weight of my feelings.

You push forward under the covers, seeking my eyes in the darkness. "Remember when we were younger and we'd hide under the covers for hours, pretending it was the end of the world and we were hiding in a cave together?"

"Yeah." I smile.

"Remember how we'd talk about what we'd do if we were the only people left in the world, and you said you'd rob all the candy stores in the world?"

I chuckle. "Forget robbing banks—I want candy."

"The end of the world," you snicker. "What a horrible thing to fantasize about."

"Yeah," I mumble in agreement.

We're both quiet for a long moment, remembering. "What

would you do if it were the end of the world?" you finally ask me.

And that's when I lean over under the pile of blankets and kiss you full on the mouth.

You're suddenly very quiet and still, your body rigid underneath the covers. "Dee!" you hiss. "What are you doing?"

"I don't know," I whisper back. "Why? Do you love Erik?"

"I don't love him. Don't be stupid—you know that."

"Then why are you with him?"

You're quiet for a moment before speaking. "Because he…*shit*, I don't know. Jesus, Dee, what are you trying to do?"

I don't feel like talking. I want to get my share of you before you return to Erik, so I kiss you again. Your mouth is so much softer than I imagined, wide and embracing as you begin to respond. I only have to sweep your lips once with the tip of my tongue before yours comes out to meet mine. And then they tangle together. My hands are underneath your shirt at your sides, laying flat against the warmth of your skin. "What's he doing?" I ask finally, pulling away.

"Waiting in my bedroom."

I slide my hands slowly down to the elastic of your shorts and pull them out and away from your body. The taste of you is still in my mouth, warm with the flavor of wine. "You should go then," I say.

There's so much I want to do and say, but I'm not brave enough. Then I realize you're not moving to leave. I lean over and cover your mouth with yet another impassioned kiss, and this time I lean into you with the entire length of my body. You move forward as well, and as our bodies collide you grab my hands and pull them around your body.

I pull my mouth away from yours. "Erik—-" I begin.

"It's all right." You are breathless and speak softly. "He's probably passed out. He came, like, two times."

I'm relieved he won't be bothering us, but that's not what I want to hear. "And you?" I ask, and as I push my right knee in between your thighs I can tell you're already very wet.

"No," you whisper against my mouth. With our leg up over my thigh, you shudder again, and I reach underneath your shorts to feel the wetness that has dampened the sheets and made you slick and inviting. You moan softly and squirm to get your clothes off. We pull apart, and for a moment we're tangled in the soft slide of clothing as we undress each other. And then we're pressing long and naked against each other, and the feel of your breasts against mine makes it difficult for me to breathe.

I cup your breasts and push them toward my mouth. I take your hardened nipple between my lips and lash at it with my tongue. My hand is still between your legs, finding the sensitive areas as your hips guide my fingers up and down your clit. With a sudden forceful thrust you draw my fingers deep inside you. You move down onto my fingers and at the same time seek my own breast with your mouth. Just the sensation of your tongue against my nipple is enough to send me rocketing quickly toward release. My stomach tightens as my knees slacken.

I can't imagine that Erik doesn't hear us. Everything seems so loud underneath the covers; the sound of your mouth tugging and sucking at my nipple, the sound of my fingers sinking deep into your wetness, and your frenzied breathing, which quickly overwhelms everything in the small space. Shaken and unsteady, you lean your forehead against my neck, and all it takes is the sound of your voice as you whisper my name against me, and I am overwhelmed with the aching buzz of my body. You're even closer to me, pushing against me until your body takes over and you climax with a sudden violent shudder. And then I know you must leave. I don't want to be left here alone, sighing myself to sleep, I want to hold you next to me and make love to you again. And again. I want to taste you this time, to make you shudder in my mouth. But I know there are things to be said, and I know you can't just leave Erik alone in your bedroom.

Finally, you sigh, pulling away from me underneath the blankets. "Good night, Dee," you say softly.

" 'Night," I say, pushing back under the covers to nestle in the comfort of the warm blankets. And then you disappear.

In the morning there's the problem of seeing you and how to behave. As I enter the kitchen I expect to see Erik and then you, laughing about how smashed you were last night and how you don't remember everything that happened. But you're alone, both hands hovering over a small teacup, and your expression is placid as you stare off into the air.

"So how was your night?" I climb onto the stool at the kitchen counter.

"OK," you say plainly, blinking as if you'd just noticed me.

"What did Erik say last night?"

"I don't know. He was gone when I got back to my bedroom. He called this morning to tell me he heard us last night."

Why didn't you return last night if Erik had left? I look at the counter, saying nothing for a while. "So what are you going to do?" I finally ask.

You sigh. "There's nothing I can do."

Will you regret what happened? Would you rather forget the feel of my lying naked against you? As I remember your heated body, I know I'll never be able to forget last night. For minutes silence envelops the room. This is the first time we've ever forgotten what to say around each other, and you suddenly seem like a stranger to me.

"Are you OK with what happened?" I ask finally, dreading the answer. I'm positive you'll say no.

You sigh again. "I'm OK with it. I just don't know how to feel." You meet my eyes for the first time, holding my gaze until I shyly look away. "But I will soon," you promise, smiling. "In the meantime, let me make you breakfast."

Lovely Lina
Mia Dominguez

Evangelina and I became friends the instant her family moved into the house next door and my mother went to greet them, as she always did with all of the new families. We were both 7 years old and were lucky enough to be in the same class together during our first six years of grade school. Of course, as with any other relationship we've had our disagreements, but nothing that ultimately couldn't be resolved.

Our most memorable disagreement happened when she told me of her plans to marry Daniel. The moment I laid eyes on him I didn't like him. Not for Evangelina, anyway. She was different in his presence, nervous and unsure of herself. When Daniel was around you could feel the tension in the room—thick and uncomfortable. Somewhere you didn't want to be and certainly didn't want your best friend to be. The thing I hated most about him was his wandering eye. Whether we were out having dinner, nightclubbing, or even in a church mass, he couldn't keep his eyes off other women. These women didn't have to be more beautiful than Evangelina, although it's my unbiased opinion that it would be difficult to find a more beautiful woman. Evangelina was exquisite to me, but for him she was merely a conquest in a sea of others he'd already had or would soon set sail for.

On the morning Evangelina called to ask if I'd be her maid of honor, I decided to express my concern. "Lina, I don't think you should get married just yet."

"Why not? I'm in love with Daniel."

"I don't think you're truly in love with him," I told her. "How could you be? He doesn't treat you the way you deserve to be treated."

"That's just his way. You only see him in public. When we're alone he's very different," Lina said.

"Why can't he be different all of the time? In public he's checking out everything in a skirt."

"Daniel does admire the ladies," she said, "but he loves me too."

"Don't you think you deserve a man who admires you above anyone else?"

"All men are the same, Mia."

"Then prove it by holding out for a while," I told her, "and seeing if you still feel this way in a year or so. Please, think about this before you jump in."

"I've thought about it, and I want to get married. I'm not desperate or insecure—I'm in love. We'd like to start a family soon, so we're going to get married in July."

"That's only four months away. You can't possibly plan a wedding in four months. Why the rush?"

"Daniel says he can't wait, and I don't want to let him get away, so I'm marrying him. Now, will you please be my Maid of Honor?"

"Only if you promise to really think about it for a while. I love you and I'll always be here for you. I just want you to be happy. I think you can be happier without him."

"Look, Mia, I'm not perfect, and Daniel accepts me for who I am. He doesn't care that I'm not a size 5, or that my hips are too big for my body. He likes me for me." I heard let out a big sigh.

"Lina, you're so beautiful," I said. "I don't see why your dress size would matter to anyone, especially the man that's supposed to love you. If he's so in love with you, he wouldn't show so much interest in other women."

"As long as he's looking and isn't touching, that's fine. I'm not a jealous woman." I could hear Lina's voice begin to shake. "Please be there for me, Mia. You're the only one I can count on."

"Look, I'll support you no matter what your decision. Just be careful, honey."

Practically one year to the day of that conversation, Evangelina's marriage to Daniel began to wane miserably. She couldn't confide in anyone in her family, so she and I became closer than we'd ever been. In the beginning I was simply a shoulder to cry on, a far cry from—and a poor substitute for—a husband. Over time, however, Evangelina and I got to know one another in a way we could never imagine. A passion grew between us that no one else, not even her misogynistic husband, could interfere with. Sexual intimacy between Lina and I had never entered into the equation because she had absolutely no idea of my interest to become much more than friends. No idea, that is, until she stayed over one night and I finally found the courage to share my secret with her.

We had just indulged in a shopping spree. She thought some new lingerie would help her keep Daniel's interest, although once we returned to my place, she realized it was a fool's attempt to revive the dead.

"Oh, Mia," she told me. "They're so beautiful, but I could never wear anything like this. I just don't have the body for it. I don't know what I was thinking."

"Who says you don't have the body for it? You're a knockout. If you're that uncomfortable, you can wear this robe over that teddy." The set was a luscious burgundy color, and I knew she'd look delicious in it. "Why don't you go put these on? They'll make you feel like a queen."

Evangelina looked at them for a moment. "They really are beautiful. OK, I'll try them, but only with the robe."

"Great. I can't wait to see you."

After a good 20 minutes changing in my guest room, Evangelina finally came out. I grew aroused immediately. She did wear the robe over the teddy, but it showed off her enticing cleavage. Her breasts were full and firm, begging to be adored.

"Mia, I feel foolish standing here half-naked. Can I go change?"

"Absolutely not," I shouted. "How about if I change also?"

"Sure. That'd make me feel more comfortable. Kind of like the sleepovers we had when we were little girls, huh?"

Without hesitation I leapt to my feet and ran into the bedroom. I slipped into my sheer red robe with satin trim and a pair of satiny red panties. When I returned to greet her in my new attire, she was quite impressed.

"Wow, Mia. You look great. I don't know why someone hasn't snatched you up yet. You're perfect."

"I guess I haven't met the right one, huh? Or maybe I've met the right one, but they just don't know how I feel."

"Anyone would be an idiot to reject you. You're the best."

"Really?" I hesitated for a moment, not knowing whether or not to pursue her, then decided to test the waters. "If I were interested in you, would you reject me?"

"Hypothetically, right?"

"Whatever you'd like it to be."

"Well, even though I've never been with a woman, if a woman like you were interested in a woman like me, I'd take the chance."

"Really?"

"Really."

I thought about that for a moment, allowing those words to seer into my brain. "Well, would you like to do some exploring with me?"

"What would you like to do?"

"I want to make love to you the way you should be made love to. I want to taste your skin and drink in those beautiful curves you were so blessed with. I want to experience every part of you."

"Then what, Mia…?"

"We can be together always." I realized the naïveté in that statement the minute it slipped from my tongue. But it was exactly how I felt.

Lina stared at me. "Like me and Daniel?"

"No. Like you and I. There will be no love like ours. I'll prove it to you if you give me the chance. I love you, Evangelina."

I reached out to touch her, but she was much too self-conscious to share her body with another, thanks to Daniel. He'd grown overly concerned with those few extra pounds she carried and would stop at nothing to have her get rid of them. He ridiculed and bullied her into accepting an image of herself that was nothing less than a mockery of his own shortcomings. My opinion was that he was not as repulsed by those pounds as he claimed to be. He berated her about those pounds because he knew it was the only way to keep her from leaving.

I disrobed Lina slowly and methodically, kissing her soft skin as I slipped the shiny robe off her shoulder. She sighed softly, moaning into my ear as I ran my hands over her quivering thighs and letting my tongue explore her velvet flesh. I slowly slipped the robe off my shoulders as well. My flesh was warm and waiting to experience the only woman who could bring me to my knees, not once, but repeatedly. We kissed passionately, holding each other tightly and breathing in every detail. We kissed until our desires demanded that we share our bodies with each other.

I sensed Evangelina's modesty when I made love to her. The warm hush that took over as she climaxed. The inability to open her eyes as she nuzzled my breasts. The way she giggled as we held each other close afterward endeared her to me even more now than ever.

I was entranced by her modesty. She had no idea how beautiful she was, didn't realize the power she possessed that was always taken for granted by the wrong men. The next night we shared was the night I realized that my infatuation was truly love. Evangelina was absolutely breathtaking. She was all woman. Not in the sense of today's "ideal woman": too thin, plastic, too cosmetic. Evangelina was a throwback to the '50s bombshells like Rita Hayworth, Marilyn Monroe, and Jane Russell.

The next morning, I put the coffee on and started warming the water for our shower.

"Lina, why don't you join me in the shower?"

"Can we keep the lights off?"

"Why can't I admire you?"

"I'm just a little shy," she said. "In time, I'll get over it."

"Anything you say, honey. But you have to know that I think you're a beautiful lady. You have nothing to be ashamed of. Nothing at all."

"You're too sweet for me."

After turning off the light switch, Evangelina followed me into the shower. She attempted to cover her body by crossing her arms."

"What are you doing?" I asked her.

"Oh, Mia. I hate my body. Please don't look at it."

"Come here, babe." I pulled her toward me. "I don't want to make you feel uncomfortable." I had her turn around, with her back toward me, so she wouldn't see me watching her.

I ran my hands across her fabulous curves, her succulent breasts, the wonderful fringe surrounding her sweet lips. I wondered why Evangelina was so ashamed of what I had longed to touch for so long. She had given me the gift of perfection, yet I wasn't allowed to fully indulge in my innermost fantasies because she didn't feel worthy of my desire. There was an urgency I felt to make Evangelina realize she was the one for me: Her full Latina hips, the tiny bulge of her belly, and her wonderfully thick thighs all begged to be adored.

I kissed Evangelina's neck with soft kisses, running my tongue across the nape of her sexy skin. "I don't know what he told you, but he was wrong. Very wrong," I whispered in her ear, as I leaned into her with my body, brushing my warm pussy against her round bottom. Again I whispered, "You're too good for him. You're too good for either one of us." I leaned into her more and more, until she began to bend.

Evangelina was in the perfect position to receive me. I rubbed my swollen clit against her delicious ass. She held onto the faucet as the friction grew between our bodies. She moaned, belting out a shrill I've never heard before.

I reached for the soap, working up a lather between my hands then rubbing it over her body. After switching the shower massage on, I washed the soapy suds from her precious skin, stopping at her clit. I switched the setting to pulsate. As the water danced between her aroused lips, she closed her eyes.

I turned voyeur as Evangelina plucked the massager from my hands and held it to her skin. It took only seconds for me to lose control of all my senses, watching the pleasure creep between her smooth, silky thighs. As she climaxed, the massager fell to the floor. Evangelina stepped toward me, pulling me in at the waist.

"I love you, Mia."

"Why?"

"I bare my heart to you, and you ask me why?"

"I just want you to be very careful of what you say," I told her. "I'm so in love with you. I've never loved anyone like this."

"But I love you too. Please believe me."

"I believe you love me. But I also know Daniel has done a lot of damage."

"Mia, I may not be over all the damage the Daniel's done, but believe me, I'm over Daniel."

Evangelina held my face in her hands. She looked deep into my eyes as she held her mouth over mine. Her breath grew warmer on my mouth with each passing moment. I sent my tongue out to play with hers, engaging in lingering, precious kisses. We washed each other. I fell to my knees, parted her moist lips, and delved my tongue deep into her sex. Slowly, she joined me on the floor, only now with no hang-ups and no boundaries. All of the places I wasn't allowed to explore were now open and available to me.

Evangelina screamed as she climaxed repeatedly, while my fingers wandered in and out of her silky pink lips. I couldn't stop thinking about how she had been so uncertain of her beauty. She wasn't able to make love in the nude, but in just a few days she was able to direct what she wanted. We basked in every minute we shared before time ran out and we needed to leave for work. I daydreamed of Lina all day, concocting ways I could make her feel special. Then the telephone rang.

"This is Mia."

"Hi, Mia."

"Evangelina! How are you, honey?"

"Mia, I'm fine. Daniel's here. He was sitting in my office when I walked in."

I grew incensed with jealousy. "Well, tell him to leave, Lina. Tell him you don't need him."

"I can't do that—he's my husband."

"I realize that, but I love you."

I prepared myself to hear what I knew I eventually would; I just didn't think it would be this soon.

"I love you too, just not in the way you would like me to love you. I'm not going to say these past couple of days were a mistake, but I need to be with Daniel now. He's sorry, and he's willing to forgive everything if we can get back together."

"Forgive what, Lina? The fact that he drove you into my arms with his infidelities? Or the fact that now he's got something to hang over your head? Which one is it, Lina?"

"I won't argue about this."

"What about us?"

"There can't be an 'us' because I'm married." Lina hesitated. "I also think I'm pregnant."

"What?"

"I don't think we should see each other for a while," she told me.

"Why? Twenty-two years of friendship gone?"

"I'll always be your friend, but not for a while. Let some time pass, then we'll talk things over. OK?"

"No, Evangelina. It's not OK. I love you." I wanted to confess my love as no other ever could—no novel or song or poem could express the depths of my love. Then Lina interrupted me.

"Mia, I'm hanging up. We'll talk soon. And, if you love me as you say you do, you won't do anything to break up my family." She dropped the receiver, and in that instant, my heart broke.

Although I never gave her my word, I couldn't call her because I was Lina's friend first, and above everything her happiness was my main concern. Perhaps, if I was a true friend, I wouldn't have allowed the lines of friend and lover to have become blurred in the first place. It was a difficult lesson to learn, but sometimes lessons are so strong that you learn them in an instant. And in this instance, the lesson was driven to my very core with the pain of knowing that the one person I love more than anything doesn't feel the same and never will.

Darrah Le Montre

Her boyfriend was into weird shit.
Not just the typical S/M stuff: whips, handcuffs, a little pain.
Her boyfriend watched videos that made her cringe;
he wanted her to do what he watched.
There were some that could only be filmed in certain countries,
'cuz it was illegal to do the sorta sex they did
here in the land of the free.

She told me the first time they did it, he was so happy
'cuz she role-played.
Big deal,
she role-played.
They were in his bedroom in his two-bedroom apartment,
and his roommate and his roommate's girlfriend, I never knew
their names,
they weren't home.
So they had sex in that room on his mattress on the floor.
I guess she pretended to be dominant.

She was the first person to show me how to kiss
and she gave me such huge hickeys I had to tell my mother
I burned myself with the curling iron.
Curling iron?
Curling iron…

Rochelle

We sat on the steps of the fire station and practiced giving hand jobs
on our forearms.
Twisting, jacking off
our forearms
in front of the place where the boys honk horns to plow through
intersections
to save burning houses and burning buildings.
I once smoked pot with my best friend Kristina in the back of a
church—
what's worse?

He grew more and more demanding.
He wanted her to piss on him and tie him up,
squeeze his nipples between her manicured fingers—
the ones that felt me up.
In her bedroom coming down off Valium and skinny dipping,
Frenching.
She started to get worried and told me so.
Break up with him! I can't. Why? Break up with the asshole!
Maybe I will. You should…fuck him! I hate living at home—
My folks are driving me crazy. You can stay with me. Maybe.

I was over there, in that room one day,
sitting on the mattress on the floor,
watching videos,
drinking a beer.
She wanted me to fuck her boyfriend.
She'd do him, then she wanted to watch me do him.
She had this look in her eyes
I didn't trust.
I couldn't tell whether she was turned on or the devil.
I fucked her boyfriend and watched her eyes
the whole time.

She called me a couple years later.
She met a guy, a "rich" guy, and was moving to Hawaii.

Tale of Two Fag Hags
Karen Lillis

Dear Kiera,

What do you mean I never told you about my *first time*? I thought I had. But OK, I'll tell you about the first time I was (as you so delicately put it) "inside a woman." So here's your bedtime story…

It was my best friend, Laura, back in 1992—actually, New Year's Eve 1991, but it was two in the morning by the time we did it. I had just turned 21 a month before, and so had she; two restless Scorpios. At the time we were straight girls, bi-curious, questioning—but most importantly we were fag hags of the highest order; it wasn't just a lifestyle but a vocation.

Her body was more like yours than mine—more Cancer than Scorpio—petite with generous curves, especially at the hips. She was a dedicated femme like you too. She loved eyeliner, and eyeliner loved her strong eyes. She had a straight-banged bob cut that framed them beautifully. She was doing the Louise Brooks look, and she wore it well. You would have liked her.

I don't know if you could even imagine or picture the scene I was a part of then. It was like the early '90s New York club scene—Kenny Kenny and James St. James, Lady Miss Kier and Deee-Lite—the flashy glamour, the high camp, the devoted mimicking of the supermodels, the rooms full of divas trying to out-diva each other. Only we were in Virginia. In a tiny city or a big town (depending on how you look at it) in the center of the state, which felt like the middle of nowhere. The glamour fags and their glamour hags—we existed in what felt then like a little oasis amidst the frat boys and the flowered-dress sorority sisters, the Bible-beating Born-Agains, the righteous Republicans, the neoclassical architecture, the Deadheads, the hillbillies, the farm folks, and the old timers in their pickup trucks. We went dancing four nights a week; it was our main priority. On off-nights when there wasn't a dance floor to be found we'd dress up in our trashy finery and go to the 24-hour Amoco Food Shop where we'd sit with our cheese fries and Diet Dr. Peppers, cracking up about everything, laughing ourselves stupid.

Not that we were always outside all of it: Laura herself was from a farming family in Southern Virginia, and half of my friends had thick Southern drawls. It was nothing at the time, but it's funny looking at it now from my Queens, New Yawk, perspective.

I found Laura and Seth at the same time, the summer between junior and senior years of college. Seth was our fag. Without him, we two fag hags wouldn't have met, for we existed through our relationships with gay men. Seth might not have agreed; he wasn't like some of the men in this scene who wanted women friends who were always coiffed and dressed to the nines. Seth didn't play with our hair or ooh and aah at the latest Linda Evangelista spread in *Vogue*.

The worst of the fag-hag relationship involved all the low self-esteem and competition of straight women, with none of the so-called rewards—like sex or truly relating, breaking down the barriers between the sexes for the sake of impassioned communication. Seth was different. He was a good friend, but Laura and I were pretty stuck in hag mode at the time. This was our scene: fags who spent their time lusting after cute straight boys (whom they hoped might be closeted) with hags who spent their time lusting after the cute fags (whom we hoped might be bi). What a mess. But we'd lived under the shadow of AIDS ever since we were sexually active, so it's probably no coincidence that we let the rush of dancing and impossible crushes stand in for a sex life.

Like I said, I met them in the summer—probably at the Friday night acid-house dances. One hot night that summer a bunch of us ended up pool-hopping, and the pool-hopping turned into skinny dipping. Both were preceded by a game of Truth or Dare that we played in Laura's apartment. I was always petrified of that game. I remember getting a Truth question, something like "Is there anyone here you'd like to fuck?" It was the first moment I realized I had a crush on Laura. But I was scared of my feelings (or was it just her that I feared, with her powerful Scorpio eyes and her mocking laugh?) Rejection by a beautiful woman is a potent sting you don't have to have experienced to know. I offered a believable lie instead of a truth; I played the hag and told them it was Seth I wanted to sleep with.

Then I shot Laura a look to find out how perceptive she really was: Did she see through my bluff? Did she want to?

Laura smiled coyly and blew smoke out of the corner of her lipstick lips.

Anyway, the skinny-dipping. It was a rare moment in the context of it all: Everyone removing their costumes, letting their poses become liquid; being naked and wet isn't exactly glamorous. But it was July, and the heat and languid humidity were giving Mother Nature an edge over gay-boy etiquette. We peeled off sweaty layers and jumped in.

It was 3 A.M., our favorite time of night, the perfect moment for a clandestine swim. I don't know what was the worst thing that could have happened to us, but the illegal nature of our playtime felt like a substitute for sex itself—we let ourselves be titillated by the threat of getting caught even as we asserted our fearlessness. I mean, *Please, queen,* we did scarier things than this on a daily basis. Existing as a queer in the Bible Belt was far riskier than violating a pool curfew, and believe me, to be a fag hag in Virginia was the same as being queer. The only people who didn't think of us this way were our fags themselves, for whom we represented a heterosexual norm they could latch on to.

Swimming: I kept sneaking glances at Laura's body, her curves unveiled, her nipples pale pink against her far paler Scottish-Irish skin. The chlorinated water hid the wetness that was happening between my legs as I watched her rounded thighs, lit by underwater lamps, wriggling around me, parting enough to reveal the dark hair between them. We dealt with the nervousness by splashing water, squealing, and swimming away.

I guess it was Christie who finally sent our tension over an edge.

Once we'd found each other in those summer nights, the three of us were inseparable: Laura, Seth, and me. We met Christie sometime in the beginning of the school year, the only self-proclaimed lesbian who clubbed with us and also the first true femme lesbian we'd ever known. We couldn't believe her at first—classically feminine, impeccably preppie down to the add-a-bead necklace; a thick, Southwestern Virginia drawl—she could have passed for any soror on campus. But she was outrageous. She had all these characters she'd made up with her hometown girlfriend, who was tall and burly like a tree; they'd launch into these different accents and make us howl. They shared a language all their own. Their euphemism for *lesbian*—because in Virginia in 1991 we still spoke in code half the time—was *big girl*, which Christie would always say in this deliciously vulgar tone of voice. *Bisexual* was *bilingual*.

Their hands were always in motion—wandering over skin, darting inside clothing; that's the other thing I remember about them.

I wonder now what they thought of us—the titillated yet petrified "straight girls." I remember the time they took us to the LBQ meeting. I was the only one who said she was "questioning"—the others pleading hetero to the bone. Even "bisexual" sounded frightening to us then. Sadly, we'd take a stand for our fags but not for our own lesbian desires. I wonder what they thought of me, the dyke-in-waiting. Was it obvious to them then?

Anyway, after we found Christie it seemed like something was always waiting to happen.

My 21st birthday fell on a November Wednesday, which was dance night at the New York–style bar downtown. It was not a gay bar per se but attracted a certain glam-queer crowd. Our friend Hunter, a flamboyant queen from Miami whose favorite outfit was a pair of sequined hot pants and platforms with no shirt, was DJing. He was a brave boy—we nicknamed him Diana, Goddess of the Hunt.

We were in a celebratory mood. The champagne flowed. My girlfriends and I dirty-danced three at a time with our arms around each other, though it was all for show—that is, to show our fag friends that we weren't *always* pining for them (even though my friends mostly were).

Then the music stopped abruptly, and the whole bar started to sing "Happy Birthday" to me. Caught by surprise and looking for a place to hide, I responded by leaning over to kiss Laura before the song was halfway through, and got lost inside her mouth, our tongues entwined. Drunk, five of us girls made out for the rest of the evening. But later we acted like nothing much had happened, certainly nothing emotional.

It was New Year's Eve before Laura and I would kiss again.

This time, on the dance floor at D.C.'s biggest gay club on the biggest night of the year, both of us were dolled up in short dresses. Playfully, one of us stuck a thigh between the other's legs, and this time I felt the dirtiness of the dirty dancing. We followed the music, riding each other's thighs with more and more fervor, until the pleasure build-up was too much for me; I asked her pointedly, "Do you want to go outside?"

We headed to the edge of the sandy volleyball courts where the dykes congregated during warmer months. A high wooden fence surrounded this "backyard" of the club, benches lined the fence at the ground level and barbed wire topped it above, separating us from the volatile southeast neighborhood beyond. We lay down on the endless bench and started kissing.

While our tongues darted around in each other's mouths, our hands wandered over each other's curves. We mirrored each other's curiosities, our hands venturing at the same time down below, each lifting the other's skirt, rubbing over nylons, then finding their way over elastic waistbands, past coarse hair, finally reaching wetness. With one finger each, we stroked and explored the other's velvety inner skin.

Seth and his new boyfriend were off on some dance floor or in some bathroom stall, I don't know. Laura and I had reached a crucial point, where we felt an urgency to explore something more than just each other's bodies, more than what can be explored on a volleyball court. We jumped into a cab and hightailed it back to the hotel room the four of us had rented for the night, hoping for a little privacy before the boys came home.

But once it was just us and the crowded scene was far away, I got scared of Laura and our intimacy. I didn't know where her emotions lay; I still feared that mocking laughter of hers. Maybe I was mostly scared that she was just a straight girl who wanted to experiment—and that she assumed the same of me. I wasn't out to myself then, and yet I sensed that my desire was something different than hers—something deeper and with more dangerous consequences.

It's so strange to look back on this now. I remember how Laura sat over me on the bed, annoyed with me while I lay curled around myself, my back to her, and feigned sleep. I guess what I was shielding from her was not just my sex but my heart.

But in the morning, waking next to her—Seth in the other bed already wriggling under the covers with his boyfriend, our intimacy safely interrupted—I was all longing again. I watched her sleep— her tiny features so doll-like, her bobbed hair only slightly tousled by a drunken slumber. After long moments of anxious hesitation— as if I feared that the stroke of midnight had returned Laura to a reasonable straight girl and left me a dyke in heat, I finally peeled back a strap of Laura's black satin nightgown and began to move my fingertips lightly across her skin. Her eyes didn't open but she seemed to sigh delightedly in her sleep.

I kept daring: I took her breast in my mouth. Under my tongue, her nipple rose as hard as it had in the December cold the night before, and as her body slowly came awake, mine did too.

No longer two girls in dresses, now I was in pajama pants and a T-shirt, all the better to play butch to her femme. I climbed on top of her, slid one arm underneath the small of her back and held her there as she arched and offered her breast to my lips. I couldn't get enough of this soft flesh, her hardening nipples—I was ravenous for her, sucking by instinct.

It was Laura who feigned sleep this time, her eyes still closed, her body too turned on to resist. I didn't dare kiss her lips, she didn't offer them to me; I tongued her neck in long strokes while she turned her head away from me. Her limbs responded differently, rocking against mine. I held her by the rounded edges of her hips while I sent my thigh between her legs, against her satin-covered lower lips, with far more delicate attention than in our frenzy the night before.

Unlike those courtside explorations, Laura was no longer acknowledging any female parts of me; I was her Romeo and my own thrills were vicarious. As I sucked Laura's nipples raw, my own, hard as nails, ached more with every flick of my tongue. Blood rippled in waves through my cunt as I caressed hers with the weight of my thigh.

My movements were guided now by the force of my own hunger, which seemed to match Laura's. My clitoris longed for touch; I moved my leg to tease Laura there, lightly brushing over her satin with my knee. Her head was thrown back and as I felt a new ache, a new pleasure coursing through me, I heard something in her breath change. Too self-aware to conspicuously change the position of my body since Seth and his lover were sitting up now and smoking in bed, I threw my leg into Laura with a new fervor, with all the finesse and erotic force I could.

It was hard to discern whose body I was feeling and whose I was imagining. I pressed my thigh against her as if to satisfy a throbbing in my own full lips, full clit. I heard Laura's breath draw shorter and shorter while I began to teeter on the edge of consciousness, pressing my pulsing vulva into Laura's leg, picturing the wetness I had touched in her the night before. I came crashing back into my body as Laura grabbed the edge of her pillow and let out a muffled cry.

Then she sort of shoved me off her, though our legs were still wrapped up together. We lay there pretending sleep awhile to disperse the awkwardness.

That was the first and last time. We stayed close friends for several more years, but after that nothing else happened between us. I vaguely remember confiding in Seth afterwards, and Seth telling me to save my energy for a girl who liked girls. But I wouldn't be ready until quite a while later, as you know.

Instead I let myself dwell a few more years in the fog of ambiguity. I internalized Laura's version of what happened between us that night—her silent insistence that we were just horny, kinky straight girls—that nothing had *changed*.

But I had changed, even if I couldn't yet say so.

I started to masturbate the very next day—being inside a woman had opened up something new and infinite in me: This image of being *inside* was utterly delicious, totally freeing. Suddenly I wanted to be inside *all the time*. If I was a late starter at the art of self-pleasure, I made up for lost time—indulging as often as I could. So, maybe I had lost Laura, but I soon became my own best lover, a one-woman lesbian couple. And that's not an unhappy ending.

So, you wanted to know about my first time—that was it. And if you ever need any more bedtime stories, I'm happy to oblige…

I'll see you soon, girl!

XO,
Karen

A New Beginning

Jennifer Rivers

"You can't live like this, Jen," she told me. "You can stay in our guest room until you get on your feet. I *want* you to live with me."

I held the phone to my ear and listened to the long distance fuzz in the background. My heart swelled with love for the woman who had been my best friend for over four years. She was offering me everything. A change…an escape…an adventure. I had only to accept and the hell I'd been living through for the last month would disappear. I dipped my head and allowed warm tears to flow down my cheeks.

"Jen?"

The breath rushed from my lungs. "OK, I'll move to Washington."

"What?"

I smiled through my tears. For years, April had wanted me to live closer to her, but something had always held me back: my ex-fiancé, money, my job. I'd hurt her numerous times by falling back on promises, but now I was ready for a new beginning.

"I said I want to come live with you."

Silence.

"Are you changing your mind?" I asked with a nervous chuckle.

"Never. You know I've always wanted you with me, but I

never thought it would happen. I'm afraid to believe you."

I closed my eyes and pictured the way she probably looked as she talked on a phone several states away. No doubt she wore her characteristic flannel shirt and jeans, her feet propped up on the coffee table, the TV on to distract her with some Real TV moment. I could easily envision her intense green eyes fringed with black eyelashes, thick dark-brown hair, and freckled complexion. My body remembered her softness and how she seemed to slip inside me whenever we hugged.

"I understand," I whispered, feeling the pain I heard in her voice as though it were my own. I had many regrets. "I know there's a lot between us that needs healing, but I can't imagine a better way to accomplish that than in person. You've always been my best friend...even when we weren't talking. I've never stopped loving you."

A broken sob echoed through the line. "Neither have I. I tried to forget you, but it never worked. I will always love you, Jen."

I traced the stitches on the quilt I'd thrown over the bed in my grandmother's apartment. Nothing I'd done in life felt as right as moving to Washington did.

Excitement, hard and fierce, erupted behind my ribs. "I'm coming this time."

Silence.

"April, I'm coming."

"I believe you," came her husky whisper.

I shivered, tingles racing from the roots of my hair to the tips of my toes. I frowned, wondering at the peculiar sensation. Perhaps I was coming down with something. "Have you talked to Adam?"

"Yes."

"What did he say?"

"There wasn't anything for him *to* say. He's my husband, but when it comes down to it, I make the decisions. Besides, his friend stayed with us for a year, so he wouldn't dare disagree."

I laughed, knowing how truthful April's words were. "I'm glad. Then it's official. I'm coming."

"God, I can't believe it's really happening. I love you, Jen. I know I keep saying that, but it's the truth. I can't wait to hug you."

Again, the shivers arched down my back. This time they were more intense. We'd talked several times of the sexual feelings we were beginning to feel for each other, but I doubted anything would come of it. We were both scared to follow through and quickly passed it off as curiosity whenever it came up in conversations. "Neither can I."

April giggled. "All right. Let's figure this out. When are you coming? Tonight?"

I laughed, enjoying the excitement I heard in her voice. How long had we dreamed of living closer? Probably years. I could still remember the excitement in our voices when we'd shared visions of shopping, watching movies, and going on vacations together. It seemed our wildest dreams had always revolved around each other and it had taken three years, but our dreams were finally coming true.

A loud pounding rattled the wall, nearly sending several knickknacks plummeting to the floor. I scrambled off the bed. "April, I have to go. My grandmother is banging on the wall. She needs something." Someone in my family should have stood up a long time ago and made the decision to put my grandmother in a place with people who could care for her. I agreed to move in on a temporary basis six months before but had reached the end of my patience. I love my grandmother, but I couldn't go on like this.

"All right. I'll be home all night if you need to talk. Hang in there, and just think about coming to live with me."

I smiled. "I'll think of nothing else."

Several days after I arrived in Washington, April and I finally had a moment alone. We lay on my bed in her guest room, the moonlight illuminating our bodies. A soft breeze pushed through the window and ruffled April's hair, bringing with it the scent of her perfume. I breathed deeply.

"I can't believe you're here, Jen. I didn't think you would come." April glanced at the quilt, her eyes shadowed with the pain I had dealt her many times during our turbulent friendship. "I guess I've been let down so many times…"

I reached across the bed and rested my hand over hers, hoping to comfort her in the only way I knew how. The softness of her skin surprised me, as did the enjoyment I found in touching her.

She sucked in a ragged breath. "Jen?"

My gaze darted to hers. In her eyes, I saw the same confusing emotions I was feeling at that very moment. Curiosity, wonder, attraction, and love.

Encouraged that I wasn't alone in my feelings, I ran my palm over her fingers until she entwined them with mine. I held tight, hoping the closeness would fill the emptiness inside of me that screamed for this woman.

Her gaze grew tender. "I love you, Jen. Thank you for driving all this way to be with me."

A warmth I'd never experienced swelled in my heart, followed by a sense of happiness that caused tears to prick the corners of my eyes.

I'd finally found my home.

I gazed into her eyes and smiled. My life would forever be entangled with this woman, this soul mate of my heart. How could I have lived my entire life without knowing this existed?

"I love you too," I whispered.

She smiled, tears welling up in her eyes. I quickly decided holding her hand was not enough. I moved across the bed and threw my other arm around her, desperate to give her all the things we'd been unable to convey over the phone.

I buried my face in her neck and felt her arm slip around my hips, holding me close. Time seemed to cease as we lay in bed, content simply to be in each other's company. I'd forgotten how easy it was to love her and how wonderful it was to have her in my life. I think she may have forgotten as well because she seemed to cherish every moment as much as I did and her grip was as tight as mine. We were afraid to let go, even for a moment.

Years had passed since we'd last talked in person, but we'd picked up exactly where we'd left off. Our lives had gone through major changes in those two years, but our hearts still managed to beat together. We were the same people who had met in 1996 and created an unbreakable friendship.

For the first time in my life, I wasn't afraid to love.

I met April's gaze and smiled hesitantly. Our increasing level of intimacy was making me breathless with desire, and I suddenly had an overwhelming urge to touch her—everywhere. She returned my smile, her eyes darkening suggestively.

I quickly conjured up something funny to say to ease the tension between us, but her warm breath fanned across my lips, silencing me. I became aware of the soft breasts that were pressed against mine, and I took a shaky breath. What was happening to me? Why did I suddenly feel light-headed and on fire? And why on earth hadn't I felt this before with the men in my life?

With a sigh of surrender, I gave myself up to the moment. I couldn't explain these feelings, and perhaps I wasn't meant to; perhaps this intimate moment with my best friend was a lesson in disguise. I suddenly felt as though I was beginning to open a part of myself I did not know existed.

April's trembling hand closed over my breast. I arched my back as tingles like nothing I'd ever felt before swelled through my body. How could I feel this for a *woman?* I couldn't deny that I did, and deeply. As her fingers searched and found my nipple, I sucked in a breath. Every nerve ending in my body rose to the surface, waiting agonizingly for her next caress. I was well beyond the point of no return. I no longer had any doubt that this was also something April desired. I couldn't stop and wasn't sure why I'd want to.

April's mouth pressed against mine, soft and coaxing one minute, then hard and demanding the next. I arched into her, wishing she would touch me everywhere at once, yet knowing I would die the most amazing death if she did.

I stiffened as pure sensation exploded through my body. My

nerves seemed to intensify, turning to the one area April caressed with exquisite tenderness. As her fingers inched up the inside of my thighs to tickle the soft hair at the juncture of my thighs, I didn't breathe. I waited, tight, trembling for her touch. I was not denied.

I moaned as they pressed inside, deeper and deeper until they filled me. My body spasmed, my hips bucking until I felt her fingers slipping in and out with each of my thrusts. The breath rushed from my lungs. I twisted on the bed, the sheets tangling around my legs. I was oblivious to anything but this wonderful woman who had opened me up to a truth I had always known existed.

I cried out when April's tongue delved inside to replace her fingers. The touch of warmth on the sensitive flesh sent lightening through my limbs. I trembled as the sensations heightened to a frightening level. Making love to a woman was an emotional and physical tangle of souls. I had never experienced anything like this and felt myself falling in love...despite the consequences.

I raised my head and watched her between my bare thighs. Overcome with desire, I let my head fall back to rest on the pillow. "Oh, God, the things you are doing to me," I whispered hoarsely.

She entwined her fingers through mine, a touch so gentle and promising I wanted to cry. There was no separation between us; the outside world ceased to exist. I found myself slipping into a new world. I stiffened against her, so tight with desire I thought my bones would burst from my skin if I didn't find release. I strained against her hands, thrust my hips, clenched my pillow in my hands, and yet I didn't find my release.

Just when I considered stopping her, a white light exploded above my head, showering me in pleasure. I trembled as wave after wave washed over me. And then it happened again. I turned my head into the pillow, my moans louder. I collapsed against my pillow after my intense orgasm, welcoming the quiet chirps of the grasshoppers outside. I became aware of the sheets against my naked skin, my best friend's hands on my thighs, the scent of sex in the air.

Humming in places I didn't know existed, I opened my eyes.

April smiled down at me, her eyes filling with tears. Unable to do anything else, I began to cry too. She crawled up the bed and held me, softly brushing her fingers through my hair until the tears stopped. "Did I hurt you?"

I shook my head. "No, it was just so...so beautiful."

"I'm glad."

I rose up on the bed and pushed her back on the pillow. "It was beautiful, and I want you to know just how much." I kissed every inch of her body, tasted her soft skin, caressed her breasts, and teased her nipples to hard peaks. I murmured in her ear and traced the pink line of her earlobe with my tongue until she panted my name.

As I slowly discovered the magnificence of her body, inch by inch, I was taken with all that I knew about her and all I had discovered that night. I touched her, listened to her moans, knew what she was feeling and reveled in the knowledge that I was able to return the pleasure she had given me with *my* fingers, tongue, and desire.

I kissed her passionately, tasting the sweetness of her mouth and the excitement in her tongue. When she clawed at my arm, drawing my hand between her thighs, I did not stop her. I slid inside, the wet satin skin clinging to my fingers. Wanting to taste her, I kneeled between her legs. I flicked it with my tongue on her hard spot, amazed at the slightly salty sweet taste of her. A taste I enjoyed above all others.

April's orgasm was long overdue. She tensed on the bed, her back arching, her body shivering with her orgasm. She cried out my name, and as I crawled up the bed to hold her, I knew this wouldn't be the end. The sight of the sweat-dampened hair at her temples, her flushed cheeks, and brilliant green eyes were nearly my undoing. She was the most desirable person I had ever met, and I knew I would treasure every day we had together.

Little did I know we would have forever.

Lucky Stones
Jules Torti

Do you remember that night out at Beckley Beach? Our mouths sweet with the sugary taste of toasted marshmallows? There were a million stars in the sky that night, and just a sliver of a pale moon slowly inching across the evening sky into dawn. It was the first time we kissed, and the first time either of us had ever kissed a girl. I remember that night perfectly, how we rolled your dad's '76 Malibu out of the driveway and pushed it halfway down Willow Street just after 2 A.M. I thought for sure your dad would catch us and chase us down Willow with the shotgun he kept beside the bed. I had to come over that night, though. It was too late to phone, but I had to tell you. I couldn't eat, couldn't sleep. Shit, I couldn't even breathe without thinking of you.

I turned back a couple of times, backtracking down the street, hesitating, afraid of what I would say when I saw your face smiling at me from the upstairs window. I rehearsed my lines to a lonely lamppost, but my actual performance wasn't exactly a romantic reenactment of Romeo and Juliet, was it? I was worried sick that your silly dog would wake up and start barking like mad if he heard me throwing pebbles against your window. I worried about waking up your mom too. She would tell my mom about me at the Catholic Women's League meeting over tea and tiny triangle tuna sandwiches, and then what? So, I whispered to you from below your window, under the arms of the red oak we climbed so many times as kids, "Let's elope."

I wanted to elope with you when we were five years old, when we were first introduced by our mother's at the Valentine's Day Tea at the parish center. You looked so adorable in your red velvet jumper, complete with matching ribbons tied neatly around your blond pigtails. I made plans then, that day, while we ate pink cupcakes decorated with cinnamon hearts, that we would hitch down to Antofagasta. I spotted Antofagasta on our warped globe (that sat with its broken axis up in the attic because my stupid brother hoofed it off the roof into the neighbor's pool); it was in the Atacama Desert. I decided that'd be a good place for us to go. Antofagasta, Chile. I don't think I could even pronounce such a word back then, but it sounded exotic and full of adventure.

That night you suggested we go to Beckley Beach instead of Chile because it was late and all the gas pumps in town were closed. I had packed some stuff in my backpack anyhow, just in case you changed your mind. You know, essentials, like my dog-eared copy of *Rubyfruit Jungle*, some peanut butter, a bag of marshmallows, a bottle of Crown Royal I'd stolen from my parents' liquor cabinet, and a copy of *Penthouse*. Jesus, my brother was so pissed when he found out I took the August issue.

When we got to Beckley you picked the spot, down past that old deserted cottage that got wiped out by the floods a couple of years back. Down by the point where we used to skip flat stones as kids for hours and have picnics with fried chicken, mom's pickled beets, and deviled eggs. There was a fire pit there, and in the cool autumn air, we welcomed the warmth of the fire.

We didn't talk too much at first. Well, we talked about school and superficial stuff like the weather. Like what a loser of a math teacher Grenke was. We laughed about your brother getting caught smoking a joint with Jeffrey Oglivie in the girls change room. Mostly, though, we were quiet, content to eat marshmallows, smiling with satisfaction as each one burst into flames. We liked our marshmallows the same, burned black, the entire sugary shell like a skin of ash. The fiery swigs of Crown Royal made us a little more giggly as the moon moved toward the west and the tide rolled out. I suggested we go searching for lucky stones. I still have the one you gave me when I was 7; I keep it in my wallet, enjoying the smooth feel of it now and again when I'm alone and thinking of you. No one believes it's a bone from a fish's head, with the perfect L engraved in it. I tell them it's from a sheephead fish and it's lucky, but they scoff at me.

Instead of looking for lucky stones you wanted to look at the *Penthouse*. I was a bit shocked by your assertiveness, but I agreed, nervously and excitedly. We had looked at my brother's magazines before, when we were younger, and he still hides them in the same place: in that box his model car came in, the '69 Mustang. Pushed to the back of the wall, underneath his bed, hidden behind the bunched-up sickly brown corduroy shirt grandma gave him for his birthday.

I stoked the fire, tossing on a couple of fat, sun-baked pieces of driftwood. Already you had delved into the magazine, a glossy blond centerfold hanging out. "She's got huge tits!" you remarked. "Do you think mine will ever get that big?" I hoped that they wouldn't; yours seemed just right to me. "Whoa, is your crotch that hairy?" I felt my face growing hot and crimson with embarrassment. Maybe I was sitting too close to the fire. No, my crotch wasn't that hairy, and I wanted to show you, or invite you to look, but I stuffed my mouth with a marshmallow instead and took another swig from the bottle.

I leaned back, casually, pretending not to be that interested in the revealing photos lit up by the flames of the fire. I wanted to seem calm, cool, and collected to you, not a stuttering, sweaty-palmed, heart-pounding wreck. I wanted you, not the glossy blond bimbo with silicone tits. I poked my marshmallow stick into the fire until the tip was glowing. "What do you think it'd be like?" I asked, turning my head in your direction, braver now from the Crown Royal.

"What?"

"You know. Being with a woman. Kissing a woman."

"I dunno. Why?"

"Never mind," you said. "No, actually, I just wanted to tell you…well, shit. This would be easier than words…"

At that moment I leaned forward, suddenly acquiring an overwhelming amount of confidence, and kissed you, much to your surprise. Your mouth opened, accepting the advance of my tongue. I closed my eyes, like they do in the movies, and felt the pleasure of your tongue gently caressing mine, like we had done this so many times before. This was definitely easier than words.

We had to laugh for a little bit. We were only 16 and this was all new to us. We both had boyfriends, but they didn't seem to matter right then. Our bodies moved closer, flannel and denim separating our skin, but not for long. You made the first move, your hand diving into the front of my jeans, searching. I repositioned my body, lying back onto the cool sand as your fingers touched my slippery lips. My underwear was damp—it had been for most of the evening.

My hands slipped under your tank top, delighted to discover you weren't wearing a bra. I pulled your shirt up above your breasts and sucked each nipple as you explored the soft folds of my skin. "This feels so right," you whispered, "so natural." I agreed as my tongue slithered down to your navel.

"Is this OK?" I asked as I unbuttoned your Levi's. You nodded, trusting me.

Grinning, I pulled your jeans down to your knees to find that you weren't wearing any underwear either. My tongue immediately found your clitoris, my nose burying deep into your heavenly scent. I asked if you wanted me inside you, and you said yes, just one finger. But I waited before I slipped it in, afraid I might hurt you. Instead, with a careful tongue I lapped up the sweet cream that lubricated your pussy.

The sky began to brighten as the tide returned to the shore. The fire flickering to coals as our bodies continued, grinding slow and hard into the sand. First me on top, then you on top. We took turns kissing each other, desperate for more, over and over, until we finally surrendered to tiredness. We curled up together, denim and flannel unbuttoned, my hand tucked into the back of your jeans. I smiled as I felt a lucky stone in your back pocket.

Does your dad still have his old Malibu? Did he ever find out about that night? Think you'll be in town anytime soon? How are the kids? Say hi to Matt for me—how long have you two been married now? I wonder if you've ever told him about that night. I haven't told anyone. Do you still have your lucky stone? You think maybe we could go to Beckley sometime, toast some marshmallows? The sunrise is supposed to be gorgeous.

Shit, I miss you.

Coffee Girl #6:
The First Time I Kissed a Girl
Rebecca S. Rajswasser

The first time I kissed a girl was an eggnog cappuccino with a ribbon of caramel. I was 24 years old and living just east of Florida's armpit. Her name was Sarah. Now wait, I can't do that. Nope, I cannot tell a black-cherry lie. That wasn't really the first time I kissed a girl. It was the first *real* time, though—the first bona fide lesbian fresh-ground-beans-and-steamed-espresso time. OK, so the first, first time I kissed a girl was a few years earlier, in the cinnamon-sprinkled-in-the-Mr.-Coffee-filter years. Her name was Kate.

It was my first day at college. I was so high on that please-let-me-out-of-adolescence angst that I didn't notice how weak the cafeteria coffee was. I don't remember how I met her, exactly, but she was unlike anyone I'd ever met and everything my friends had warned me about. Kate. She was boylike, sort of butch. She carried her coffee in a big plastic mug, and she took me under her wing during orientation, walked me through the registration process, and wooed me right into my first college keg party. She told me she could introduce me to Madonna. What would you have done?

Coffee Girl #6: The First Time I Kissed a Girl

The party was a quick stop. We got drunk, then stumbled together to my first college dance. Kate gave me my first shots of tequila. We didn't dance much. Later, Kate lifted her head barely off the table and said, "You want to kiss me, don't you?" I'd only had a few shots of tequila, but all of a sudden I was spinning inside. I figured she knew what she was talking about, so I went with it. "Uh, yeah?" I shrugged and sputtered like one of those automatic drip pots that doesn't stop spitting out brew after you take the carafe out of the cradle. Kate must have been feeling a little like that too. She went into a tiny tirade on how she was no good for me and I shouldn't get mixed up with her. I don't remember what happened next, except brushing her hair away from her face, and walking outside with her to wait for her cab. We sat on the grass and made out. It was astonishing. Like the first sip of a hot Irish coffee on a cold, blustery Winnie-the-Pooh kind of day. I lost my cat eyeglasses that night, and in the morning I completely lost my wits.

Cliché, I know, but it did feel like I was kissing me. I couldn't put my finger on why it felt so different. A mouth is a mouth, and yet… I called my high school guidance counselor, he talked me down, and that was that. Maybe the best parts of sex and attraction are all in the mind the way the best part of a good cup of java is all in the aroma.

I spent the next eight years figuring I must not be a lesbian; girls just didn't like me. Maybe it was the string of boys I carried around like a security blanket.

Eventually, I got sick of pretending, sick of Sanka with Sweet'N Low. One fateful day, I spied a flyer for a Womyn's Prom put on by the LGBSN at the local university. I decided right then that it was time to find and sow my Sapphic oats. I left my then-boyfriend alone with the TV and drove to the Metropolitan Church. Gotta love a church that'll host a dyke dance. I think they even donated the cookies.

Back to the dance. That's where I met Sarah. The coffee-ice-cream-with-Kahlua-syrup Sarah. She was a delightful imp. Cute as a Costa Rican picaberry bean, all dressed in her brown and camel circa 1940-something suit complete with hat and little white gloves. She paid attention to me, and I was instantly smitten. We exchanged numbers. My first, on purpose, on the cusp of lesbianism positive action.

I rode my bike home that night on a new kind of high, Sarah's number tucked in my back pocket. It was the best night I'd had in months. I didn't tell my boyfriend anything about it.

Sarah and I met up a few nights later. She was wonderful. I went to her house after school one day, perky as a percolated pup. Tucked away in a tiny wooden townhouse village that said to me "bungalow colony," it was perfectly quaint and covered in quirky kitsch. She had clocks of various shapes and sizes all over her apartment, all set to different times. She had closets and closets of clothes in every possible color, style, genre, and time period. I had no idea when or where I was. I liked feeling lost in her world.

One night we went out dancing. After a few rounds of "We Are Family" and the like, Sarah suggested we "get some air." We took a little walk to the park a few blocks away. The one between the bar and my house. The one my boyfriend could have walked by at any minute. I didn't care. I was with Sarah, standing under the full Florida moon, talking and laughing and being girls together. We rode the swings and the seesaw. We climbed around and sprawled ourselves under the jungle gym. We scrambled to the top and jumped back down again. And then she kissed me. It was like summer camp behind the bunkhouse, out on the dock after curfew, free swim on the tanning rock behind the drooping white pine. That kiss was like a key turning in a long-locked door. A door that, once opened (in that oh-so–Jill Sobule moment), could never be closed again.

Not too long after, Sarah took me to the movies. We saw *Dolores Claiborne* and on the way home we talked about kissing girls, coming out, and to be or not to be with boys. We did a lot of things together over the next couple of weeks, mostly getting high, hanging with friends in her apartment, going dancing, and eating late night pancake feasts at Denny's.

But because she was my first *real* kiss, she will always be my barista—the one who poured me solely, solidly, fluidly, and piping hot into the big plastic mug of lesbian love. Eventually, like within a few short weeks, Sarah let me know that she was not interested in me "in that way," but before long, and not on purpose, she introduced me to my next first: my first "real" girlfriend. Sylvia was a thick and steamy espresso panther with a gentle, quirky twist of lemon on the side...but that is another story, and another cup of Joe.

My First Love

Lisa N. Cacciabaudo

I met her online. It was January 26, 2001, when she responded to my personal ad on PlanetOut.com looking for friends. She wrote:

> Hello! I live in Tennessee, and I'm looking for an online pen pal. I love talking to people from all over the place. We seem to have a bit in common, and I thought you might be fun to talk to. If you're interested, E-mail me back. I hardly ever check this account, but I check my AOL account daily. Hope to hear from you soon!

I received her message the next day while I was checking my E-mail at work. It was a Saturday, and I was the only supervisor around, so I pulled up AOL Instant Messenger and added her screen name to my buddy list. The door creaked open, and she was online. I IM'd her, and we chatted for a bit that afternoon. I didn't see her online for a couple days after that since our schedules were so different, but soon we'd be up chatting until 4 or 5 in the morning for days on end.

Her name was Barbara. I called her Barb. She had one previous relationship with a woman about 10 years before, dated men for a while, got married, and was now in the process of a divorce.

She was 33 years old to my 26, but we were both new to the lesbian scene, so it balanced out our age difference.

I couldn't stop talking to her. I never wanted to say goodbye even when I could barely keep my eyes open. She made me laugh so hard it hurt to smile. She teased me in my naïveté, sending shivers down my spine with her flirtatious comments. Once she wrote that if I ever needed anything, even just to talk, I should call her. She gave me her home and cell phone numbers. I gave her mine. The next morning as I was getting ready for work, the phone rang. I nearly jumped out of my skin. I knew it was Barb. I answered, and she returned my greeting in her Tennessee twang. "I'm sorry I'm calling; I couldn't resist."

Whatever we talked about on the phone that morning wasn't too terribly significant. I joked with her about her accent; being from New York, we couldn't possibly have sounded any more different. She babbled a lot, thankfully, because I was too nervous and tongue-tied.

After that, we alternated calling each other and chatting on AOL. Our friendship quickly moved on to something else. We talked about the possibility of meeting in person. I was living in Indiana, so it would have meant a seven-hour drive for one of us. We set a date, and then I freaked out, telling her maybe it wasn't such a good idea yet. It was too soon; I wasn't ready. I didn't want her to have any major expectations. I mean, driving all the way from Southern Tennessee to meet up with me in a hotel seemed so sketchy. I didn't want to give her the impression that I do this all the time; I am not that kind of girl.

I was very much attracted to her personality, and we flirted so much, arguing back and forth about which one of us would have to make the first move, but I didn't want her to think that I was necessarily going to jump into bed with her. This happened two or three times—we would discuss a date, then I would back out.

Finally, late one night, after we'd been talking for a couple months, I blurted out, "Well…maybe it would just be better if we didn't plan it out so far in advance. Then maybe I wouldn't have the opportunity to get so nervous." She was silent for a minute then mumbled something about the rental car places opening up in just a few hours. She asked if I would send directions, and that was that.

I was excited to meet the woman I had been pouring out my soul to for the past several months. We got off the phone while she did some research—calling about the car and hotel. She called me back, telling me she would sleep for a few hours and then go pick up the car. It was settled. She asked again for the directions and said she would check her E-mail in the morning and talk to me online before she headed out. She would arrive here between 6 and 7 P.M., call me to tell me her room number at the local Holiday Inn, and I would go meet her.

I went to bed and hardly slept. The next day I hung out with friends and tried to keep my mind occupied. I sat around fidgeting, watching a movie, and pacing my apartment. Finally it was getting close to 6 P.M., so I decided I'd better get ready to go.

In the shower I debated whether or not to shave. If I did shave, I was making a conscious decision that something might happen between us physically. But I had never even met this woman! I threw caution to the wind and shaved my legs, my armpits, even my labia. I washed and conditioned my hair with Clairol Herbal Essences—her favorite scent. I dressed in my black second-skin-satin panty and bra set from Vicky's Secret, blue jeans, and a black turtleneck. I looked in the mirror, held myself upright, and repeatedly told myself that I was ready to meet her.

When the phone rang after 7 P.M., she apologized, saying she had gotten lost and driven around Bloomington for 45 minutes before finding the Holiday Inn. I nervously laughed and asked what room she was in. "OK," I said, "I'll be right over."

My stomach was in knots and my heart pounding when I pulled into the hotel parking lot. I rode the elevator up to her floor, walked slowly to her door, and stood outside it for a moment trying to relax. Finally, I knocked and she let me in.

It was awkward at first. I felt so nervous. She was sitting on one side of the bed with her legs stretched out watching TV, and

I sat on the chair far away from the bed. She laughed, "Do you want to go down to the bar and have a drink?"

"I brought some beers, but they're in my car." She didn't even like beer, but I thought one or two might help me to calm down. "Let me go get them."

This time when I walked in from the car, my pace was quicker than before. I wanted to get back to the room, hoping our online chemistry would translate to real life.

We had discussed watching the season premiere of *The Sopranos,* so she had made sure to get a hotel that had HBO. Once the show was about to start, I moved onto the bed next to her, sitting up against the headboard. She was lying down. I finished one beer and started a second. After *The Sopranos* was over, we small-talked and decided to order in a movie. We watched *Charlie's Angels,* and as the movie went on I felt more and more comfortable and moved down onto the bed, slowly inching my way closer to her.

Finally, I reached over and took her hand, lacing my fingers through hers. We lay there holding hands, massaging and rubbing each other's hands with our thumbs. It just felt so natural, so right, unlike anything I had ever experienced before. I began to fall asleep in my comfort with her. I rolled over onto my side, taking her hand with me so her arm fell across my body and over my stomach.

The movie ended, and I teased her about the massage she had been promising me for the last several months. To my surprise she said, "Roll over." I did and she moved up beside me, rubbing my shoulders with expert hands, working all of the tension from my body as she went. It felt so good having her hands on me.

She worked her way down my body, being careful not to do anything inappropriate. This was just a casual massage. Her hands were irresistible, and I felt myself nodding off. I'm not certain how long I slept, but when I woke up she was turning off the lights and getting into bed.

"Are you awake?" I asked her a few minutes later.

"Yes… Do you want to stay the night? I've already set the alarm, just in case. I didn't want to wake you."

"Sure," I said. "I'd like to stay. I think I'm too tired to drive home."

"Sounds good."

I went into the bathroom, washed up and changed into my pajamas—a carefully chosen red satin, long-sleeved, button-down top and pants. When I climbed back into bed, I curled up into the curves of her body, spooning with her.

I had been so sleepy during the movie and massage, but all of a sudden I felt wide awake. My heart began to race and flutter. I held her hand close to me, so scared to make a first move. I moved her hand closer to my breast a millimeter at a time, or so it seemed. I felt her arm tense as I guided her thumb with my hand so it slowly stroked my nipple. I moved closer in to her and leaned my head back toward her ever so slowly.

When my lips met hers for the first time, a shiver spread through my body like an electric charge. Her mouth was so soft, so sweet. Her kiss delicate, tender, passionate. I turned around to face her and she began to unbutton my shirt. She laid me on my back and moved her mouth to my breast, licking, sucking, and nibbling. I almost forgot to breathe. She seemed to take much pleasure from my breasts, endlessly stimulating them until I was gasping for air.

Her hands roamed all over my body. She rubbed me through the material of my pants, stirring a fire deep within me before pulling them off. Her fingers explored—first one, then two— alternating between massaging my clit and entering into me. She moved down my body, parted my legs, and probed me with her tongue. She licked and lingered and I silently moaned with pleasure. Never before had I enjoyed having someone go down on me, but this time everything about it felt so comfortable, so familiar.

She kissed her way back up my body to my breasts, nibbling on my nipples until I thought I might explode. It was the most exquisite pain I had ever felt in my life. She kissed my lips with urgency and insistence; I enjoyed the taste of me on her tongue. She stroked my body and moved her hand back to my pussy, making it moist once again before parting my lips with her fingers and entering me, slowly thrusting in and out. I was too tight for a third finger. "I'm sorry," she whispered in my ear, and I answered her with a kiss.

I turned over on my back, and Barb again went down on me, bringing me closer and closer to delirium. My body began building toward a climax; I was swept with pleasure as my first non-self-stimulated orgasm hit me in waves and spasms of bliss. My body loosened and released its tension. We lay holding one another for a while as my body continued to shake and tremble, and then I rolled over and fell into a deep sleep.

I don't know if I ever thanked her for that amazing first experience because the next morning, my nervous awkwardness returned. But to this day, when I think about our dream-like heavenly night, the night my friend initiated me into the world of lesbian sex, I get chills. I think I'll E-mail her this story right now.

Summer 1985, The First Time
Maria V. Ciletti

The early morning light peered through the tall leafy oaks; it was already hot outside, and the humidity hung in the air like a wet dishrag. My freshly pressed white uniform was already sticking to my back. As I crossed the parking lot, a candy-apple-red Mustang barreled toward me, way too close for comfort. The driver slammed on the brakes just in time to avoid rendering me quadriplegic. She sheepishly emerged from the cockpit, sunglasses perched on the top of her sandy blond hair.

"Sorry about that. Are you OK?"

"Yes, I guess so," I coughed, watching the dust settle around me.

"It's my first day here, and I didn't want to be late. Hi, I'm Reagan," she said as she extended her hand. "Are you really OK?"

"I'm fine. A little shook up, but fine," I answered, rubbing the dirt off my hand to shake hers. "I'm Mina."

While she pulled her car into a parking space, I clocked in and headed to the second-floor nursing unit. Although I was only an LPN, I was in charge of the unit that day. After my shift report I was preparing the medications for the first pass of the day when the elevator doors across from the nurse's station yawned open and out stepped the nursing supervisor with the maniac who had just tried to kill me.

"Mina, this is Reagan," the supervisor said. "She's starting orientation today and is assigned to your unit for the next two weeks."

Wonderful, I thought.

Reagan smiled shyly, a silvery smile. She wore braces on her teeth, which made her look much younger than her 24 years. I must admit my first impression of her wasn't very good, but I couldn't help notice she had the most magnificent ice-blue eyes I'd ever seen. She was an attractive woman with a slim figure, flawless skin, and sandy blond hair pulled back into a tight bun under her freshly blocked white nurse's cap. My mind, still reeling from the near accident, didn't know if this experience was going to be my worst nightmare or a dream come true.

That's how it all started.

After that we worked together often and she actually turned out to be a pretty decent nurse. Oh, there were a few moments, like the time she gave Mr. Giovanni his sleeping pill instead of his potassium supplement (the capsules did look a lot alike) at 9 in the morning. Or the time she freaked out because she had to catheterize one of the male residents (she had never touched a penis before). But it all turned out fine. No one was hurt, and Mr. Giovanni just took an extra long nap that day.

As summer turned into early fall, we started spending more and more time together outside of work. One of our favorite things to do was to walk on the beach of the small lake nearby. We would walk and talk for hours about anything: Our dreams, our hopes, and even our secrets. Except there was one secret I couldn't share with Reagan—I was falling in love with her. There was just something about being around her that made me feel wonderful. She was beautiful, kind, and compassionate. She would paint the female residents fingernails and trade jokes with the men. All the residents loved her.

Although we spent a lot of time together, she also found time to date this guy, who, if you want my opinion, never treated her right—although I could be a little prejudiced. He would break dates with her at the last minute, and she would come crying to me.

One date he did keep, however, was the day they spent in his dinky one room apartment. She later gave me the play by play details of their "passionate night together." I could feel the knife pierce, then twist in my heart, but I let her continue. At the end of her story, she confessed that it was nice and all, but the guy did not seem to care how she was feeling, and she didn't know what all the big fuss was about sex anyway. Then she told me that was her first time. Feeling crushed and betrayed I tried to console her, explaining "that I heard it gets better over time." I didn't know what else to say.

Time did go by, but things didn't get any better. The guy appeared less and less in our conversations. One late summer evening I asked where her guy had disappeared to, and she said that what they had together just didn't feel right. She anxiously admitted that she didn't feel she would ever find the right guy, then snickered, "If only I could feel with them like I feel when I'm with you, everything would work out fine."

Dumfounded, I managed to choke out, "What do you mean, the way you feel when you are with me?"

She looked at me innocently and said, "You know, we get along so well, we like to do the same things, we have a lot in common. If you were a guy, this would be the perfect relationship," she giggled.

"If I were a guy?" I repeated, still cautious of where this was going.

"Yes, If you were a guy, this would be a perfect relationship, don't you think? Too bad we're both girls." She snickered again, and then, with the charm of a 12-year-old, punched me in the arm.

My heart sank. I knew it was too good to be true, but thank God I didn't say anything about how I truly felt. It would have destroyed everything.

The coral sun set that evening, and the previously warm air turned cold. As we walked the beach heading toward the car, Reagan entwined her arm with mine and held on to the sleeve of my white oxford shirt. The sound of my heartbeat thundered in my head so loudly that I couldn't hear the waves breaking on the shore as we walked; the cold water swept over our feet and lapped up to our ankles. The scent of her Avon Musk perfume and Johnson's Baby shampoo permeated the air and swirled around my head, causing me to become dizzy in the moment. We reached the car. I opened her door for her, and she slid in. As I slid into the driver's seat, thoughts of it's now or never, clamored in my head. Then, throwing caution to the wind, I spoke; "You know all those thing you were telling me about that night you spent in that guy's apartment," I stammered, "you know, the physical stuff?"

"Yes…" she answered, cautiously.

"What would you say if I told you I wanted to do those things with you?"

There, I said it, it was out and…there was no response coming from the passenger side of the car. I looked over in her direction. The beautiful, peaceful face I was admiring only a few moments ago was now so distorted, I barely recognized her.

"Are you crazy?" she said. "We can't do that. We're both women."

"Well, what was that back there at the beach?"

"What was what?"

"That comment that if you could meet a guy and felt the way you feel with me that it would be a perfect relationship."

"It was just a comment," she mumbled. "I didn't mean anything by it."

"Well, what about on the way back down the beach…you locked your arm around mine, and pulled me close, I could smell your perfume…"

"I was *cold*, you idiot! Stop trying to read things into what isn't there. This is making me very uncomfortable. Please take me home," she demanded.

The remainder of the drive back to her house was in stone-cold silence. I didn't even get the car stopped in the driveway before she threw open the door and dashed into the house, slamming the door behind her.

It wasn't until a week later that I heard from her again.

"Mina, its Reagan. Can I come over?" came across the phone line.

"Why?" I answered, in the most rigid tone I could muster.

"We need to talk about what happened last week…you know, out at the lake."

"What more do you need to say?" I asked.

"We just need to talk. Can I come over or not?"

"All right, but give me a minute, I just got in from work and I'd like to clean up a bit."

"OK. I'll be over in half an hour."

"Fine." Click, then dial tone.

An hour later (she never was much for being on time), Reagan showed up on my doorstep with a six-pack of Seagram's citrus wine coolers.

"What's on your mind?" I asked her, hands clammy, heart picking up pace.

She pulled one of the wine coolers from the carton and twisted off the cap with the bottom of her T-shirt. "That stuff you told me the other day really freaked me out."

"You didn't have to come here to tell me that. You made your point pretty clear in the car."

"Wait a minute, just give me a minute."

She was pacing now, from the dining room into the living room, to the dining room again, searching for the right thing to say. "I thought about it…actually, I thought about it a lot." She let out a big sigh, pausing again to search for the right words. "I've never done anything like that…I've never even thought about doing anything like that." She reached over and grabbed another wine cooler, snapping the top off and taking a big swallow.

"I've never done anything like that either," I confessed. "I'm sorry if I made you feel uncomfortable, but the comment you made, and the way you touched me… It's like you have some kind of power over me. I've never felt that way before, and I thought that maybe you were feeling the same way too."

Summer 1985, The First Time

She came over to the couch where I was sitting, and cautiously sat next to me. She took my hand and gently pressed it to her face. Her skin was soft and warm. Hormones I never knew I had surged through my body. Breathing became difficult, and I got lightheaded. *Now is not the time to pass out.* She turned her head and softly kissed the inside of my palm. She reached for my other hand and placed it on her fully clothed breast. I thought I was going to die.

She took my face into her hands and gently kissed me on the lips. Her lips were soft and sweet. She kissed me again, more fervently now. Her hands were under my T-shirt now, stroking each breast through the lace fabric. My hands trembled as I slid them under her shirt, cupping them around her small firm breasts. Her breathing was labored now. "Can we move to the floor?" she gasped.

Once on the floor Reagan and I sat facing each other, hands moving everywhere. I tugged her T-shirt over her head and gently laid her on her back and gazed upon the most beautiful sight I'd ever seen. "You are so beautiful," I whispered, looking down at her, stroking between her breasts. Her eyes were moist and wide. I bent down and kissed her mouth, then trailed my tongue down her neck to the top of her lace-covered breast. I lowered my mouth over it, covering it completely. A long soft moan escaped from her lips. I pushed the fabric away and then took her naked breast into my mouth. It was as soft and sweet as her lips. The ache in my belly was becoming unbearable and was definitely in need of release. I moved my hands lower and caressed her legs, languidly edging to that forbidden place between them. As I inched my hand up the inside of her thigh, I could feel her heat. When I finally reached her secret place, she was soaked clear through her jeans.

I slowly unbuttoned her Levi's 501s and yanked them, along with her panties, down over her hips. Her dark pubic hair was soft and silky. Her swollen pink lips glistened with moisture and her scent, highly erotic, invaded my senses. I gently stroked the mound of hair, eliciting another low moan from her lips. She moaned again as my fingers slid easily inside her. On the brink of my own release (I couldn't keep this up much longer), I lowered my face to her, deeply inhaled her scent, then gently touched her with the tip of my tongue. She raised her hips off the floor, grinding her sex into my face, matching the rhythm of my strokes. Then, suddenly, she stopped and bolted up, clutching her rumpled T-shirt against her chest.

"Stop!" she gasped, pulling her legs together, and drawing her knees up to her chin. "I'm sorry. I can't do this anymore." She staggered to her feet, frantically searching for her discarded clothes. "I'm sorry, I'm sorry, I'm sorry. This never should have happened."

Stunned, wounded, and with a raging case of blue clitoris, I watched helplessly as she plucked the last of her clothing from the floor. I got to my feet, feeling dazed, my knees weak, and leaned against the living room wall. What clothing she did not put back on she shoved into her purse. Before she left, she came over to me, angry now, shaking her bony index finger in my face. "Don't you ever touch me like that again. You hear me? Never. And you can never tell anyone this happened—understand? *Never!*"

I watched as she left and slammed the door behind her. I staggered over to the couch, buried my head into the cushion, and cried. How stupid could I be? What had I done? And for what, a few hours—no, a few minutes—of pleasure. I had to work with this woman. What if our coworkers found out? What then? Suddenly there was a knock at the front door.

"Mina, it's Reagan. Let me in."

I braced myself for more berating and opened the door. Reagan burst in with the same fury she left with. She pushed me against the wall again, her face inches from mine, fire burning in her blue eyes.

"You can't tell anyone about this," she said. "This will ruin both of us. No one can ever find out. We only did this because we don't have any decent men in our lives—right?" Before I could answer, she took my hand, led me to the couch, and said, "Now finish what you started."

Epilogue: We did finish what we started, and it was good. It was good for a little over a year, then Reagan couldn't handle it any more. We had to sneak around because even after a year of living and loving like this, she still thought we only did this because we didn't have any decent men in our lives. I finally admitted to her that our relationship wasn't due to "a lack of a good man." I loved women and I loved her, and I wasn't ashamed of that. Unfortunately, she was. So on an icy-cold gray day in February she eloped in West Virginia with a maintenance man from the nursing home.

That was more than 15 years ago. It took me a long time to get over it. But the joy and the pain I experienced during that time brought me to the place I am today, with my soul mate, my super-hero, and the true love of my life, Rose.

A Lady in Waiting
Alison DuBois

Funny how sometimes you don't realize what you most want or need is right in front of you. It was like that with Anne. We met through a lesbian correspondence club, The Wishing Well, and from the moment we started writing I sensed a difference: She was a lady, not some aloof, snotty, or pretentious little thing. Her warmth, honesty, and caring were refreshing.

It was in the way her words flowed, almost coming off the paper. Savoring each letter, I longed to feel the same fingers that wrote them on my skin, but kept my adoration to myself.

Over the years, in our letters, we shared many thoughts and dreams and feelings of joy, sadness, disappointment. We wrote of lovers who had come and gone as well as our mutual frustration. Our confidences nurtured the friendship. We were slowly falling in love but didn't realize it.

Occasionally, we'd engage in harmless flirting over the phone. It made me wonder, but then I'd dismiss it—this was *Anne*, my faithful friend. It never occurred to me that she might be feeling something too.

As time went on, things began to unravel. Anne's last relationship had disintegrated and she was planning to return to her homeland, Britain. And relationship problems were only part of

176

her troubles—her visa had expired and she couldn't get another to stay in the States. She would have to leave.

I felt a twinge in my heart. I had to meet her. It was now or never. But I worried. She was still hurting from her last relationship, and the likelihood she'd want to get involved again so soon was remote. Regardless, I had to see this lady with the golden hair and beautiful green eyes. I had to.

Was she feeling the same?

Finally our day of reckoning came. We'd decided that I would fly down to Orlando and meet her. After my plane landed and I disembarked I stood waiting in a sea of people, but there was no sight of Anne anywhere. In my frustration I decided to have her paged. It was already 3:20 P.M., nearly half an hour after my landing time.

I listened as the loudspeaker came on: "Anne Marie Hollowell, please meet your party at the American Airlines counter." I surveyed the area for any blond women. A tall blond carrying a case and dragging a wailing toddler emerged. Well, I knew she couldn't be Anne. I spotted a heavyset woman with wheat-colored hair and knew that couldn't be my Anne Marie either.

Then, suddenly, a woman in white shorts and a T-shirt ran up to the desk. My heart skipped; it had to be Anne. I compared the pictures in my memory to the woman standing at the counter. I came up behind her and timidly tapped her shoulder. She turned to face me, and suddenly I was greeted by the most beautiful pair of green eyes I'd ever seen—clear as the waters of Lake Winoka in Canada and just as deep.

"Anne?" I said shyly. Immediately she smiled.

"What a beautiful woman you are," she said, and gave me a huge bear hug. A flush of nervous excitement spread through me like a raging river. By the time we pulled apart I was breathless, but I could see from the corner of my eye that she was also blushing. It made me happy. So, sweet little Anne was nervous also.

"Do you have luggage?" she asked.

"Just my carry-on. We can go." I was trying desperately not to notice her nipples protruding through her T-shirt.

We engaged in small talk during the walk to her car. But once we were on the road I burrowed against her. For a moment I thought I'd been presumptuous, but then she put her arm around me.

The smell of her perfume reminded me of the faint sweet scent that had accompanied all of her letters. I opened my eyes, her right breast inches from my face. I wondered what it looked like, felt like. She glanced at me.

Did she know? My face grew hot.

"Are you tired?" Anne asked, turning into the parking lot of her apartment building. She brought the car to a stop and I straightened up. "I can't believe I'm really here," I told her. She gave a quick smile before climbing out of the car. I followed.

Her place was simple, just as she'd described it. Very neat. No papers or clutter of any kind. Instinctively I fretted—would she think I was a slob? I didn't wade through messes, but my apartment definitely had that "lived-in" look.

"Anything in particular you'd like for dinner?" she asked, disappearing into the guest room with my bag. She reappeared looking like a kid in a candy store, hands tucked inside her front pockets. "Want to order in?" she offered. "I have a bunch of menus in the kitchen." She half chuckled as she pulled out a handful. They ranged from Chinese to barbecue. Lingering on the Chinese menu, I looked up.

"What do you think?" she said with a smile. In the course of trying to decide what we wanted, our fingers brushed. My heart did a flip; even my scalp tingled from the rush. "OK, I guess we're ready to order, right?"

I just nodded, looking at those perfectly shaped lips. I listened to her place the order as if she were reciting love poetry to me.

"Are you OK?" she asked me. "Jet lag?" Again I nodded. "I've got just the thing. Why don't you rest and I'll make some iced tea, hmm?" She ushered me into the living room.

"Anne, you've already done so much," I started to protest, but she came and took my face in her hands.

"It's my pleasure," she said. "You want to please me, don't you?" Please her? If she only knew.

"Thank you," I managed to choke out before she once again abandoned me.

Anne returned with two glasses and placed one in my hand. The drink was strong but good, exactly what the English are known for. I pressed the cool glass against my hot cheeks. She settled in the lounge chair across from me, tucking my legs under her. She was an incredibly sexy woman. It was easy to understand why so many had been drawn to her. We chit-chatted until the food came. But then as she spread the cartons across her table so close to me, I was overwhelmed with the urge to follow the delicate fragrance into her arms. She smiled in a knowing way, which embarrassed me, and a long period of silence followed.

"This is really good," I said, referring to the pork and snow peas in an awkward attempt to break the silence.

"Glad you like it."

"Anne, you're absolutely beautiful," I heard myself say. Where did *that* come from? A new wave of embarrassment hit me. She looked into my eyes but said nothing. All at once I felt the need to disappear. Just as I started to rise she rested her hand on my arm, holding my gaze.

"Stay. Finish your dinner. We'll talk later, all right?" Those deep-green eyes once again pulled me inside her. How could I refuse?

After dinner she tossed the empty cartons and put the remaining food in the refrigerator. "Can I help?" I offered.

"All done," she said. "But you can dance with me."

I followed her into the living room and waited anxiously while she selected a CD. Immediately I recognized the sultry, raspy wail of Melissa Etheridge floating from her stereo. Anne opened her arms. Shaking all over, I took her hand, folding into her embrace as we began to dance. Her breasts pressed against mine, my heartbeat blending with hers, her blond hair meshing with my light brown curls, her hips swaying. Soon we were notes of a new song being sung together as we created our own melody.

The satiny-skin of her cheek caressing mine, her breath so

near, made me queasy. In as much as I was intensely aroused, I was equally afraid. Anne wasn't just another woman to me. She was the woman I had dreamed about for so long. My ideal woman: passionate but proper, intelligent and funny, kind, affectionate, and loving. I'd never wanted to be loved by any woman as much as her, nor had I wanted to love any woman so completely as her. And yet I knew it would be extremely hard for me to go to bed with her because she both excited and intimidated me. She was without a doubt a woman's woman—more woman than I could possibly imagine.

When the song ended, Anne slowly moved back, looking at me intently. I wanted to kiss her, but I was afraid it was too soon, afraid of her response. I didn't want to do anything that would spoil this glorious moment.

"Alison," she said, taking my hand and leading me to the couch. "We need to talk." Her expression grew serious. I curled up in the corner waiting. "I think we're both aware of our feelings," she began. Did she just say "our"? My beautiful Anne Marie had said "our feelings." It was too wonderful to believe. I looked into her eyes, so clear but somber now. "Well?" she said. Suddenly I snapped out of my daze.

"I'm sorry. I didn't hear you. I'm sorry," I mumbled sheepishly. At first she looked miffed, but then her expression softened.

"Well, I don't think I'll ask you where your mind's been. I think I have a pretty good idea. What I was saying—are you with me?" I nodded. "What do you want to do about this?"

I couldn't respond. I couldn't help it. My eyes welled with tears. I loved this woman. It had taken us more than five years to get to this point—how could I even fathom losing it all so quickly? "I don't know," I stuttered. In my heart I wanted to say that everything would be all right. But I feared the practical realities, which made my heart sink. I couldn't lose her, not after all this.

"You live in Oregon," Anne said. "You're a citizen here, and I'm not. I have my return to the U.K. already planned," she said matter-of-factly.

"I know. I don't want you to go. Stay, Anne. I don't know how yet, but we'll work it out. We need to." In her eyes I saw a sea of emotions; she was worried too.

She scooched closer to me on the couch and snuggled me tightly. Shyly I wrapped my arms around her, inhaling her perfume, feeling her taut body resting against mine. We nuzzled our cheeks together as if it were some secret language between us. I desperately wanted to kiss her. She turned then, looking at my lips, then my eyes. Her face was like a whisper. I felt her hot breath on my skin.

I wanted her to kiss me. I needed her to. But she remained still. What was she thinking? Why wouldn't she do it? What was holding her back? Why couldn't I do it? As passionately as I wanted her, I couldn't close the gap between us.

"Alison," she started, but stopped midway, as her lips, so soft and gentle, lightly brushed mine.

A thousand tingling sensations swept my body. I was "home" in her arms but also acutely aroused. When she moved back, her eyes seemed to be searching mine for some secret. She once again moved forward and I felt those same sweet lips kiss me tenderly. My emotions were a jumbled mess as I lay trembling in her arms.

I pressed my breasts against her, slipped my hands under her shirt to feel her bare back. My fingers explored the length of her flower-petal-smooth skin, ran along the edges of her bra. Did I dare?

She gently bit my bottom lip as my fingers darted over her skin, leaving a trail of goose flesh. I nibbled her earlobe, heard her sigh softly. With equal parts of adrenaline and raw excitement driving me, I kissed her neck, making a path along her cleavage. Her body fluidly accepted my kisses and caresses. She was ready for me.

With shaky fingers I unbuttoned her shirt, which slid down her shoulders, exposing a black lace bra. I unfastened the hooks and her pert nipples stood at attention, luring me to them. Anne looked so serious. What was she thinking? Just as I was about to take one of her breasts in my mouth, I felt her hands underneath my shirt. Off it came. She briefly looked at my purple bra, then unfastened it, exposing my ample bosom.

Did she find me attractive? She had never said what she found physically attractive in another woman. For a moment I worried: Did she like big breasts? But she soon dispelled my doubts when she cupped my breasts in her hands and tenderly kissed my nipples. I drew her to me, tasted her lips, felt the depth of her passion unfolding, her breasts against mine. My fingers continued their trek along her body, following the curve of her hips, exploring her ass. She groaned between kisses.

"Oh, yes," she said again before engaging me in another series of passionate kisses. I inched my way to the dampness between her legs. Her eyes were dark and serious.

She got up, took my hand, and led me to her bedroom. She stopped at the foot of the bed, waiting for me. Hesitantly I removed her shorts and soaked panties, then backed her onto the bed. Her fingers unsnapped and unzipped my pants, then gently but firmly tugged them south, leaving my panties stranded midway between my crotch and my knees. Her eyes smiled in a devilish way as she pushed my panties down to join my discarded jeans on the floor. For a moment we lay there looking at each other, delighting in the newness of it all. I kissed her softly and tenderly, then with more urgency, until finally I pushed my tongue inside, wanting, needing to taste her completely.

Anne wasn't timid with her touch. Her fingers roamed my body as if we had been lovers for years. I began my descent over her petite but supple frame, starting with her neck, then along, around her tight breasts, watching her nipples come to life like flowers budding in the springtime. I started with one, then the other, circling the areola with my fingertip, teasing her. I gazed deep into her luminous eyes: Anne was watching me make love to her. I felt beads of sweat roll down my cheeks.

Anne's skin was a blend of salty and sweet. As I licked the

silky plane under her ribs and across her smooth hips, I was drawn into the muskiness of her secret place. As I nibbled along her matted blond curls, her legs fell open. I inched my way down, and she shuddered as I opened her. Her hips rose and fell as I licked her delicate, intimate ridge. I inhaled her scent, savored her unique taste.

We were the perfect mates—as long as she could hold out, I could continue to build her, bringing the tempo to a furious exchange of passion then back to a more subdued rhythm. All the while, her cunt expanded and contracted with each thrust of my fingers. Anne was not like most—she didn't fizzle; she could go all night like smoldering tinder. Just the feel of her on my fingers, on my hand and face, brought me close to climaxing.

I brought my lips to her clit—a dark, swollen rosebud—and licked the tender tip. Her body told me, *Yes, you're doing this right.* She gasped, writhing in joyous release. I clutched her hips, riding her until every sliver of ecstasy had left and she lay satiated and serene.

She was my ambrosia. She rested, twisting a few strands of my hair. All at once, with a crooked grin on her face, she mounted me. "Let me show you how the English do it," she said. I smiled nervously. At first she just lay there, our breasts pressed together, pelvis to pelvis, the tickle of pubic hairs on my skin. She placed feathery kisses across my face, stopping briefly for a more passionate moment on my lips before resuming her journey over my body. It was hard to relax. In as much as I had imagined this scenario a thousand times, I still worried about her reaction. Her previous partners had all been about her size—how would she respond to me? I had always been self-conscience about my size, and with Anne being so much smaller I worried even more. And yet, there we were, coupled tightly like two strands of intertwined chord. If there was any reticence on her part, I didn't sense it. Anne worked my breasts with all the skills of a seasoned lover. When she brought her lips to them I let out the sigh I'd been holding. She seemed to delight in their size and softness.

She took her time making a trail of kisses and nibbles to my crotch. As she grew closer, my body tensed in anticipation. Her breath and lips tickled my skin until she took her place between my legs. When she pushed her tongue inside me the entire room seemed to spin. And when she stroked my clit with her tongue, everything felt very unreal, a floating sensation overtaking my body.

Over the next few days we danced and dined, getting to know each other more intimately with each conversation. One afternoon she took me to Disney World, and when we returned, both wearing Mickey Mouse ears, I found myself drawn to her every movement. Following her into the kitchen, I leaned against the table. watching her fixing tea. Anne had incredibly sexy, shapely legs and a perfectly sculpted ass that took my breath away. I came up behind her and slipped my arms around her waist, planting a kiss on her neck. She trembled as I turned her around and drew her into a long, soft kiss. Then, feeling particularly gutsy, I lifted her onto my hips and set her on the counter.

Her eyes flashed with equal parts excitement and shyness. She knew what I had in mind. Instinctively she raised her hips as I slipped down her shorts and panties. I opened her shirt and bra, freeing her breasts. I licked between them as she sighed and sank back against the cupboards. Gently I tugged each nipple with my teeth and lips as my fingers went inside her.

Anne pressed my face harder against her breast, moaning and running her fingers through my hair. I gingerly slid my fingers in and out of her wet pussy. Her hips smacked against my hand with each thrust. She pulled my face to her, kissing me deep and full. Her tongue darted in and out of my mouth in sync with my rhythm. The longer we kissed, the more insistent her cries grew, echoing through the apartment. She needed release, and I would give it. I place my thumb over her and massaged her hard spot in circles. She bucked, growing tight. I held her as she started to shake, her cunt contracting in orgasm. I steadied her until her eyes focused again as she kissed me briefly.

"I love you," she whispered.

"I love you too," I said, scooping her back into my arms, resting her on my hips again as I carried her into the bedroom and laid her down. She climbed into my arms. We made love many times that night, sharing our bodies and hearts, until we lay spent. I held her, feeling a sheath of closeness all around us. I loved this woman, and knew then that no matter what it took, somehow we would find a way. Anne would stay, for keeps.

Hawaiian White Ginger
Kate Dominic

I won't say how old I was because I come from a small town where everybody knows everybody else's business, and memories are long and unforgiving. Carrie and I are both married now with children. Grandchildren, even. So let's just say it was a long time ago, somewhere between puberty and my junior year of high school, the latter being when I got pregnant and any lingering questions I had about myself were pretty much settled by default.

I don't know why Carrie and I started hanging out together that spring. We didn't have any of the usual things in common—not classes or being from the same neighborhood or being in any school clubs together. Carrie was pretty in a way I didn't notice with my other friends. For here and now, I'll say she had soft, curling blond hair and striking blue eyes. Maybe she did and maybe she didn't. If anybody there should ever read this, I don't want them to figure out who she is. So, for the sake of discussion, I'll say she had blue eyes. Her laugh made me feel so good that the skin on my arms rose up in goose bumps, the same way it did when she played with my hair, which she did all the time. Mine was long and dark, and when she twirled it through her fingers or brushed it up into French braids, I felt like I my bones were melting.

So, we hung out together—the two of us and a half dozen or so of her other friends. I didn't have anything in common with them either, but they accepted me when she did. We went to the movies they liked. We went shopping and bowling and ordered Hawaiian White Ginger perfume and bath scents from the Avon lady—all the stuff young girls in small Midwestern towns did in the last years of the '60s. And almost every week we had a slumber party at somebody's house. Usually, we went to Carrie's. She was an only child, so she had a room to herself.

Sleepovers at Carrie's were the best. We listened to 45s and read smuggled copies of *True Story* and *True Confessions* and the movie magazines her mother picked up from the beauty salon. We stayed up all night, talking about how there was no way that stuff could be true. Not that any of us knew anything about sex beyond the bare mechanics: We got our periods so someday we could have babies, and we always had to tell boys "no" so we wouldn't get pregnant before we were married, which we all know we would be, eventually. That was just the way things were.

I'd never imagined that two women could have sex. The requisite penis that made sex "sex" wouldn't be there if a man wasn't involved. So, it never occurred to me that anything women could do together could be sex. All I knew was that I was drawn to Carrie. When she invited me I joined the rest of the gang that hung out at her house. I felt good around her, especially late at night, when we'd all lie together in her room with the lights out, talking about boys and what we'd read in the magazines.

I usually ended up in Carrie's bed with her. As everybody was settling down, she'd pat the pillow next to her and laugh and tell me to climb up. So I would. I think some of the other girls got a little bit jealous since they'd all hung out with her longer than I had, and she'd never been "best friends" with anybody before. But I didn't really know them well enough to care if they liked me. I didn't even see them except with Carrie. All I knew was that I liked Carrie.

By the time school let out for the summer, she and I were

pretty much inseparable. In addition to the weekend slumber parties with the gang, I spent a couple nights a week at her house with just the two of us. Nobody cared. It was just two girls hanging out together over vacation.

Since the midweek sleepovers were on plain old weekdays, we didn't wear the cool slogan-covered T-shirts and hip-hugger panties we saved for the weekends. Instead we lay close together in our everyday baby doll pajamas, with the covers thrown back to the hot, sticky July air. I wore silky yellow with tiny bikini bottoms. The low-cut top caught between my breasts with a tiny green embroidered flower. I liked the way the style made my too-flat chest look like maybe I'd be getting bigger breasts someday. Carrie wore sheer translucent blue. I remember thinking I couldn't have worn that at my house—I had brothers who sometimes came into my room without knocking.

Carrie's nipples were pink and pointed, centered on the full, creamy mounds of flesh that were already starting to rest on her chest. More than once, I wondered what it would feel like to lift her breasts and hold them in my hands, to see if they were as warm and heavy as they looked, to rub my face against them and see if they smelled like her perfume. To me, though, that was curiosity. Like I said, I'd never imagined two women doing anything sexual together.

So it was safe for me to watch the way her hips rolled in her bikini at the pool. It was OK to laugh and blush when she told me how much older I looked in the new black swimsuit I'd finally, *finally* convinced my mother to let me buy. We rubbed suntan lotion on each other's backs and drank Mountain Dew. I watched her swim, since I couldn't. Back then I was still afraid of the water. I'd almost drowned a couple years before. Carrie swam like a mermaid, the stuff of the old 1940s movies we watched on the black-and-white TVs in our family rooms, except she was in living, breathing color. When she stepped from the water her breasts rose and fell with her breathing, and her nipples were hard against her suit.

We showered afterward in the locker room, sharing shampoo and soap.

I liked that she'd used my soap first. It almost seemed to smell like her.

That night at Carrie's house we ate pizza for dinner. Then we went back to her room to listen to records and talk. Her mom wanted to go out and asked if my parents would mind. I lied and said, "No." So she left, and then Carrie and I were alone, giggling as we danced to our favorite records—"Beast of Burden" and "Incense and Peppermints." Pretty soon we were hot and tired, and it was getting late. We had to turn the music off so we could keep the windows open without the neighbors getting mad and complaining to her mom. I went to the bathroom and came back in my yellow baby dolls. I climbed into bed and laid back against my usual pillow, watching as Carrie got ready for bed.

She slipped her hands up her back and unhooked her white cotton bra. As it slid free, her breasts fell forward, full and heavy. She put on her blue see-through pajamas again. Even with just the reading light on I could see her pink nipples peeking through her top. I knew when she sat down on the bed to read, her hem would pull up and her thighs would spread as she sat cross-legged with her magazine. I'd be able to see the hidden shadows of the folds beneath her sheer blue panties.

We read for a long time, our legs almost touching, giggling at the ridiculous love stories. When we got tired, we turned off the lights and lay next to each other. For a while we talked about our favorite musicians and which ones would be the better kissers and whether we'd be doomed to despair or live happily ever after if we married them. From what the magazines said, the outcome was pretty much a toss-up, even though we'd always been told that marriage was forever and a husband and children were the be-all and end-all of a woman's life.

Eventually we stopped talking. We lay there with our hands behind our heads and our legs spread, our elbows and knees bare-ly touching in the heat as we listened to the crickets outside the open windows. It felt so good lying there with Carrie, so natural.

I could say I was almost asleep when she moved, but I wasn't. I was awake, so aware of the comfort of her body. She said my name, just my name, just "Katy," so softly her voice was almost lost in the quiet buzz of the insects outside the window. Then she leaned up on her elbow and cupped my head in her hand. She tenderly turned my face to hers. And then she kissed me.

Her lips were warm and wet and soft, so soft and sweet. I leaned into her and let her kiss me. I let myself fall into her kiss. Her body pressed into mine, and suddenly I knew women could have sex together. Somehow, someway, they could. And if it was anything at all like what we were doing, it would feel so good.

In the same breath, fear like a cloud of demon shadows screamed into my brain. A cacophony of voices too intermeshed for me to even begin to separate howled at me to run away, shrieked that sex was something I must always run away from, and the touch of a woman was something from which I must run far and fast and never stop if I wanted to survive. So I froze. I lay there, pretending to be asleep, breathing in the scent of Carrie's perfume and feeling the soft weight of her breasts against me. When she finally moved back, I felt her hesitancy, like she wasn't sure if maybe I was asleep after all. I rolled over and made a muffled sound like I was just barely stirring from my dreams. I breathed deeply and evenly. I stayed that way, even when she gently stroked my hair and the tears rolled down my cheeks into the pillow. A long while later she rolled over and snuggled her back to mine. I tried to stay awake, but I know I fell asleep first, leaning into the warmth of her body and the dampness on my pillow.

We didn't talk about it in the morning. I went into the bathroom and got dressed, and when I came out, Carrie was already in the kitchen, dressed and setting the table for her mother. When her mom asked when I wanted to go home, I said I wanted to leave right away, that I didn't feel good.

Carrie and I didn't say much in the car on the way to my house. I think her mom thought it was because I didn't feel good.

But I think both Carrie and I knew there was no point in making plans and talking about a future that was never going to be. The next day I took a job baby-sitting for the rest of the summer. I didn't call her and she didn't call me.

When school started again, I passed Carrie in the hall on the first day. I know she saw me too, but she looked away and pretended she hadn't. I did the same. She looked kind of scared, like she was afraid I would say something in public about what had happened. But I didn't. I couldn't. I mean, no, I didn't ask her to kiss me. But it wasn't her fault I'd liked it.

Years later I could admit to myself what I'd known in my heart even back then. That fall, though, I was still too young to have figured it out. Carrie and I weren't in the same classes, and we didn't do the same things, and we didn't have the same friends. After that first day, we only saw each other once in a while in passing. Over the years we eventually came to say "hi" to each other before we hurried on. Then I got pregnant and dropped out, coming back only enough to finish the last couple of classes I needed to get my diploma before I moved to the West Coast. Carrie graduated with the class and went on to get married in town and have a passel of kids.

I didn't see her again until our 20th reunion. It was another hot July day, and the air conditioning in the VFW hall couldn't quite keep up with the humidity. I'd flown in by myself, divorced and single again, though I was seeing a man I liked enough to start wondering where things would go.

Carrie stood by the half-open front door, passing out nametags to the latecomers like me. She was as pretty as ever, a little plumper, but it fit her well. We smiled and awkwardly said hello. For just a second there was a flicker of her old smile, a sparkle in her clear blue eyes that made my belly flutter. Just as suddenly, she turned back to laughing with her friends, the same circle of friends she'd had way back then, and I walked away in search of mine.

The awards for who had the least hair and who had traveled

the farthest were just finishing. As the hoots and hollers died down, I heard crickets calling outside. Then the DJ began playing our class song, "American Pie."

I didn't expect the tears stinging my eyes. Bodies flooded toward the dance floor, and I ducked into the bathroom, grateful for the unexpected solitude. As I dabbed the tears, trying to keep from getting raccoon eyes, the door opened. Strains of the music surged in, the long version of the song. The sound faded with the closing door. I kept my head down, hiding my face as I fiddled with the spaghetti straps of the revealing black minidress on which I'd spent a week's pay, silently cursing myself for indulging in something so ridiculous. I smelled her even before her fingers slid over my shoulder, brushing my hair away so she could gently kiss the skin she'd bared.

"I still want you." Carrie's voice was low and sultry. She slid her hands up my arms. This time, when she cupped my cheek, I turned and leaned into her hand, closing my eyes as I promised myself, I was not, not, *not* going to cry anymore. But I couldn't help the tears streaming down my face. Finally I looked up and smiled, my vision still blurred and watery as I pressed my lips against her palm.

"Same perfume," I choked out. Carrie laughed, whispering "in here," as she pulled me into the handicapped stall. The minute she threw the latch, her arms were around me. We kissed like we were starving, soft and achingly sweet, but so desperate our lipstick smeared between us.

Carrie's breasts were every bit as soft as they'd been pressing against me in my "sleep" all those years ago. She slid the thin straps off my shoulders, unzipping the back of my dress and yanking it down to my waist. Even being a mother I was still small enough to go braless. Carrie slid her hands up and down my sides, shivering when I unbuttoned the front of her dress and unhooked the lacy front of her support bra. Her breasts fell warm and heavy into my waiting hands. They were bigger now, her nipples huge and round and dusky rose. I lowered my head, inhaling the scent of her perfume as I licked up the sides, swirling my tongue over the velvety tips.

I sucked her nipples until they were wet and elongated and covered with dark mascara smudges from my tears. Carrie stroked my hair, alternately laughing and moaning and whispering "shh, shh, shh" as she held me tightly to her. This time, when she took my head in her hands and lifted my lips to hers, my hands slid around her waist.

"Kiss me, please," I smiled through my tears. I told myself I didn't know why I was laughing, but I did. Ooh, I did. I loved her and I wanted her, and I kissed her like I was drowning. We didn't talk, just stood there swaying softly against each other, our bare skin rubbing together to the distant strains of the music and the whir of the ceiling fans. Even over the bubble-gum scent of the air freshener I could still smell the flowery spice of her perfume.

When her hand slid under my skirt, I parted my legs. Her wedding ring snagged for just a moment on my hem. Then her fingers slipped beneath the edge of my panties. I moaned, stiffening as she found the pleasure spot between my slippery lips. Her lips curved up, still kissing.

"This is so much better than those crazy damn magazines we used to read."

I shook when her finger slid into me. With my hands still trembling, I lifted her skirt. Under her slip, she was wearing only a garter belt and stockings. I slid my fingers over the delicate, sticky strands of hair hiding her labia.

"Ooh!" she gasped. "That feels so nice."

It did. She was hot and wet and slippery, and just touching her made me open my legs farther for her questing fingers. I rubbed her with the pad of my thumb, groaning as she slid a second and third finger into me, and pressed firmly on my clit.

"You were the first woman I kissed, Katy. But oh, hon, you weren't the last."

I couldn't stifle the cry that escaped my lips. Carrie's fingers were soft and warm, and they felt good, so good, as they slid in and out of me and her thumb rubbed mercilessly over my clit. God, I wanted her. In my entire life, I don't know that I've ever come that hard or that fast. As I shattered into her arms, she held me tightly, shaking while her orgasm took her and our lips sucked softly and gently with an unbroken kiss so tender I ached and cried all over again.

"This will be the day that I die..." The song was ending, haunting strains of Miss American Pie's final goodbyes. Carrie and I hurriedly straightened each other up. By the time the ladies' room door opened to the new onslaught of chattering women, Carrie and I were fixing our makeup and hair. Her friends came in looking for her. I don't think they recognized me. I figured that was for the best. Carrie and I exchanged a wink and I walked out the door.

I sipped a blush Chablis for the next round of awards, the biggies: the most years married and greatest number of children. Then the music started and the crowd around me once more surged toward the dance floor. As they passed, someone brushed the hair from my shoulder, a single caress, soft and gentle, that reached all the way to the shiver rising on my scalp. When I turned around, I was alone, inhaling the faintest hint of ginger in the night air.

Kerry

M. Damian

I turned to Kerry, my appointed partner in crime, sitting next to me in the classroom where we had both just attended a training session. We had been recruited to help proctor a huge exam being given the following week. "Want to go check out the testing room?" I asked her.

As we strolled leisurely down the newly renovated halls, we made small talk about working at such a prestigious school. She said had specifically come to work for NYU to get her MBA. "The salary won't get me far," she told me, "but the break on tuition is worth sacrificing little luxuries for a few years."

"Yeah, as long as you get your degree and leave," I said. She looked at me strangely, and I gave a wry chuckle. "I'm a lifer. Came here for my AA, stayed for my BS, got an MA, and *still* haven't left. Don't let that happen to you."

"Well," Kerry replied brightly, "my plan is to get my MBA and then get an accounting job with a big firm like Merrill Lynch. There's no way I'm going to work for $30,000 a year with minimal benefits."

"The perks take away some of the sting," I drawled, thinking of all the gorgeous female students I saw on a daily basis, but I kept that to myself. I knew her, but not to the degree where we had shared sexual confidences; I certainly didn't know if she was gay, so why go there? Not that it mattered if she was or wasn't— I mean, we only saw each other at work.

During the intervening week until the test, we firmed up plans to meet early Saturday morning at the complimentary breakfast buffet provided in the student lounge so we could pick up our test materials and be set up when the test-takers stormed the room.

Test day was gloomy, dark clouds roiling overhead, their contents drowning the sidewalks and streets. I drove into New York City and parked in front of the building; Kerry was training it in from Jersey. I got there first and immediately grabbed us a table by the window. The place was quickly filling up; Diane, the head proctor and general supervisor, had gotten more than 200 people together to help out this year.

Suddenly, Kerry broke through the crowd, smiling apologetically. "Sorry, Marie, but this rain! It's horrible out there. I thought the train would never get here." She looked slightly bedraggled. She stayed at the table while I got her a cup of hot tea and a bagel with cream cheese.

While she ate I greeted people I knew with a bemused expression on my face. I could tell by their curious looks that they were wondering whether Kerry and I were an item. I'm very out at work, so I was tickled watching as they tried to figure it out.

The test was set to start at 9; in the 30 minutes we had, we prepared the room for the test-takers. I stayed in the background while Kerry and a hall monitor stood at the classroom door and checked the ID and calculator of each person coming in; when that was done, I read instructions for the test-takers to follow. Once the testing was officially underway, Kerry quietly sat at the desk and finished the clerical stuff that needed to be done. I was thankful she was so capable.

Now that all the checking in and checking up was over and done with, we had just shy of three hours to watch 14 people take a test. And let me tell you, the only thing worse than *taking* a test is *watching* someone take a test. We weren't permitted to talk, read a book, or have any snacks or beverages in the room. After an hour of rigorous scanning to make sure no cheating was going on, Kerry leaned over and whispered sotto voce, "Let's play Hangman. OK?" I heartily concurred.

The morning session slowly ebbed away. At high noon the test-takers went off for their two-hour lunch break. Kerry and I gathered up the test materials, dropped them off, picked up the box lunch provided for the proctors, and headed back to our classroom. Along the way I met a male coworker, and he joined us; our lunch break was a lively three-way exchange of amusing anecdotes concerning the morning's session.

After a repeat of the morning's settling in, the afternoon test began. This time it was harder to stay focused, but I wasn't bored anymore—not after I saw Kerry's nipples harden beneath the fabric of her shirt. The room was cold with the air conditioner running on high. I quickly averted my eyes, but then I started to fantasize about what it would be like to take those young firm peaks into my mouth. I mentally slapped myself to stop this line of thinking and tried to concentrate on the job at hand. But I simply could not take my eyes off her beautiful red hair, her hazel brown eyes, her soft lips.

When the afternoon session finally ended and we had dismissed our group, Kerry walked around the room collecting test booklets and answer sheets from the now-empty desks. She was dressed in tight faded jeans, white leather sneakers, and a black cotton blouse. As she bent over the desk toward me, the neckline of her loose blouse dipped down, and I could see she wasn't wearing a bra. Her milky breasts hung in front of my riveted eyes like two ripe melons waiting to be plucked. I held my breath as she smiled and asked, "Don't you want these?" It took me a moment to realize she was referring to the answer sheets she had collected. To my embarrassment I felt myself getting aroused. Guiltily dragging my eyes down, I practically snatched the materials from her hands and hurriedly started putting everything in order.

After we dropped off our test materials our day was done and it was time to head for home. As we stood in the lobby, however, Kerry's face took on a look of urgent concern. The deluge that had begun in the morning was still pelting the city with full force. After she made a quick call on her cell phone, I learned the reason behind the look. "My mom said the river overflowed. The streets are a foot and a half under water." I stared dumbly at her. River overflowing? Where the hell did she live, on Tobacco Road? "I can't get in; they can't get out. And the trains aren't running anyway."

"Does this happen often?" I asked, the city girl in me wondering what it was like to live with a river so close it could flood the streets of my neighborhood.

"Only when it rains like this," she replied, glumly pointing out the window. "Fuck! What am I going to do now? I won't be able to get home until who knows when. Where am I going to stay?"

I could tell she was upset. Who wouldn't be, stranded in a strange city? "You're more than welcome to have my spare bedroom for the night." My gallant offer was met with a grateful smile.

We waited for a lull in the storm, then ran the half-block to my car. When we got to Staten Island, we stopped first at the mall, a scant mile from my house, so she could buy some necessary overnight things (toothbrush, pair of panties, etc.), then I drove to Pathmark, where we got some comfort food. The wind had picked up intensity, twisting tree limbs into grotesque shapes behind a gray curtain of rain as I pulled into my driveway. By the time we dashed the 20 or so feet to the house, we were both soaked. "The main bathroom's upstairs," I told her when we got inside. "I'll get you something to change into and then I'll throw your wet clothes in the dryer."

While Kerry was changing, I followed suit and changed into dry togs. I had just bought the house and hadn't really had anyone over yet, especially not an overnight guest, so I stumbled around the kitchen trying to do the best I could while she sat at the table, watching my every move. That didn't help my awkwardness, but eventually I managed to put hot food and cold drinks on the table.

Kerry

Dinner conversation consisted of our day together and people at work we both knew. But my mind kept straying as she talked, remembering her low dip over the desk when she was handing me the test papers. A slow flush chased up my face as my X-rated thoughts reemerged. And unfortunately, it was a perfect night for sex, with the storm's fury adding a wild backdrop.

"Some storm," she suddenly commented, as if she were reading my mind. And truth be told, I wished she was. But like I said before, I didn't know about her so I just dumbly nodded and gathered up the plates.

The rest of the evening passed swiftly. We were both so tired from having gotten up at 4:30 A.M. that by 9 both of us were yawning. "Want to call it a night?" I asked. We were watching a tape of the Sopranos, and every time the camera panned the exotic dancers in the Bada Bing Club, I tried to act as nonchalant as I could. Not that I was even *seeing* the strippers on the screen. Instead, Kerry's breasts returned in all their remembered glory to torment me anew. The sooner she was upstairs in the spare bedroom, the better for me. I'm not made of stone.

I showed her the spacious guest bedroom with its four-poster bed, then wished her good night. I was sleeping downstairs in the family room until renovations were finished in the master bedroom. I turned off the light then gratefully crept into bed, exhaustion quickly closing my eyes.

The next morning dawned gorgeously sunny, and after breakfast I drove Kerry to Jersey and that was that.

On Monday morning she E-mailed me, thanking me for letting her stay with me. Then a strange thing happened: She started E-mailing me more than once or twice a day. This went on for weeks, interspersed with phone calls and occasional lunches. After four months, she asked me in an E-mail if I would like to play host again, saying she had had such a good time the night she had spent with me. Maybe next time we could go out to dinner, she said—her treat!

I looked at her message through narrowed, suspicious eyes. Was she flirting with me? "Are you flirting with me?" I E-mailed back.

"Only time will tell," came her enigmatic reply.

What?! She's gay? Bi? How come my gaydar hadn't picked up on it? Maybe the flashing of her breasts in my face had been deliberate. I decided to test the waters. Each successive E-mail got more and more flirtatious until finally we broke into sex territory—yeah, she wanted to be with me. Would I do her? Well, I've had better invitations for sexual encounters, but the thought of fucking her wouldn't let me hesitate. I picked up the phone (we were at work) and whispered "Yeah" in her ear.

Friday night she drove up from Jersey and met me in the hallway with a single red rose. I was nervous with first-kiss thoughts. That was always my sticking point: Once that was out of the way I knew I'd be fine, and so, taking the bull by the horns, I kissed her full on the mouth. I knew she was taken aback because she hesitated, but as the kiss got more involved, so did Kerry.

When we broke apart, I led her up three steps into my bedroom, anxious to get my first full *legal* look at her breasts. I had her blouse off in under a minute, her bra off 30 seconds after that. "They're beautiful," I whispered in awe. "Now that I can see them all," I added impishly.

"Well, how else was I going to get you into bed, unless you had a brief peek at the merchandise," she quipped back.

That's when it hit me—I'd been played. "You wanted me to have sex with you back then?" I yelped. "Then why did we just go through months of playing footsie?"

"I didn't want you to think I was easy," she replied primly.

When I took off her clothes, I finally found out what the comment about "natural" redheads meant. Her red pubic hair was soft as down, nestled between creamy thighs. Her skin was baby-soft smooth, her nipples dusky red in their hardness. She lay back on the pillow amid the glow from three candles while music conducive to the mood played on the stereo. She was quite the picture. Soft, innocent, sweet—

"Well? Are you going to do me or not?"

Screech. So much for the innocent image. Well, always give a lady what she wants, eh?

"Where are you going?" she asked when I got off the bed.

With new music more conducive to raw sex pumping from the speakers, we started to rock.

A couple of weeks passed. Kerry would come up to my house for the weekend and we'd only get out of bed to eat. Now that we were comfortable around each other, Kerry's sexual imagination took flight. The third weekend we were together she showed up with a bag full of sex toys. I was shocked—she just didn't look the type. "You want me to use *that* on you?" I warily eyed the black leather harness and eight-inch dildo she pulled out of a shopping bag.

Even though I had never used toys before, it was easy to get into the groove (no pun intended) with the lifelike soft rubber cock. Kerry helped me put on the harness, and while she spread out beneath me, I eased myself between her legs, the artificial hard-on I was sporting trying to poke its head into her cunt almost without my help. When she felt the smooth head graze her nether lips, she sucked in her breath and I watched in joyful amazement as her nipples tightened into hot, hard knobs. "So this is what baby wants," I sing-songed into her ear. "She wants me to ride her, doesn't she?" With her lower lip caught between her teeth, she nodded rapturously.

Well, hell's bells! Why not?

I guess it's true what they say: Still waters run deep. And Kerry wanted it—deep. I slathered the wiggly prick with edible lube Kerry had brought along. "Mmm," I said, "strawberry." Once it was greased up, I grabbed the slippery little varmint in my right fist and eased its contoured pink head into her; her hips thrust up at it eagerly. "Whoa, girlfriend," I laughed. "Don't worry. I'll let your cunt deep throat the whole thing. Just give me a minute, OK? This is all new to me."

"Please, baby, please," she whimpered.

I drove my own hips forward, felt my fake prick slide easily inside her. She let out a gusty sigh of satisfaction. Then I started to ride her, pulling most of the eight inches out and then quickly stuffing it back in again, churning in and out of her. We were eye to eye—and I saw desire mounting with each thrust I made. My own excitement was on the rise, building up inside me, making it difficult for me to swallow. My clit was stiff, my breath coming in ragged gasps. I liked this new side of Kerry!

When her ass started coming off the bed to meet my every plunge, I pulled out, the cock wet and slimy with her juice. "No, no, please no," she said in a strangled whimper.

"Open up, baby, I'm comin' in," I said as I slithered my body down until my mouth was where my dick had so recently been. I kept rimming her pussy, enjoying the shudders my tongue was letting her experience. My nose intermittently nuzzled her inner lips as I made my tongue rigid and imitated the motion of my newly appended dick: In and out, in and out, until I pulled out and headed for her clit, letting the flat side of my tongue glide over her.

"Expose yourself," I commanded. When her clit was fully exposed, I shot my tongue out in a snakelike flick. A deep moan came from Kerry when my moist tongue kissed her burning clitoris. Fastening my lips around it, I alternated noisily sucking on her nub and unmercifully flogging it with my tongue. The faster I whipped it, the more frenzied Kerry got. Her thighs were clamping themselves on either side of my head: I knew she was close to coming. As her moans grew more frantic, I kept up a steady beating of her clit, knowing my reward would come soon, very soon.

"I'm going to come, Marie. I'm going to come for you, baby." She chanted this over and over until finally her legs stiffened and her back arched up. I kept my mouth firmly attached to her. When her body went slack, I knew she was finished.

She lay there, breathing heavily while I crawled up alongside her. My own breathing was kind of heavy too as I threw myself down next to her. My rubber cock jiggled back and forth in the harness, obscenely spearing the air. I felt stupid wearing it now that the main event was over, but I kept it on. Kerry had a quick recovery time: I knew I'd be deep inside her again in no time.

Kerry

We made good use of the toys that weekend and the following weekend too. I found out Kerry had a penchant for getting plugged from behind, either standing beside or kneeling on the bed. I must admit, I liked it too; I liked standing or kneeling behind her as either my artificial friend or my own fleshy fingers probed and delved deep inside her body. But our fun didn't end there. Her bag of tricks also contained a blindfold, handcuffs, and two different size vibrators. And she wanted me to use everything.

"I want you to dominate me in bed," she panted. "Do whatever you want to me." She was spread-eagle on the bedspread, her feet tied to the bedposts with strips of sheet, her hands handcuffed above her head, the blindfold securely over her eyes. She lay there, a feast for my eyes and my mouth. Climbing up and over, I went into the 69 position. She let out a gasp of surprise. "Eat it," I growled. It only took a moment to feel her soft mouth on my pussy. I enjoyed feeling her lips nibbling my cunt lips, feeling her tongue swirl over my erect clit. Using the tips of my fingers, I pulled back her outer lips and began stroking her pulsing clit with my tongue. The fact that she was virtually helpless under me added to my enjoyment. I kept pushing my ass farther back, making sure her tongue hit my clit just right. "Stroke it. You know how I like it." I could hear her silken hair whisper against the pillowcase as her head moved up and down, her tongue stroking the length of my shaft. It felt so fucking wonderful I almost lost my concentration. Almost. With my head buried between her legs, I lightly grazed her with my tongue, knowing how sensitive she was. But it wasn't until I blew hot breaths on her rosebud asshole that she went wild, letting out a deep animal groan while she ravenously attacked my cunt, thrusting her tongue deep inside me. It took all my strength of will to stay focused on pleasuring her while she pleasured me so...well, pleasurably.

My middle finger massaged her clit with a circular movement as my mouth alternated between licking her and blowing on her sweet rosebud. Her deep moans made me doubt if she could withstand this assault much longer. I could tell by the way her body was beginning to thrash around underneath me that her orgasm was very close.

I shifted to maximum stimulation overdrive. Positioning myself for ultimate tongue and finger-fucking caused me to move out of the range of her mouth, but I wanted her to have a climax she'd never forget! I heard low squeals of disappointment that she couldn't reach me, but it was quickly replaced by gasps, moans, and "Yes! Yes! Yes!" Sweat was pouring down my face, blinding me, but I kept going, knowing she was seconds away from exploding.

My hard work paid off—she stiffened, momentarily straining against her bonds, a muffled scream drove itself into my brain and her body started to spasm, once, twice, three times. I felt her stomach muscles under me, tense-release, tense-release, tense-release. I knew then just how powerful an orgasm she was in the throes of. "Stop, stop," she gasped, and I immediately did. Once Kerry orgasmed, she was highly ticklish.

After a few minutes I summoned the strength to untie her; that's when I saw 'it.' I had heard about it, but had never seen it: female ejaculation. I saw the huge stain under her ass and knew she had enjoyed the ultimate orgasm. (And I'd be lying if I said I wasn't damned proud of myself for giving it to her.) Two minutes later we were both in deep unconscious sleep.

The next morning over leftover Chinese food in the dining room, Kerry suddenly looked at me and said, "I'm in love with you." The forkful of lo mein stopped halfway to my mouth.

I didn't expect it. Neither of us had even gotten close to the L word, and now here it was, out in the open. "Why?"

"Because you're you."

Well, folks, I'm sure you thought this story was leading up to a happy ending. And it was—for a while. Kerry and I fell in love and planned the future, you know, the house together and the whole nine yards. Unfortunately, not all dreams are meant to be realized. Two and a half years into our relationship, she surprised me one day by calling me up and saying, "I kissed someone else." It was out of the blue and I went understandably ballistic. When we both calmed down, we tried to make a go of it again, but knowing she cheated on me changed my feelings for her. The second breakup was permanent. Our future just wasn't meant to be.

Sigh. She's with the other woman now and I'm single. Any takers?

Dreams

Zonna

Think about it: If dreams came true, we'd all walk around with our eyes closed, compiling wish lists of fantasies to take us through the next millennium. Or better yet, we'd never get out of bed at all. So I didn't go in much for dreams—though sometimes the idea of lying in bed with my eyes closed all day was really appealing. I wasn't the type to play the lottery or to sit by the radio trying to win big bucks on Thousand-Dollar Thursday. Unlike most of my friends I didn't watch *Who Wants to be a Millionaire?* while repeatedly dialing the special contestant number during the commercial breaks, and I doubted if I'd ever get lucky at Atlantic City, so I didn't bother going. I wasn't particularly gifted at anything; didn't have any hidden talents like an amazing singing voice or an eye for photography. I couldn't paint to save my life, and I hadn't started writing yet, back then. I could cook a decent meal and I was pretty good at scrabble, but I was fairly certain neither one of those abilities was going to put me on the map.

So aside from dreams of fortune and fame, what else do people fantasize about? Why, love, of course. Unfortunately, I hadn't had much success there either, though I still found myself hoping that would change. Oh, I'd had a few lovers over the years, but no one I'd even faintly considered spending the rest of my life with. Usually I'd meet someone I felt comfortable with, we'd date for a while, the sex would be nice but nothing spectacular, and soon we'd both lose interest and drift apart. The breakups were always amicable. I was friends with most of my ex-lovers. I guess there had never been enough passion involved in any of those relationships to warrant a nasty split. We'd just both get bored after a while. And that's no reason to kick or scream or throw clothes out the window. Whatever it was that made a relationship fresh and exciting and able to constantly renew itself, I hadn't stumbled upon it. And by the time I reached 25, I figured I probably wouldn't. But deep down inside, that was my secret dream—a recurring one.

Even so, I was fairly content. It was a very level kind of existence—no drastic highs or lows, just lots of middles. My life was my life, and I accepted it. I assumed I'd meet someone someday and we'd both be ready to settle down. The time would be right. Things would fall into place. Blah blah blah. Or not. I could imagine myself happy enough bouncing other people's babies on my knee or attending commitment ceremonies for all my ex-lover friends. It wouldn't be a bad life, just a little lonely, perhaps. There are worse things than lonely.

And that probably would have been the end of the story if my best friend in the whole world wasn't a lunatic.

Matty and I had been friends since third grade when she'd beaten up a group of boys on the playground for calling me "Four Eyes." Ever since then she'd made it her business to save me, even though she was usually the one in trouble. I guess like all good friends we looked out for each other, although she'd never admit to needing any help from anyone. In the 17 years I'd known her I'd found her four jobs, paid countless overdue utility bills, rescued her from two crazy girlfriends hell-bent on carving their initials in her ass, and even bailed her out of jail once (don't ask). I think she'd slept on my couch more than any other piece of furniture. Matty was everything I wasn't, and then some.

"Don't hog all the popcorn," Matty grabbed the bucket, managing to spill most of what was left all over the sofa and my lap.

"Now look what you did!" I jumped up, wiping frantically at a rapidly widening blotch.

"What's the big deal? It's just popcorn."

"It wouldn't be such a big deal if you hadn't poured half a stick of butter all over it."

"So? It's just your pajamas."

"But these are my favorite pajamas," I pouted, staring at the big yellow spot discoloring half of Pooh's left cheek.

"So, now they're your favorite pajamas with the stain on them. Lighten up, girl."

Matty cleaned up the rest of the popcorn, attempting to hide the spatters on the couch with a pillow. I saw but didn't say anything. I felt stupid enough about being so upset over a pair of Winnie the Pooh pajama pants. I wasn't going to whine about the cushions as well. I made a mental note to buy seat covers and tried to let it go.

I couldn't help being grouchy, though, and Matty noticed.

"Are you that upset about a dumb pair of pajamas?"

"I'm not upset," I lied.

"Oh, God…" she sighed.

I changed the subject. "I can't follow this, can you?" The movie had continued playing through the entire popcorn debacle, and I was hopelessly lost.

"Rewind it."

"It's after 11 already."

"So? Are you going to turn into a pumpkin at the stroke of 12?"

"The movie is due back by midnight."

"All right, so it'll be a little late."

"It's on my card."

"I'll give you the three dollars, then. Jeez."

"That's not the point, Matty."

"Well, what *is* the point, exactly?" She sounded exasperated.

I didn't want to have to say it. I knew Matty would think it was ridiculous. The truth is, I didn't want the video club to think I was the kind of customer who couldn't return a tape on time. "I—I just want to bring it back. It's not very good anyway."

Matty looked at me like I was crazy. Then a smile started to creep across her lips. "You don't want the video people to yell at you."

"Don't be silly. They wouldn't say anything. They'd just charge my credit card."

"No, that's it. You're afraid those little 16-year-old clerks are going to think you're a bad customer or something!"

"I don't care what they think. And they're not 16."

Matty laughed so hard she couldn't get up from the couch.

"That's not it!" I knew my face was red; I could feel my ears getting hot.

"OK, OK..." Matty wiped the tears from her eyes. "If that's really not the issue, then don't rewind it."

"What?"

"Don't rewind the tape—that is, if you really don't care what they think."

I felt cornered. I had never returned a tape without rewinding it. It was thoughtless and needlessly annoying for the next person who rented it. Besides, it was against the rules. "That's just stupid," I argued, grabbing the remote.

Matty broke out in another bout of uncontrollable giggles.

"Just shut up, OK?"

"Sure, sure. We'll just take the video back now."

I slipped out of my ruined pajamas and pulled on a pair of jeans. I caught Matty staring at me from across the room. She looked away quickly when I caught her eye.

"What are you looking at?" I asked her.

"I never noticed what nice legs you have," she said, a little gruffly. She sounded embarrassed, but that was impossible. Matty was never embarrassed about anything.

"Well, you've seen them a hundred times."

"I know."

"At least I shave mine once in a while," I teased.

"Whatever."

I felt funny taking my top off in front of her when she was in this strange mood, so I just pulled a sweatshirt over Pooh's head.

Matty seemed disappointed.

"Ready?" I asked.

"Let's go."

Matty parked in front of Blockbuster, and I slid the tape through the little drop-off slot. The boy behind the counter turned around and waved.

"Happy now?" Matty smirked, folding her cell phone as I got back in the car.

"Yes. Who was that?"

"A wrong number."

She pulled onto the highway, headed in the wrong direction.

"Where are we going?"

"It's a surprise."

"Matty, it's almost midnight."

"It won't take long."

"I have to get up early for work."

"So do I."

"Yeah, but you're used to dragging your ass all day. I'm not."

"Chill out. I'll write you a note."

"Can't you just tell me where we're going?" I practically whined.

"I'm buying you a pair of pajamas."

"What?"

"To replace the ones I wrecked."

"Oh, don't be ridiculous!"

"No, they were your favorite pajamas, and I'm going to buy you a pair just like them."

"Matty, no stores are open this late."

"Ah, but I have connections."

She turned off the highway and aimed the car for the Kmart parking lot.

"They're closed."

"I have a friend who works here. She'll let us in through the back."

I knew better than to argue once Matty had made up her mind about something. It was easier to just do what she wanted and hope for the best.

We drove around to the rear of the store, where Matty's friend was holding the door open for us. So that's who she'd been on the phone with. It was totally weird being inside the huge store when it was so empty. There were a few workers stocking the shelves here and there, but it was pretty desolate. We found a pair of nearly identical pajamas right away, and I headed for the checkout. Then I realized the inherent problem with this crazy scheme.

"How are we supposed to pay for these?"

"Don't worry about it," Gina, Matty's friend, reassured me.

"Well, then you can just put these back. I'm not stealing them."

"OK, OK." Matty reached into her pocket. She gave Gina $11 and told her to keep the change.

We left the same way we'd come in and got back in the car. Just as Matty was about to turn the key, a security guard pulled around the corner, heading straight for us.

"Shit," Matty hissed.

"What do we do now?" I was frantic. We didn't have a receipt or even a Kmart bag to prove we'd paid. Do they arrest you for stealing $11 worth of pajamas in the middle of the night? I imagined the worst.

"Kiss me," Matty ordered.

"What?"

"Just do it."

Our lips collided, and I felt Matty's tongue explore my mouth. Suddenly the guard tapped on the glass with his flashlight. Matty rolled down the window.

"Why don't you take it home?" he suggested, more politely than I would've guessed.

"Yes, sir," Matty replied, in her most sincere voice.

The ride home was quiet. Too quiet.

I kept reliving the kiss. It couldn't have lasted more than a few seconds, but I remembered so many details, it seemed like it must have been longer. There was Matty's lips pressing against mine; then her tongue, pushing it's way in. I remembered the little jolt I'd felt when the tips of our tongues touched. I could almost feel her arms pulling me closer, as my nipples stiffened under my sweatshirt. I recalled the way her hands had caressed the back of my neck as she kissed me harder. All this in a matter of moments.

Something told me I shouldn't have liked it as much as I had. Matty was my best friend. In all the years we'd known each other, I'd never even considered sleeping with her. Sex was the one thing friends don't share. It was against the rules. I knew that. I wondered if Matty did.

When we arrived back at the house, she followed me inside, still not saying a word. It was stupid for her to drive all the way home, since she lived about half an hour away and it was already 1:30. I threw her a sheet and a pillow, thanked her for the pajamas, walked into my bedroom, and closed the door behind me.

Ten minutes after I shut off the light, I heard a soft knock on the door.

"What?"

"Can I talk to you for a minute?" Matty stood silhouetted in the doorway.

"Matty, it's late."

"I know."

"I have to get up in four hours."

"I know. I just—I need to talk."

"OK." I sat up.

"Can I get under the covers?"

"Sure."

She slipped in beside me. "Are you wearing your new pajamas?"

"Yes."

"Let me see."

"Matty, I thought you said you wanted to talk. What do you want to talk about?"

Silence, which, in the presence of Matty, was most unusual.

"Hello?"

She fidgeted. "Back in the car."

I tried to swallow the lump that rose in my throat. My hands were sweaty. "Back in the car, yes? Try to speak in complete sentences."

"When I kissed you, I liked it. Did you?"

I decided to answer honestly. "Yes. You're a good kisser."

"So are you. I wouldn't have thought so."

"Excuse me?"

"No—you know—I mean, you're so uptight and everything. And you hardly date."

"Thanks a lot." I was getting miffed.

"No, No. I'm sorry. That's not what I want to say. I guess I just didn't expect to like it so much, is all. I never thought about kissing you before. I feel kind of weird. I never considered you a sexual being."

Great. That made two of us. "Did you come in here to insult me?"

Matty ran her hand through her hair, something she did when she was upset or confused. "No. I came in here to make love to you."

"What? Have you lost your mind?" I pulled the covers closer. This couldn't be happening. And yet I wanted her to touch me. I wanted to feel her hands and mouth on me. But more than that, I wanted to take her, to make her tremble with desire. I wanted to watch her face as she cried out with pleasure. Would it be as exciting as our kiss?

"This is wrong," I protested weakly as she pulled the sheet away to expose my new pajamas.

"No, it's not." Her lips brushed against mine. Again, that jolt of electricity that went from my teeth to my toes, making a few key stops on the way.

"What about our friendship?" It was my last attempt at sanity, before giving in to the need that was growing with every breath.

"Nothing can change that. This'll be fun. I can make you feel so-o-o good... Besides, you owe me for the pajamas. Now you can pay me back."

That broke the tension and made me laugh. We embraced, Matty's body topping mine. It felt right. We kissed harder, our tongues twirling together in a dance of lust. Each kiss left me hungry for more. Matty's lips moved to my neck, and I felt her hands caressing my breasts. My nipples were so hard they ached. I sighed as she took one in her mouth, teasing the tip with her tongue.

I tugged at her T-shirt, yanking it off over her head. Her full breasts spilled out; she held them, just inches from my face. I leaned forward and captured a nipple between my teeth, knowing from Matty's many tales of torrid conquests that she liked it a little rough. Her eyes closed as I sucked harder. I reached up and pinched the other one until she moaned, a low throaty sound. I pulled her shorts down and ran my hands over her ass and the backs of her thighs. Soon Pooh was a forgotten heap at the foot of the bed and we rolled together, skin on skin.

Matty moved her hand between my legs and held it over my cunt, cupping me. She didn't go inside, and it drove me nuts. I could feel myself getting wetter by the minute, wanting her to touch me. She smiled, aware of what she was doing. I tried spreading my legs farther apart to move her hand closer to my clit, but she was on to me. Laughing, she pulled it away all together and returned her attention to my tits.

I was throbbing.

"You bitch!" I sat up, pulling Matty over my knee, and gave her a sharp smack on the ass. I knew this was a particular turn-on for her, and I also knew she didn't expect it from me. I spanked her again, and she gasped in obvious approval. I slid my hand down the crack of her ass to her cunt and entered her from behind with two fingers. I began a slow rhythm, in and out, feeling her hips moving with me. It was so hot, watching her gyrate like that, knowing I was the one turning her on. When she started to move faster, I held back, making her wait just a little bit longer. Finally, I gave in and let her come. She shook with the force of her orgasm, grunting and squeezing my fingers from the inside. I lay her back on the bed and kissed her as she calmed down.

"Wow," was all she said.

She pushed me back against the pillow and started kissing my stomach and thighs. I was still half-aroused from watching, and it didn't take much to get me back to full throttle. She lowered her head between my legs, and I felt her warm breath on me. She parted my lips and started to lick slowly on either side of my clit. I felt it swell up instantly, begging for her tongue to touch it directly. She continued to tease me until I pleaded with her to let me come. Then she lifted my ass, took my clit in her mouth and sucked. I came so hard I started crying. Matty held me in her arms, and that's how we fell asleep.

We were lovers for the next four months. It was like having one foot in heaven and one in hell at the same time. It didn't last, of course. Dreams never do. Eventually, you wake up. And when we did, there was screaming and kicking and clothes thrown out of windows. I miss her, both as a friend and a lover. Never before or since have I shared something so passionate. But now I do buy the occasional lottery ticket. After all, I got lucky once. And there's a bus that leaves for Atlantic City from the corner diner every Saturday. I've got a ticket right here in my pocket. Hey—you can't win if you don't spin.

Spring Term
Robin Perry

Spring term. 1972. Second Saturday of my second term at boarding school. I was sharing a room with only one girl, and after 16 years of rural isolation I loved being part of a large, almost exclusively female, community. Still, it was difficult for me to adjust to the lack of privacy, and I missed the sanctuary of my own bedroom. At least I'd have the room to myself for the next few days since my roommate Jo was in the clinic with the stomach flu.

Our room was predominantly deep cream—ceiling, walls, bedspreads, and basic furnishings. The big sash window was curtained in heavy cotton in faded blue-gray, and the floorboards had that rich glow that comes from generations of waxing. We had each brought a colorful rug and bright posters, but still the cream-motif dominated. That day, however, after the hustle of morning classes and the bustle of the dining hall, it soothed me.

I slung my book bag into the closet and opened the window to let in the warm breeze and happy chattering from the birds in the great chestnut tree in the center of the quad. I loosened my tie, opened my collar, kicked off my shoes, and shed the thick tights that were part of our winter uniform. Ah, the relief! I stretched out on my bed and closed my eyes, letting the light, warmth, and gathering energy of spring embrace me. Now, what to do this weekend? And with whom? One of the joys of being here was that there was always something going on and someone who wanted to join in for the fun. I'd go and find them soon, I thought drowsily, the girls who'd become my friends since September.

The sound of the doorknob turning slowly lifted me from reverie. I felt someone enter quietly. Perhaps if I kept my eyes shut they'd think I was asleep and leave me in peace. I heard a murmured consultation. Two people. I sensed them approach the bed and kneel, one on either side of me by my head. Someone brushed the hair clear of my right ear, leaned close, and whispered, "Are you asleep, Robin?"

My lips twitched at the familiar voice. Her warm breath, her almost-touch, sent hot shocks through me. End of pretense. I opened my eyes and met Tatiana's near-black ones. Flicking my gaze to my left I saw my other closest friend, Peta. Her light gray eyes brimmed with anticipation, but she remained silent. Tatiana whispered again, "We want to see if we can make you come just by nibbling your ears."

Something scary but delicious clutched at my entrails. Wow! Where had this idea sprung from? At 16 we had a healthy interest in sex and discussed it quite often as we did myriad other topics. Well, Tatiana did most of the sex talking. She claimed to have slept with several men and delighted in sharing the details with anyone who cared to listen. She wasn't a bit shy. Everything about her was bold—her lips, her breasts, her hands as they moved in the air while she talked. The thinner, smaller Peta was a little shy but eager to appear worldly and claimed that she planned to "do it" as soon as possible.

As for me, I was mystified but intrigued by what any woman found sexually attractive about men. I had plenty of boy friends, I just couldn't imagine wanting to get sexual with them. My yearnings were for the beautiful bright girls around me. And some of the staff. And other women I'd see on campus. Or on the street. Or in the mall. You get the idea.

But my friends and I didn't really talk about *my* objects of desire. They didn't seem interested. It didn't make them wary of me, though. We touched, cuddled, walked arm-in-arm, lay close for hours reading, massaged away aches after a hard day, went skinny-dipping in the swimming pool after hours, showered together, and washed and brushed each other's hair. But my tentatively expressed sexuality was basically dismissed. Yet here they both were—my two closest friends. I was acutely aware of our breathing in the utter stillness in the room, the contained energy, the prickle of apprehension felt at a remote border crossing point.

"Well? What do you say? Shall we try it?"

I felt excited but hesitant. "You mean now? Here?"

They'd closed the door behind them, but there was no lock. This was risky. Tatiana brushed a thin, tapered finger through my hair, tracing the shape of my ear. Every nerve in my body responded. "Let's try it," she murmured. Only her breath, her words caressed me. My eyes closed; my caution evaporated. The low sound in my throat wasn't consciously made. She began.

She spread her hands on the bedspread beside me then lipped the outline of my ear with her tongue. Slowly, surely, alternating lips and tongue she worked inwards. Sensation centered on my right ear but tendrils of arousal wound along my limbs down my trunk, drawn to the heat rooted in my loins. I'd often imagined what it would be like to touch and be touched by someone with sexual intent. I'd felt strong desire for other women and fantasized about making love with them. Neither exercise came close to the power of the real experience.

I'd always thought that my first adventure would unfold with someone I loved and who was in love with me. Not just a friend, however close. Certainly not two of them at once! And not out of the blue like this.

As Tatiana's tongue began probing, Peta gave my left ear a swift lick then began following the same slow pattern Tatiana had. Pleasure pulsed in stereo. My cotton shirt felt cold against my nipples. The heat between my legs built to white. The soles of my feet grew ticklish. I clawed the bedspread, snatched for breath, ceased speculating. Peripherally I felt Tatiana and Peta raise their hands and bridge them above me. Each took an earlobe between her teeth and pulled gently. I tried to stifle my cry of climax. Perhaps I did because no one burst in to discover what the hell was going on. I opened my eyes. We looked at one another.

"That was amazing," offered Peta, looking as stunned as I felt.

"Mmm…" I managed.

Tatiana laughed, cupped my jaw with a hand turning me toward her, and kissed me on the lips. The combined touch of lips and hand created a fresh surge of desire. I'd been passive long enough. I reached across, furrowed my fingers through her hair, and kissed someone sexually for the first time. Did my lips feel as pliant as hers did to me? Did I taste as sweet? Did my tongue feel as tentative, as daring? Would our friendship survive these revelations?

Peta ended the kiss by tugging me gently back to supine. "Let's move on," she said as she unbuttoned my shirt. We had all seen each other naked many times but never before had I sensed in my friends the faintly alarming ripple of primeval hunger which I then felt in their focus on my breasts. As one they bent to suckle. My body somehow harmonized the different rhythms they adopted.

Tatiana's daring hand stretched down to my foot. I jerked at the contact. By the time she reached my thigh, every hair on my body was raised. As she stroked lightly across my knickers, the pleasure came close to pain. Peta rolled me onto my side and unfastened my skirt. Together they drew it and my knickers off, slowly, sensuously. Tatiana crouched between my legs. The touch of her mouth was ineffable and as I felt her finger ease into me, I came so powerfully that my pleasure was shaded with concern that the force of my thrusts had hurt her—or that I'd pulled her hair out in clumps. The pulsing sensations continued for so long that I grew frightened and tried to stop them.

In the ebb, mumbling anxious inquiries and apologies, I pulled her up my body till I could look into her eyes and kiss her mouth. My first taste of myself on her lips was fascinating. It sparked an urgent desire to taste her. Clumsily I shuffled sideways pulling her under me. She was wearing a silk kimono. The friction of it against my skin and the heat of her body through it as we maneuvered was delicious. We laid each other bare. Her skin, genetically designed for life in a hot climate, was sallow after years in temperate Britain. Her breasts were huge and squashy, the areola pinky-brown and bumpy, her nipples plump and inviting. So many times I'd wanted to touch them, take them in my mouth. I began to suck. Excitement escalated.

"Don't take too long, babe. I don't need warming up. I'm hot already. I want it fast."

Eagerly I slithered down her trunk and took my first lick. The delicacy of her scent, her taste, our physical reactions, the medley of sensory information rocked me. I lost balance, steadied myself, resumed with lips, nose, tongue, teeth, fingers. She felt so intricate, so fragile inside, yet fundamentally strong, resilient, flexible. I wanted to go slowly. There was so much to discover, assimilate. I wanted to revel in it all, in her, in me, in us together.

"Oh-h-h, speed up. I want it now. Now! Don't make me wait."

Abashed, I sped up. In seconds she pulsed around my fingers and gripped with astonishing strength for such soft tissue. Abruptly, her arced body relaxed. She released my fingers and she drew me up into her arms for a long hug. I had no idea what to say so I kissed her neck, stroked her back and waited. Eventually I risked eye contact. Her eyes glowed with delight and affection.

"I knew you'd be beautiful."

"How?" I was intrigued. How on earth could one tell such a thing?

"Ooh…the way you move…and that look of yours, so-o-o… *langoureuse.*" She rolled the French word out, ruffling my hair, grinning.

"Well, you're…voluptuous and…astonishing." Remembering Peta, I turned, "And you are…" Peta had gone. I had no idea when she'd left. I turned back to Tatiana, troubled.

She shrugged. "She probably felt left out once we really got going and decided to leave quietly."

"Will she feel hurt, do you think?"

"No. She only wanted to do the ear thing really. Don't fret, she'll be fine."

"Are you sure? Perhaps we should find her? Apologize?" I suggested.

"Can't you think of anything else you'd rather do just now?"

"Well, yes. But…" The dinner bell rang. It reminded me that I was hollow with hunger. For food. For more of her. But I needed to know that Peta was all right too. What if she felt jealous?

"I need food. Aren't you starving? Let's eat."

Her look was lascivious, teasing. "Mmm, let's. What is your pleasure?"

I blushed. "Food first. Then…" I gathered my courage. "Then I'd like to bring you back here and…" I traced her ear with my thumb and forefinger and pulled on the lobe. "Maybe have seconds? It…uh…depends on how hungry you are."

She shivered and pecked my nose. "Let's do just that, Robin. I want a lot more of you too."

We hurried to dinner and were joined by Peta, who chatted happily with us and our table companions. She showed no sign of offense or jealousy but embarrassed me by repeatedly smirking and sending us blatant "I know what you've been up to and you owe me the details" looks. Tatiana merely basked.

She and I spent as much as possible of the rest of the weekend in bed. We scattered laxative granules in the corridor. They were invisible in the dim light but crunched underfoot, which gave us a few seconds warning of any approach to the room. The cultural imperative toward physical modesty and shame in females helped too. A cry of, "Just a minute! I'm not decent!" greeting a knock on the door was respected, even by Peta who showed no further interest in lesbian sex.

Once Jo returned, my liaisons with Tatiana were more difficult to arrange, but Jo was willing to swap rooms, at least sometimes, so that we could be together. And for my final year I was given a single room. The holidays were hardest, but during most of them we managed at least a weekend here, a week there, days and nights schemed for and treasured. We remained lovers until I went to college and she returned home. A year later she got married. She told me she'd never stopped sleeping with men. After all, she had to marry, didn't she? Did she?

I was heartbroken but accepted her choice. There seemed to be no alternative. We wrote for a while but that petered out. We had increasingly little in common, after all.

Years later we literally bumped into each other in a theater foyer in London. I was delighted. Initially she seemed thrilled to see me again and then…something locked down in her, and she became…patronizing. She seemed anxious to keep me away from her female companion. It was horrible, awkward. I felt that her reaction was unnecessary, ungracious. She knew I accepted our breakup and that in the future we would be neither lovers nor friends because she didn't want either. Why dishonor the memories? Or each other?

A third of a century later my body still remembers her touch and the feel of mine on her and my vision of our relationship as a mosaic which enabled us to move from being friends to lovers and back again, at least for a while. A variable pattern always fragmented, never truly whole.

I don't regret a minute of it, and I hope she doesn't either. But I doubt I'll ever know.

Waking Elizabeth
Kimberly Streible

I woke to the sound of screeching tires and the loudest profanity I had ever heard. My first thought was that my father was trying to intimidate the front lawn sprinklers into working again, but I'd crawled into bed after 11 and had distinctly heard his low rumbling snore coming from my parents bedroom. I lay silently in bed staring at the black ceiling, the room a swirl of dark shadows. Sharp images flashed through my mind: the curve of a woman's shoulder, her slender back, a twisted figure behind a dark purple curtain, tiny fragments of a dream that fell away as my eyes snapped open. From what I could recollect, the dream was quite interesting. I was at an all women's nudist colony, *and* I was happily invisible. It was a good dream, voyeuristic and good.

I waited a few seconds, wondering if I'd actually heard anything at all. The Kelleys' German Shepherd was barking. He'd heard it too. At least I could take paranoia off of my resume. His guttural warning echoed across the pavement, reverberating in my room, where shapes began to slowly appear: The tall dark legs in my dream became the outline of my bookcase and swirling dark circles turned out only to be my clothes strewn across the bedpost.

The sound had come from just below my window, I was sure of it. I *had* heard screeching tires and an angry voice shouting

"Fuck!" There is no mistaking the word "fuck"—when you hear it, you don't forget it. I could see it in my mind: a horrifying scene unraveling in our very own driveway—a dead body tossed like a rag doll at our doorstep, the remnants of some grand mob war. I would have to shake Dad awake to tell him about the carnage. It would take days to wash away all of the blood.

I kicked the sheets away and, while nearly severing my toe on the corner of my desk, reached the window. The sidewalk was painted by a warm yellow light at the end of the driveway. The street lamp buzzed with electricity and insects swarmed around the glow like clumsy guardians. It had rained while I was visiting the nudist colony and the pavement was slick, reflecting the faint glow in small puddles like sheets of glass. To my dismay, there was no bloody corpse, no carnage. And as my eyes swept over the small street that separated our homes, the hope for a mob war became suddenly futile. But, this was better than a mob war, better than the nudist colony. Much better.

She was standing on the sidewalk. Her hair was damp from the rain and her arms were crossed in front of her chest, not in defiance, but from the cold. She drew her shoulders to her neck and stood silently facing our driveway, as if she were waiting for something, or someone. I could see her clearly under the street-lights and my heart leapt to my throat.

Rachel Wylan had lived across the street from me for over eight years. We'd sold lemonade on the corners after church on Sundays and kicked soccer balls down the street, bouncing them off Mrs. Landers's row of oak trees. We let Barry and Chris Vern chase us down the street and laughed as we climbed into our fort in my backyard and shut the small wooden door in their faces, NO BOYS ALLOWED painted neatly on the outside of the door in hot pink. We'd used a whole bottle of my mother's nail polish. We slept in that fort, curled up in our sleeping bags talking all night with only my father's flashlight between us. Rachel was my best friend; she had been since I was 7. She was, and I was quite certain of it, the biggest crush of my life.

I didn't really know what to think of it at first. Was I just jealous of her? Was I comparing myself to her? Was it some sort of hormonal imbalance? Maybe every girl had fantasies about their best friends. It was probably a symptom of irregular puberty glands, or something. Finally, after six months of nightly dreams, sweaty palms, a queasy stomach and a case of the stutters, I had come to face reality: I wanted Rachel Wylan, not the way my father wanted the Yankees to win the pennant, but more like the way a tree wanted water. It was a sheer need in me. I felt it in every fiber of me, and although at age 16 it seemed confusing and sometimes weird, it was the strongest feeling I could ever remember having.

Rachel didn't know anything about it. I mean, what was I supposed to do, confess my desire on a banner and hang it outside my bedroom window? I could see it now—she'd step outside her front door, faint from embarrassment, hit her head on the wooden stairs, and die from a cranial blood clot. The whole neighborhood would have me convicted of sexually deviant manslaughter. I already knew that the sex dreams meant I was going to be some big lesbo when I grew up, but I wasn't really ready to start broadcasting my latest personal discovery. My dad would go nuclear and probably force me to see a psychiatrist. I would have to reveal all of my secret desires and strange fantasies to a balding middle-aged man who would tell my parents I had a twisted personality and a borderline social disorder. My mom would start drinking red wine for breakfast and my dad would mow the lawn at night and during rainstorms. I would become Elizabeth the Lesbo, Lizzie the Lezzie: feminist, martyr, lesbian.

"Beth?" Rachel said suddenly, her voice cutting through my thoughts.

I looked out at the sidewalk, startled. She was no longer there; she was standing just below my window on the wet grass. The street was quiet now, and the German shepherd had given up his struggle to alarm the neighborhood.

She looked up. I could see her squinting at me.

"What the hell are you doing?" she asked, her arms still crossed. She was wearing a maroon sweater.

"What am I doing? I was sleeping. Did you hear someone yelling?" I asked, leaning out the window, my stomach resting on the windowpane.

"Oh, that," she said simply and looked down at her feet. She kicked at the wet grass and looked back up at me. "Can you come down?" she asked, hugging herself.

"Sure, go to the front door," I replied. And that was it. I would have leaped out if she'd asked me too, but instead I withdrew from the window and started toward the hall. I was wearing my sweatpants and my brother's hockey shirt from seventh grade. I crept into the hall and headed down the stairs, listening to the faint sound of my dad snoring, and I knew that unless the government sounded alarms warning of a coming bomb raid my parents wouldn't wake up. I walked through the kitchen and unlocked the front door.

She was standing on the porch, her dark hair pulled back behind her ears, still slightly damp. She looked back at me, her brown eyes black without the aid of light, then stepped past me, her arm brushing mine, her hair rushing by like a dark breeze. She smelled like apples. She always smelled like apples. One night after sleeping at her house, I showered the next morning with apple-scented shampoo. I stood in her shower, letting the warm water fall over me, my nose stuck to the rim of her shampoo bottle.

"Does your dad have any of his cigarettes lying around?" she asked, walking into the kitchen and leaning slightly on the counter, her legs crossed now and her arms at her sides.

"Yeah, he hides them in the junk drawer." I flung open the drawer and saw a pack of Marlboro's sticking out from underneath a stack of garbage ties. I grabbed them and tossed them on the counter. "So what was going on?"

"Cool," she said, and snatched the pack quickly, drawing out a cigarette. She patted her jeans, dug into her front right pocket, and produced a lighter. Her fingers were so amazingly slender.

She popped the cigarette in her mouth like an aspirin. "Well, you heard the asshole, that's what you heard," she proclaimed, the cigarette bouncing between her lips.

"What asshole?" I asked. I was staring, but then I was always staring. I don't think she noticed, at least she never seemed to.

"Chris," she stated simply, as if I should have already known. She lit the cigarette and the bright orange bulb ignited. "We went to Stanford's tonight."

Stanford's was our local drive-in theater. They got rid of the old metal speakers and trash cans and changed the name to Stanford's CinemaTec, instead of the Nightly Watchman Theaters.

"OK," I said. She acted as if I should know exactly what she was going to say next. Sometimes I actually did. It came from years of study, but I really had no idea what had happened with the asshole.

"He's such a little dick," she began. The cigarette was out of her mouth, and she started moving around the kitchen. I followed her movements, watching the orange orb trailing through the dark kitchen like a miniature flare. "How long have we known them? Like since we were 9 or something."

"Seven," I said.

"Yeah, we are friends with them. Not close, but friends. We go to the movies tonight, as *friends*, and he tries to stick his hand up my sweater."

I drew in a quick breath and my face suddenly felt hot.

"I told him no way, and he got totally pissed." She sucked at the cigarette. "He drives me home and starts mumbling under his breath. He called me a tease." She stopped and placed her hand against her hip. "A tease. A tease, how? I was probably just inspiration while he whacked off on the toilet for God knows how long."

I looked away. It wasn't the toilet for me, but rather my bedroom, or sometimes the shower, but never the toilet. And girls didn't whack themselves, we caressed, yes, that's what we did. We caressed ourselves. I was sure I never imagined her the way Chris must have either; sweaty and moaning beneath me like some cat in heat. She was always much more exotic and usually surrounded by a warm yellow glow. In my dreams she was angelic, and she wanted me too.

"I told him he was just a desperate geek, and that did it." She laughed, one hand on her hip, the other floating aimlessly in the air, the cigarette between her fingers. At that moment she looked like a picture, poised, positioned, and perfect. She was quiet for a moment, and then in a low voice she said, "I was really glad when I saw you in the window."

"Yeah, well at first, I thought it was my dad cussing in the front yard again." I said, and giggled. Everyone knew my dad swore like a sailor, but he really was the harmless type. Vulgar, but harmless.

She laughed. I loved the way her mouth moved when she laughed. It curved and stretched at the corners, smoothing out her round lips.

"Your dad is a trip." She looked down and smiled. "You look cute in that hockey shirt."

I laughed. All I heard was a silly, uncomfortable croak spill from my lips, but I was trying to laugh, trying to push the comment aside and get back to reality. Uncomfortable, secretive, tortured reality.

She leaned over, bending at the waist, and I felt her lips against my cheek. They were soft, softer than anything I'd ever felt. My heart began to beat so rapidly I was afraid she might hear it. I could feel my cheeks burning.

"Where can I put this?"

She held up the cigarette. The orange glow was a blur and I had to push the words past my lips. I felt as if I were speaking a foreign language.

"In the sink," I replied. My voice sounded like some distant memory.

The water hissed and whined and the orange glow disappeared. I was resisting the urge to touch my cheek, where she'd kissed me. My hands were at my sides, rolling my sweatpants between my fingers. She moved in front of me and suddenly her hand was on my shoulder. My body felt tingly and warm. She leaned forward and I could smell apples again. My head was swirling, and my knees swayed. I wanted to say something but was desperately afraid of embarrassing myself. And then she kissed me.

Her lips pressed against mine and my stomach spilled on the floor. A warm pulsing energy filled my cheeks and moved down my neck. Her lips were full and wet and slid over mine so smoothly and slowly. My heart pounded my chest, threatening to break through my rib cage and seize her. She moved back, our lips parted. I saw the tip of her tongue and watched her lick her top lip and smile. I needed to recover my intestines from the kitchen floor, but I dared not move for fear of slipping on them. I stood so perfectly still I began to fear I might be frozen like that for an eternity.

"Are you OK?" she said, and brushed back a strand of her hair that hung loosely down her shoulder.

I swallowed hard and tried to find my voice. I was mute! Lost to me forever was the art of speech. I would forever use my hands and grunts and squeaks to communicate.

"I didn't mean to scare you, or freak you out. I thought it would be OK." She took a step back and waved her hand. "We can forget about it. OK?"

Forget about it? My foot rushed forward, and I stood inches from her. I was in control again. Who cared about my intestines? I could get a transplant, couldn't I?

"No," I said. And my hand touched her hair. It felt like silk. It was thick and still slightly damp. I ran my fingers along her jaw-line and then over her cheek. I could feel her beginning to smile.

I lunged forward and kissed her. I covered her lips with mine, resting my palm against her neck, holding the moment like a candle in the dark. She was kissing me back; I could feel her moving her lips against mine. She opened her mouth and slid her tongue over my lips. My tongue danced with hers and I could feel a million fluttering wings take flight in my abdomen. She moved her hand along my side and electricity pulsed through me. I began to kiss her more fiercely, and I was trembling slightly. I tried to steady myself, but there were too many sensations passing through me at once. I just wanted to continue kissing her, feeling her warm, wet tongue sliding against mine. I didn't care to eat, or drink, or sleep again. Just this—her lips against mine, her breasts swelling against mine, until my entire body peeled away and dissolved like an orange.

I slid my hand under her maroon sweater and across her stomach. She buckled and pulled me tightly against her. She was giggling and then I could feel my own stomach roll forward in bursts of laughter. I was still functioning, moving, feeling, laughing like a human being, even without my intestines.

"Can we go up to your room?" she whispered, as if suddenly our secret were out.

I nodded my head and we were on our way up the staircase. The carpet was soft against my bare feet. As we reached the hall, my dad's boisterous snoring set us to giggling again, and we quickly stumbled into my room. I closed the door and let a string of laughter roll over my lips, muffling it slightly with my fist. She fell on my bed and I rushed to join her.

We lay face to face, our heads lying against our palms, smiling widely. I felt mischievous, as if we were breaking curfew or looking through dirty magazines. But this was better. Much better. Her eyes looked like dark pools, and before I could utter a word we were kissing again. I felt her hand under my shirt, caressing my side and then my stomach. She ran her hand along my rib cage and then slowly over my breast. I caught my breath and broke our kiss. A moan escaped my lips as she ran her fingertips over my breasts, lightly pinching my nipples between her fingers. My fingers and toes were tingling as the pulsing sensation shot through my body. I could have powered the entire neighborhood.

Rachel began kissing my neck. I could feel her tongue making circles against my skin. My hand moved slowly into the small space between us, my fingers finding the folds of her sweater. I grasped a piece of her sweater in my fist and started to pull it up. She sat forward, her arms rising into the air. I pulled the sweater over her head and let it fall onto the bed. Her hair fell brazenly onto her bare shoulders; it was so incredibly sexy. I felt as if I had a permanent smile fixed to my face.

She wasn't wearing a bra. Her breasts were full, and her nipples were light pink. I ran my fingertips over them slowly, feeling them harden under my touch. I could feel my panties begin to slide against me. They were wet and hot. My sweatpants felt like heating pads against my legs. With one hand, I grasped the band of my sweatpants and pushed them over my hips while keeping the other hand firmly on Rachel's breast. She reached out and helped me get them to my ankles, where I kicked them away. Then she unbuttoned her jeans and slid them over her hips. It was a smooth, sexy, luxurious movement that made my heart leap uncontrollably. I removed my hand from her breast long enough to fling the hockey shirt over my head and onto the floor.

We pressed our bodies together. I could feel her breasts against mine while our tongues were dancing again. There was a pulse beginning between my legs, slow and steady, separate from the one in my chest. Our legs caressed one another, and I raised my knee, feeling it rub against the outside of her panties. It was warm and wet. I pushed forward and ran my hand down the small of her back. She lurched forward in response and my lips were against her neck. I ran my hand under her panties and caressed her gently. Her ass was firm and beautiful like the rest of her. I ran my hand over her hip and felt her soft pubic hair under my fingertips.

I kissed her shoulder and moved slowly to her breasts, circling her nipples with my tongue. I had no idea what I was doing but was lead on with every inch of her body. Her skin tasted of salt, and her lips and nipples were sweet like fruit. She moved her hands under my panties. I didn't have any sense of time or space. My bedroom disappeared. The dark shadows were nothing but a distant memory.

I tasted her nipples while her fingers moved in a circle between my legs. My toes curled and my body shivered. I tickled the wetness between her legs, and felt the hardened bulb pulsing between her lips. I circled my finger over it and she released a slow, low hum. We moved against one another, our sweat mingled, our fingers moving with an excited quickness.

I felt a quick sharp wave of electricity begin in my abdomen. Her body stiffened against mine and shook slightly. I could hear her humming and moaning against my shoulder. The jolt pulsated through my body. My toes, fingertips, and tongue tingled and I too shook against her, holding her tightly against me, the sensation washing over me like an intense wave and then releasing me. We lay limp against one another, letting the bed become substance again, supporting us. Her skin glistened with sweat.

I could hear her short gasps of breath. She rolled onto her back and stare at the ceiling. My heart still felt like a racehorse caught in my chest.

"I'm so hot," she said.

"Me too," I answered, and rolled off of the edge of the bed. "I'll turn on the fan."

I flicked the switch to the ceiling fan and fell back into the bed. The fan began to whirl and hum above us. The cool air felt incredible against my bare skin. Just then we heard a short snort, followed by a long guttural growl. We erupted into laughter.

"How can your mom stand that?" she asked between giggles.

"They've been together for 15 years. Besides, my dad has always secretly wanted to live the life of Arnold Schwarzenegger, and I think he does it in his sleep. He's never been content being a regular man with a smoking and cursing habit," I joked.

She laughed and said, "You're really funny." She turned onto her side and looked at me with a smile. "You're always coming up with these wild comments. I've always loved that." She paused, and ran a single finger over the curve of my shoulder. "Why didn't we do this sooner?"

I laughed. "Fear," I answered, and she nodded. We were both smiling again. "Fear of rejection, fear of the unknown. Fear that Chris Vern would secretly videotape us and broadcast it live at Sanford's midnight showing."

We laughed, then kissed and touched again; kissing longer, reaching farther, our bodies drawn together like two synchronized swimmers. We watched the sun seep through my window, and although I wanted the night to continue for eternity, it actually looked beautiful: The slanted yellow beams crisscrossed through my room like rainbow arms. We snuggled and giggled. My dad rapped on the door and asked us what we were up to. We just laughed and rolled together under the sheets. He wasn't ready to hear that I was a fledgling lesbian sprouting my wings for the first time, so I gave him the lazy, bored "We're not doing anything, Dad" response and with a grunt and shuffle, he was on his way.

I didn't really know what was happening, but I knew that it felt good. I wanted to wake up like this every morning. And to think it all started with someone yelling, "Fuck!"

High Count
W. Lynn Smith

Terry had long hair, really long hair that ended somewhere past her waist, jet black and shimmering, iridescent in the sunlight like the sheen of a crow. She wore it in "the popular style," parted in the middle and pushed behind her ears.

Terry wanted to be a hairdresser, and as her best friend, I was often her guinea pig. She'd comb and brush and stroke and pin up and roll and curl and braid, leaving me with a tender scalp and a hair brush full of long, auburn head hairs.

I don't recall when, but at some point those hairdressing sessions became far more than girlish play. Goose bumps would rise along my arms as her fingertips gently brushed the nape of my neck. Gathering the weight of my tresses, she'd lift a handful of hair, humming tunelessly to herself.

Her mom's round hand mirror would jiggle in my grasp, and I'd surreptitiously study my friend's determined expression in the smudged surface. Terry would squint her eyes and grip the tip of her tongue between her front teeth, intent. I would feign impatience over having to sit still, while secretly reveling in the brush of her body, her smell, and her gentleness.

I was always careful to not let my reactions or feelings show in my expression. "Queer," "faggot," and other verbal darts were often thrown in the emotional upheaval that marked our puberty. And for us and I suspect most of the kids we knew, being accepted as part of the group was far too important to risk.

We were both 10 years old when we first met at the neighborhood bus stop where new friends might be made and old scores settled. My two brothers and I were new to this coastal Florida town, trying to fit in.

One day at the bus stop, Terry interjected herself into yet another scuffle between me and the neighborhood bully, a tall, mean-faced boy of 12. I recall her shouting at the bully and threatening to sic all four of her brothers on him if he so much as laid a finger on me. That was enough to defuse the situation. Later on the bus I had a chance to thank her for speaking up for me. "That's OK," she replied shyly. "I know what it's like to get picked on. Here, come sit beside me," she added as she patted the empty space on the bus seat.

Terry asked if I had met any other girl friends, and I admitted sheepishly that I hadn't met anyone very friendly. She was sympathetic and promised to introduce me to some of her friends. "Although I don't know many girls," she warned. "Most of them just want me to introduce them to one of my brothers, and I won't do it. So don't ask, OK?" I assured her I wasn't interested in any of her brothers.

Although I was only 10, I'd figured out that I might be very different from most kids. I had fooled around with a few boys and also an older neighbor girl who taught me the basics of foreplay as we kissed and fondled each other. I knew I would rather spend time with her than with the boys.

By the time I met Terry I was beginning to suspect my interest in girls extended beyond just being friends. Looking back I think I was afraid of being so different. I know I was insecure, and I'm certain I took great pains to avoid doing anything that would cause Terry to distrust my motives.

Shortly after we both turned 14, Terry reached a full-blown puberty that was frightening to me in its intensity—her black, glowing tresses, dark brown eyes, pearly white teeth, and gorgeous figure made adult men stare. She topped off the package with an impish, flirtatious personality and a devilish grin no one, including me, could resist.

Terry's family lived a few blocks away from mine. Most of our time together was spent at her house—a noisy and loving, if crowded, household.

Terry and her sister Susan shared a tiny bedroom. Susan was two years our senior and had little tolerance for our "childish" ways. However, the three of us would often sit on the twin beds sharing a cigarette purloined from Terry's parents, waving the smoke out the open sash window. When I'd spend the night, I'd squeeze into Terry's bed and we'd stay up late, giggling and talking until Susan would bark, "OK, that's *it!* Shut up, or I'm telling Mom!"

Terry confided to me that she had starting having sex with her boyfriend David. I was frightened for her, as several of our classmates and older girls in our school had become pregnant. But Terry claimed that she and David were careful to always use a condom. "And besides," she once said, "I usually give him a hand job or a blow job anyway. It's faster and safer," she'd grin. I wasn't amused.

As the summer of our 15th year approached, I felt torn by angst and jealousy. Terry was spending all of her free time with David. I knew damn well what they were doing, and I didn't like it one bit.

Fed up with my pouting and ill humor, Terry arranged for me to meet Joey, a friend of David's. I went along for the ride and to be near Terry. Much to my surprise, Joey wasn't half bad—cute, tall, and shy. We actually hit it off, although probably not in quite the way Joey imagined. Nonetheless, we four were soon double-dating every weekend, riding around in either David's mom's car or Joey's dad's new dark-blue T-bird.

One summer night we were all hanging out on the beach, drinking cheap wine under a full moon. At some point, Terry and David sneaked off into the dunes, leaving Joey and I alone. I fretted.

"Aw, forget about 'em," Joey advised, when he sensed my sour mood. "Let's make out too, then we'll all go get some ice cream, OK?" So we made out, which went about as far as heavy petting. I'd fantasize about Terry and Joey would get a hard-on. Our relationship was based on mutual frustration.

A couple of weeks later I was spending the night with Terry, something we hadn't done for months. Susan was baby-sitting somewhere all night, so we had the tiny bedroom to ourselves. After dinner dishes were cleaned and the house tidied, Terry's brothers and parents retired to the living room to watch TV and we headed to the bedroom to smoke stolen cigarettes, drink Cokes, and gossip.

Terry stretched out on her little bed, lighting a cigarette and gazing up at the ceiling. Susan's radio played softly in the background.

Terry usually preferred to talk about David, about their plans to get married and live in an apartment together after high school. I was surprised when her opening question was about Joey.

"How does he kiss?"

"Um, not all that great, I guess," I replied cautiously. I didn't know where this line of questioning was going. "Why?"

"Well, David kisses like a dream," she exclaimed. Then seeing my darkening expression, she frowned. "What's wrong?"

"Nuthin'," I pouted. "Well, it's just, uh, I mean, I guess I don't want to talk about kissing." I hoped that would end the topic.

Terry sat up on the edge of her bed and faced me. I drooped; my arms were on my knees. I suppose I looked generally unhappy.

"Aw, honey, don't be so sad," she cooed as she reached out to give me a hug. "You know I love you. And I love David too. It's just different, that's all. Don't be jealous. You're my best friend."

I remember feeling mollified by the hug and her entreaties. And I remember us talking about kissing, and how boys kiss differently than girls. And I remember telling Terry that Joey really didn't kiss well at all and that I was getting tired of coaching him.

"Well, how do you kiss him?" she asked. I tried to explain, and she suggested I show her.

"Show you?" I asked, dumfounded. "You mean, like, um, demonstrate? On you?"

"Yes, silly, on me." She seemed exasperated. "Come on, show me how you kiss him. I can tell you if you're a good kisser or not. Then you can show him how I kiss you back."

Logic was definitely missing somewhere, but I wasn't going to argue. In spite of the fear I had of the strength of Terry's attractiveness, I let her start the kiss. I kept my eyes open, watching hers slowly close, her dark lashes settling softly on those high cheekbones.

"Don't open your eyes." She broke the kiss, leaving me puckering while she whispered. "Here, let's try again."

Darkness. My heart raced. The sound of blood pounding in my ears. Her lips were softer than anything I could possibly describe. My lips felt dry, but just then she flicked their surface with her tongue, sending barbs of fire down my spine and out my fingertips. My hands clutched her shoulders. Her head twisted, and our lips collapsed into each other. Our teeth lightly clicked. She giggled; I moaned and opened my mouth slightly to allow her softly exploring tongue to penetrate farther. I inhaled through my nose, my chest heaving as if I was running full tilt. My fingers moved to her face. I ran my palm along her jaw line as I relaxed farther into the kiss, the exploration. Our breasts barely brushed together, and my nipples hardened to painful intensity. I'm feeling, sensing, breathing more than I have ever before in my lifetime. I was lost.

"Whoa," Terry whispered hoarsely. I sat upright on the edge of the bed, slowly coming back to reality, leaning toward her as she leaned back. My hands dropped abruptly from her shoulders. I gazed into her eyes; she stared back, her expression confused and slightly...slightly afraid. I cleared the lust from my gaze and reached out to take her hand. She shifted just out of reach. I heard her inhale a ragged breath.

"I'm sorry," she whispered into the darkened room, her face averted. "I'm sorry, Lynn. I didn't mean…"

"What? Didn't mean what? What's wrong?" I was confused and starting to anticipate rejection. I wish I hadn't let myself go so completely. *She knows I'm queer and I want her,* I thought.

She shifted again, facing me, with tears in her eyes. "I know what you want. I mean, I thought I knew, but I never—well, I never meant to lead you on. Oh, shit." She shook her head, then looked carefully into my eyes. "Lynn, I guess I've always known you like girls. And I know you like me. But I never thought, until now, that you felt about me like I feel about David."

I sat in stunned silence.

Somehow we got through that night. Terry slept in her bed; I slept in Susan's. We talked: Terry said she understood how I could like girls but that I should give it a chance with guys. I know she tried to understand but simply couldn't.

That summer we drifted apart. A few months later my parents divorced, and I moved several hundred miles away upstate. Terry called one day—she was pregnant. I drove to her house, and we talked. It was as if we had never been estranged. The storm caused by her out-of-wedlock pregnancy was mostly over, overshadowed by her doctor's concerns about Terry's high white-blood-cell count. My mom managed to get Terry's doctor on the telephone, only to be told that Terry was diagnosed with leukemia and her time was short.

I still have dreams of Terry lying in her bed those last weeks, thin and pale, taking my hand and telling me to stop crying, everything is going to be all right. It's all right that I love her. It's all right that I like girls. She's had a good life and is tired, and ready to see God. Just take care of her mom and dad and Susan. The boys will be OK on their own. Then falling asleep, peacefully, drifting away to another place where I can't follow.

And the kiss? I've only actively, deliberately recalled it once in my life—just long enough to write this story.

Like Sunlight
Lisa Chen

Amanda, I say softly, so softly my voice is like the breeze, a whisper against her trembling skin. Amanda, I want you to do something for me.

Her navy eyes look back at my brown ones. Her curly blond hair tangles with my silky black hair until you can't tell where she begins and I end. I look at the skin of our arms lying pressed together; her deeply summer-tanned white skin, my smooth cream color that I rarely allow the sun to touch, per the dutiful obedience of a lifetime spent being my mother's daughter. Amanda's breath rustles sweet and gentle past my ear when she answers, Yes.

Can you kiss me, I say. Here, and here, and here, and I touch the places I want her to kiss me on her body, showing her where she can ignite me, start a slow boil that will build and froth and bubble over, carrying us both down a path we did not know we could follow.

I touch her soft breast, feel the taut nipple beneath her thin tank top, rub it in circles with my little finger until her breath comes fast and ragged, until she grasps my hand with her own and says in a low growl, Stop. Let me do that to you.

Oh, I gasp, as the force of those few words makes my cunt swell and heat almost unbearably, makes me drip wanton juices down my leg inside my jeans. Okay, I say weakly. I am still amazed that this is happening, that we have never before explored this leaping passion, this skin-on-skin heady rush, this unexpected meeting of one body with another.

You do want me, don't you, Lisa? she whispers, hesitating a moment, looking into my eyes again, perhaps searching for doubt or fear.

Yes, I whisper back, no indecision, and she reaches her fingers for my breast, takes my nipple between them, rolls it around, pulls on it gently, then harder, listening to my moans and seeming to find satisfaction with them. Slowly, so slowly, she pulls my shirt up, then maneuvers it over my head and off so that I am lying half naked on her bed.

Amanda, I begin to say, but she stops me with a hand over my mouth, which I kiss and lick, and she puts her fingers inside my mouth, letting me suck them wet, rubbing them over my lips when she slips her hand out and brings it down again to my breast, this time to the bare skin. The wetness touching my hypersensitive nipple draws out a shuddering groan, and another, and another, and she does not stop touching me.

You are so beautiful, my friend, she says, and she puts her head down to my breast, takes my nipple in her mouth, between her teeth, licks little circles around it like I did to her nipple with my finger earlier, and I almost hyperventilate, except that she raises her head for a split second and murmurs, Ah-ah, you stay present, before putting her head down again and seriously going back to work. I wonder if it is possible to pass out just from the delicate sound of someone's voice.

Now kiss me here, I say a while later, and I guide her hand down to my shivering belly, to a place just above my pubis. She lightly, almost thoughtfully skims her fingers across my skin, and it jumps and quivers in response, and I say something inarticulate, and she smiles lazily at me.

Just you be patient, Lisa. Don't get greedy on me just yet.

Greedy. I am surprised by the smoothness of her skin, her tongue, her hair against my chest. I do not have time to be greedy;

I am just trying to understand and adore every second of what is happening.

Her lips on my stomach shock me into saying her name, and the sound of her name hangs in the air like a statement, a reminder of who she is, and she looks at me, questioning silently. Don't stop, I say, looking at her hard until she drops her head again.

Touch me here, I whisper much later, and I place my own fingers against the crotch of her pants, feeling the swollen labia pressing eagerly against the fine linen material, feeling the warmth and wetness waiting for me between her legs, the legs I have covertly watched for so many years. I imagine how she will taste on my tongue, salty and sweet, and I am so overcome by a rush of shooting sparks seeming to fly out of my head that I think I do pass out for a split second.

Let me take off your jeans, Amanda says, her voice a velvet swirl in the dimness of the room, soothing me, arousing me, turning me about and sending me spinning through an array of sensations I have so long wished I could experience with her.

Sure, I say, attempting a steady voice, failing miserably. I listen to Amanda's husky laughter, years of cigarette smoke in her lungs. She slips the denim easily down to my ankles, starts to pull them all the way off, pauses for a moment, then leaves them where they are.

Spread your legs as wide as you can, and her voice is a command that makes my heart rattle and sends electric shocks down my skin, from my bare arms all the way down to my imprisoned feet. I do as she says, feeling like the dutiful Chinese girl again, taught to obey, can't say no to my friend, this woman loving me, teasing me, capturing me and doing with me what she will. The very thought of doing whatever she tells me to do pings around my brain, makes those electric shocks that much more powerful, makes me stutter, Okay.

My knees ache when Amanda pushes them down against the bed, spreading me open, naked, vulnerable to her smoldering attention. I start to breathe fast, shallow, making my mouth dry, my lips sticking together. I am so excited I can hardly think.

Amanda! I yelp when her lips touch my labia lips, tickle around the wetness for my clit, find the little nub and kiss it. Her tongue reaches in too, melts my clit like so much butter under the hot sun of our southern home. I feel engorged, desperate, like a bitch in heat writhing on the bed. I only want her to keep doing what she is doing, never stop, Never stop! I cry out, and I hear her chuckle against my skin, my slick wet pubic hair, and she does not stop.

Her tongue darts in and out of my slick wetness, plays with my clit, then her lips replace her tongue and roughly kiss me, burying her face into my cunt, into my trembling legs, then her tongue returns, and it cycles and cycles, and I spiral up higher and higher, reaching toward some sort of pinnacle that dances just out of my reach, and suddenly I am there, and the light flashes in my eyes, and I open my mouth and holler and yell and cry as wave after wave of enormous, indefinable pleasure grips my body and holds it hostage. I feel my pulse beating in my flesh, feel it pounding in Amanda's mouth, which does not let go of me until she has sucked the last possible tremor from my shaking body.

Gently, carefully, she removes her lips, her tongue, works her way up my body with the sweetest of kisses, the last of which is planted on my mouth, and I can taste myself, sort of spicy and earthy, like the herbs in my garden, like my entire garden and the rich soil it springs from. She holds me until my breathing settles, until my pulse has stopped bouncing wildly, until the haze clears from my eyes.

My turn, she says simply, and her voice leads me, guides me into giving her the same pleasure she just gave me.

Much, much later, when she is contentedly lying back on the bed, she almost shyly asks, Will you please love me? I gently say back, I already do, and she snuggles down in my arms, her breathing steady and low, and I realize she has instantly fallen asleep. I smile, kiss the top of her curly hair that is like sunlight, and hold her close. I do not plan on letting go.

Contributors

J. Devon Archer lives in Denver, where she works as a paralegal. She shares her home with her life partner, three dachshunds, and a golden retriever. She's currently finishing her first novel.

Rachel Kramer Bussel is a freelance writer in New York City. She writes the Lusty Lady column at ctomag.com, the Tight Spots column at Lesbianation.com, and Rachel's Kiss and Tell at www.erotica-readers.com. She is an editorial assistant at *On Our Backs* and a contributing editor at Cleansheets.com. Her writing has been published in the *San Francisco Chronicle, Curve, Diva, Playgirl, BUST, Lambda Book Report,* and in several anthologies, including *Best Lesbian Erotica 2001* and *Best Women's Erotica 2003*. She revised *The Lesbian Sex Book* (Alyson, 2003) and cowrote *The Erotic Writer's Market Guide* (Circlet Press, 2003). Visit her Web site at www.racherkramerbussel.com.

Lisa N. Cacciabaudo is a 26-year-old New Yorker living in Bloomington, Ind., where she recently earned an MA in musicology at Indiana University. She hopes to return to the East Coast and pursue her interests in social work, gender studies, and singing.

Lisa Chen lives in San Francisco, where she is working on her first novel.

Maria V. Ciletti is a registered nurse working as a medical administrator. She recently finished the novel *The Choice*. Her short story "The Green Poem Book" appears in an anthology sponsored by Little Professor Book Stores, and her article "Vaccines and Reimbursement: Physician Beware" was published in the August 2001 issue of the Ohio State Medical Association's monthly publication *Practice Essentials*. She lives in Niles, Ohio, with her partner, Rose.

Contributors

M. Damian resides in Staten Island, N.Y. When not penning erotica, she struggles away at her detective novels, one of which has been accepted for publication.

Mia Dominguez was born and raised in Los Angeles, where she lives with her son and cat. Her writing appears in *Philogyny* magazine and the anthologies *Skin Deep* and *Wet*. She's hard at work on her liberal arts degree.

Kate Dominic is the author of *Any 2 People Kissing* (Down There Press). Her stories have appeared in the anthologies *Early Embraces III; Herotica 6* and *7, Best Lesbian Erotica 2000* and *2002; Best Women's Erotica 2000, 2001,* and *2002; Tough Girls;* and many other anthologies and magazines under a variety of pen names. She still wears Hawaiian White Ginger from time to time.

Alison DuBois is a Dutch-American writer working on a book called *She Kissed Me*, a pictorial and documentary of lesbians and kissing. Her work has appeared in a number of anthologies and literary publications, including *Hag Rag* and the *Womyn's Press*.

D.M. Gavin lives in the Washington, D.C., metro area with her partner of seven years. She works in the nonprofit sector as a director of publications and has a full-length book in progress with Women's Work Press.

Margaret Green lives in Southern California with her girlfriend of five years. This is her first published story.

Beth Greenwood's stories can be found in *Of The Flesh, Sweetlife,* and *Faster Pussycats*. Beth herself can be found hitting on soda jerks in small-town diners across America.

Brenda King, a computer programmer, lives in Milwaukee, where she's hard at work on a mystery novel, *Kiss the Sky*.

Contributors

Toni Rae Knight was born in Nigeria in 1978 and moved to the United States at the age of 6. Years later she studied business and creative writing at St. Andrews College in Laurinburg, NC. She started writing erotica as a way of exploring her own sexuality, as well as themes of race, class, and sexual identity in lesbian relationships. She now lives in Maryland, where she is working on her first novel and a comic series based on some of her work.

Karen Lillis is an artist and writer living in New York City. She is the founding editor of the Xerox press named Words Like Kudzu and the anthology *Venus in the Mirror*. She is the author of the novel *i, scorpion: foul belly-crawler of the desert* and the short story collection *Tough Broads and Classy Dames*, both from Words Like Kudzu Press.

Lee Ann McCann loves all things Celtic, card games, and fresh warm French bread. Her work has been published in the National Library of Poetry, *Seasons of Change*, and *Pathways*.

Darrah Le Montre is a writer and performer trying to stay warm in Boston. When she's not reading at an open mike night or involved in progressive queer performances, she's hard at work trying to publish her first book of poetry. Keep your eyes peeled for this firecracker at a lesbian event near you.

Jesi O'Connell lives in Utah, where she hikes, meditates, and writes as often as she can. Her work has appeared in the anthology *Awakening the Virgin*.

Katie L. Parker is happily partnered for life, living under the palm trees of California. She is working on a short fiction collection and often thinks about writing a novel set in Australia.

Gina Perille lives in Jamaica Plain, Mass. She works as a project consultant for a firm that does strategic planning for arts and culture organizations throughout the United States. Prior to that, Gina worked as an Equity stage manager at several professional regional theaters. She writes reviews and other articles for *Bay Windows*, New England's largest gay and lesbian newspaper.

Robin Perry was born and raised in Wales, currently lives in London, and is trying to juggle the demands of being a mother, a (long-distance) lover, and a writer.

Bernadette Rafferty is a nonconformist, well-traveled, vegetarian wannabe, long-haired dyke who much prefers animals to people (particularly dung beetles, who are just *so* determined and focused). She's passionate about caving and paragliding but still hasn't found what she's looking for. She lives in Melbourne, Australia, but that could change at any moment.

Rebecca S. Rajswasser works as a receptionist for a very swanky company. She supports her habits and vices by working as a relationship coach privately via E-mail and telephone and in person, and as the facilitator of the Java Love 101, 201, and 202 workshops, which she created. Her writing can be found in *Faster Pussycats* and *WeMoon 2001,* at www.shadesofgrey.com, and in the 2001 *Sexy NYC Guide*. Feel free to E-mail her (lovediva@juno.com) for more information about Java Love or just to sing her praises.

Jennifer Rivers lives in Portland, Ore., with her partner of three years and considers her day job to be her hobby and writing to be her profession. She dedicates this story to the love of her life, April, the woman who inspires her, nurtures her, and opens her heart and mind to all things new and previously unimaginable.

Monica S. lives on the West Coast with her lover and their two dogs. This is her first published piece.

Contributors

W. Lynn Smith is a Florida-based marketing executive and writer who dreams of retiring to travel and write fiction. She and her partner, Lisa, are cared for by their Siamese cat, Spooky. A selection of her travel tales appears online at Lesbianation.com.

S. Katherine Stewart spends most of her time reading queer theory, writing about poets who haven't breathed in 350 years, and forcing undergraduates to read things they never thought they'd like. She lives in Illinois with her partner and a requisite number of ungrateful cats.

Kimberly Streible, originally from Louisville, Ky., now lives in Phoenix. Her short story "Steven's World" was awarded First Place Fiction and published by *Traveler Magazine* in 1991. Her work has also appeared in *So What* magazine.

Karen T. Taylor has been writing kinky erotica for several years because it got her dates with really interesting people. Now she's married to author-editor Laura Antoniou, and not only edited the fourth volume of Laura's Marketplace series, *The Academy: Tales of the Marketplace* (Mystic Rose Books), but also contributed stories to the book and collaborated on the Marketplace short story collection *Slaves of the Marketplace* (Mystic Rose Books, 2002). Her writing appears in *First Hand Personal* (Down There Press), *Friday The Rabbi Wore Lace* (Cleis Press), *Best Bisexual Erotica 2* (Circlet Press), and *Best Transgender Erotica* (Circlet Press).

Jules Torti had an English teacher who told her that her writing was like a whitewater rafting adventure instead of a calm paddle on a placid lake. What's wrong with that? Her dirty work has appeared in *Beginnings, Early Embraces 2, Awakening the Virgin, The Mammoth Book of Erotica,* and *Hot & Bothered 1, 2,* and *3* (Arsenal Pulp Press). Jules lives on the river in Dunnville, Ontario, where she owns a massage therapy clinic called The Upper Hand.

Contributors

Zonna is old enough to be Britney Spears's mother (and the less said about that, the better). You may have seen her stories in the anthologies *Skin Deep, Dykes With Baggage, Early Embraces, Hot & Bothered II* and *III, Tough Girls, Shameless,* and *Moment of Truth.* When she isn't writing she's usually changing her cat's litter box.